THE
RULE
OF
THREE

THE
RULE
OF
THREE

A NOVEL

E. G. SCOTT

DUTTON

DUTTON

An imprint of Penguin Random House LLC
penguinrandomhouse.com

LIBRARY OF CONGRESS CATALOGING-IN-PUBLICATION DATA

Names: Scott, E. G., author.
Title: The rule of three : a novel / E. G. Scott.
Description: [New York] : Dutton, [2022]
Identifiers: LCCN 2021049978 (print) | LCCN 2021049979 (ebook) |
ISBN 9780593185445 (hardcover) | ISBN 9780593185476 (ebook)
Subjects: LCGFT: Novels.
Classification: LCC PS3619.C6623 R85 2022 (print) | LCC PS3619.C6623 (ebook) |
DDC 813/.6—dc23/eng/20211015
LC record available at https://lccn.loc.gov/2021049978
LC ebook record available at https://lccn.loc.gov/2021049979

Printed in the United States of America
1st Printing

For Fiona and Brian

THE
RULE
OF
THREE

PART ONE

The spiritual path is not a solo one; choose
carefully who you decide to walk it with.

The Rule of Three, Sawyer Selwyn

PROLOGUE

"Nine-one-one. This call is being recorded. What's your emergency?"

"*Plea . . . he . . .*"

"I can barely hear you. Can you speak up?"

"*Help.*"

"Do you need the police or an ambulance?"

"*I think there's someone in the house with me.*"

"What is the nature of your emergency?"

"*My husband.*"

"What's your name, ma'am?"

"*Oh God. There's so much blood.*"

"Where are you right now?"

"*I'm hiding . . . I'm in a closet.*"

"Okay, try to breathe. Are you hiding from your husband?"

"*No.*"

"What is your address?"

"*Thirty-four Saltmeadow Lane, in Kingsland.*"

"Are you injured, ma'am?"

"I'm *not.*" *(sobbing)*

"Can you tell me your name?"

"Vicky."

"Good, Vicky."

"I just heard something. An explosion."

"Okay, stay calm for me, Vicky. Is your husband conscious?"

"No."

"Is he breathing? Did you check for a pulse?"

"I heard something in the dark. I ran away."

"That's okay. You did the right thing."

"I . . . I . . . I . . . think he's been shot."

"What makes you think he's been shot? Is there a gun in the house?"

"There's a hole in his chest."

"Don't hang up. Help is on the way."

"Please hurry!"

"Do you think you can get out of the house safely?"

"I . . . I . . . don't know."

"Vicky, stay with me."

"Please, don't hang up. I'm so scared."

"I'm not going anywhere."

(Whispers) "Did you hear that?"

"Did I hear what?"

"There was a crash. Someone is out there."

"Stay on the line."

"Oh God . . ."

"Vicky, are you there? . . . Please tap the phone or make a noise if you can . . . Vicky, are you all right? . . . Hello?"

CHAPTER ONE

WOLCOTT

"MRS. BARNES?" SILVESTRI and I have cleared the house and, finding no one on the premises, have called the widow inside. She's seated next to me on the one-armed chaise lounge in the lavishly appointed parlor near the front door of the home, several rooms away from the scene we've been called here to investigate. My partner stands off to the side, leaning against the priceless Steinway in the corner.

We'd only been on the clock for around fifteen minutes when the call came in about the incident at the Barneses' home. A spate of car thefts in the tonier sections of Stony Brook and its surrounding towns have accounted for the bulk of the department's cases in recent weeks; individuals hot-wiring luxury cars and taking them for joyrides before abandoning them in remote locations. Silvestri and I clocked in tonight shortly after one such call came in and were relieved we'd dodged that bullet. Now here we sit, on the eve of the Fourth of July, kid-gloving a woman whose husband's been murdered under this very roof.

"Please," she manages, in a trembling, shock-soaked monotone. "Call me Victoria." Her gaze rests somewhere against the far wall, without a fixed point to anchor it. She blinks slowly, heavily, as if having been drugged. Yet even in her current state, her rangy frame maintains a naturally formal posture, suggesting a woman long accustomed to an easy elegance. She's quite striking; chestnut hair flowing to her shoulders, emerald eyes bright amid the emotional turmoil, barely a thread in her tailored designer ensemble out of place. Her hand involuntarily finds mine, and I feel her palm pushing back against my knuckles, fingers floating, as if trying to stave off the tragedy that's befallen her. "I'm sorry I panicked," she says. "On the phone earlier. With the operator. The fireworks must have spooked me."

"Completely understandable, given the circumstances," I say steadily. "Victoria, we know you've been through quite an ordeal. Would you be able to run us through the events of the evening as best you can?"

She blinks deliberately, still dazed, and turns her eyes to mine. "I, um, was over at our friend Monica's with my sister, Laura. We hold our book club there every week while the husbands play poker here." Her eyes shift in the direction of the den, like a character in a horror film turning their attention to a closet that's just produced an unexpected sound. "We kind of lost track of time, and then Terry texted to say that they were wrapping up for the night."

"Uh-huh." I nod, subtly slipping the notepad and pen from my pocket. "And who were the 'they' in this case?"

"Oh, um, let's see; my husband, Terry Barnes. Spencer Nichols— that's Monica's husband. And then Laura's husband, Gil Mathers. My brother-in-law." I've got my pen at the ready as she ticks off the names, though I barely need to jot them down; Terry Barnes, the former congressman and very-well-connected resident of Kingsland—and probably the lowest of the three on the notoriety scale—who managed to court his own share of controversy in certain sectors by staying in the good graces of the NRA with his staunch support of pro-gun legislation. I flash momentarily to the gruesome scene in the den and flinch at the morbid irony. Next up is Spencer Nichols, the disgraced former CEO of Galapagos, Inc., the geotracking company that touted the groundbreakingly small scale of the nanotech it developed—devices tiny enough to fit on the head of a pin, I remembered reading. Nichols was all over the news last year after Galapagos was found guilty of defrauding investors; and last but certainly not least, Gil Mathers, the deliriously successful motivational speaker whose career was undone after video leaked of him at a party, surrounded by drugs and underage women, drunkenly belittling the very people who looked to Gil for inspiration to better themselves.

"Okay," I say. "And was that everyone in attendance, Victoria?"

"As far as I know," she answers, nodding slightly. "They sometimes had other people sit in, but that was the core group."

"A regular get-together, then?"

"Yes." She nods. "Every Sunday evening."

"I see. Now, you mentioned your husband having texted you after the game wrapped up. What time was that?"

"Let's see." She retrieves a cell phone from next to her on the chaise with a shaky hand and taps the screen. "Um, 10:32."

"Okay," I say, making a note. "And how much time would you say elapsed between that text and your arriving home?"

She raises a hand to her forehead and kneads the skin with her fingers. "Around thirty minutes, give or take. Terry always let me know when the boys were finishing up their last drink of the evening—the 'nightcap text,' I call it. I usually built in half an hour before I left Monica's house to walk back here."

"I see. So the Nicholses live nearby."

"Yes, they're both close. My sister lives around the corner at 88 Dogwood, and Monica's down the road from her at 22 Bayberry. We can all walk to one another's houses. Comes in handy when we've, you know, had a bit." She tilts her wrist back lazily.

"Of course," I say. "Now, when you returned home this evening, did you have a sense that anything was noticeably amiss, before you discovered your husband?"

She blinks hard and blots the corner of her eye with the back of her wrist. "I, um . . . the front door was cracked open. Just slightly ajar. I assumed that whoever left last hadn't latched it all the way, you see? But then when I . . ." She bites her bottom lip.

"I understand," I say, saving her the pain of having to recall the moment out loud. "And you haven't touched anything in the house, moved anything?"

"No, I just . . ." Her mouth hangs slack. "No."

"Okay, good. We know you've had a terrible shock, Victoria. We're going to get you out of here in just a minute. Do you have a place you can stay tonight?"

"Yes, I can . . . sure."

"Good," I say, nodding to Silvestri, who dips into the hallway. "I'm going to have one of the officers take you down to the station to file an official report. You'll tell them what you told me. Then they're going to swab your hands for gunpowder residue, so that we can go ahead and eliminate you as a suspect. Standard procedure. Once that's done, they'll drive you to wherever you're going to stay for the night. Does all of that sound okay, Victoria?"

"Yeah." She nods absently. "That's fine."

"Great." Silvestri returns with the uniformed officer as I rise from the chaise lounge and help the widow to her feet. The officer leads her out of the house as my partner and I start down the long hallway, in the direction of the den, to get a look at the scene while we wait for forensics to show up.

⁌

"Let's see what we can see." Silvestri snaps on a pair of nitrile gloves as we survey the room. The wall to our left appears to be a shrine of sorts to Barnes's hunting habit. A bolt-action rifle with a scope affixed to it sits on a display rack, surrounded by a series of photographs depicting Terry and his hunting buddies in camo outfits and flanked by big-game carcasses. As I scan the images, I recognize a number of prominent figures—celebrities, politicians, and a few CEOs of major corporations.

In the center of the den, on a round oak table set on a sprawling carpet, lay the remnants of tonight's game—a deck of playing cards set to the side with loose cards fanned out, faceup, in three separate piles. Next to each pile sits an empty crystal tumbler rung around the inside with the golden residue of the half-empty bottle of twenty-year-old Pappy Van Winkle that stands next to the deck of cards. My partner lets out an impressed whistle.

"Treated themselves to the good stuff, eh?" I ask, stretching my fingers inside the gloves.

Silvestri nods. "You don't drink this for the taste, pal. You drink it for the price tag."

"Well," I say, taking in the splendor of the room. "No expense spared, I guess."

"Nope. And it looks like it was a party of three, like the wife said."

"Right." We cross the room to the magnificent hand-carved desk, where I finally take a good look at the body sitting lifelessly in the leather office chair behind it, head slumped to the side. I've only ever seen Terry Barnes via his image in the papers and find that encountering the familiar figure in person has the effect of compounding the usual disorientation that occurs when coming across a body sapped of life. Absent are any signs of the brash, charismatic personality that had announced itself at every turn. Death, the great leveler, has robbed him of his presence, leaving a meek husk in its wake.

As I study the corpse, it occurs to me that Barnes is smaller than anticipated, and the impression of him I'd developed through photos begins to click more clearly into place: the seemingly spring-loaded tension he carried himself with; the confrontational gleam in his eye, suggesting a mix of suspicion and insecurity; the clean-cut good looks and arrogant smirk that gave him the appearance of a guy you'd love to get in the dunk tank at a county fair.

The chest is a mess; whoever shot him got him right through the heart, it looks like. Blood has bloomed across the entire front of his pink polo shirt, and the backspatter has stained the top of the desk in a reddish brown half circle. I walk around to get a look at the rest of the body and notice the framed photo propped on the desk—an image of the happy couple, now tinged with tiny projectiles of blood.

As I scan the scene, my eye catches the edge of a cell phone wedged between Barnes's thigh and the side of the chair. I carefully pluck it out, bag it, and drop it into my pocket. I check the back of the chair and find the remnant of a slug poking out of the leather. "Bullet went clean through him," I tell Silvestri.

"Okay." He nods, crouching next to the body. "Hey, take a look at this." He points to the arms, hanging limply on either side of the chair. "There's barely a trace of blood on the hands or forearms, considering all the blowback. It's like he was relaxed when he got plugged. No defensive reflexes."

"Never raised his hands. Barely saw it coming. He knew whoever it was who shot him."

"Right. Single pop, nice and clean, from . . ." He stands and crosses to the front of the desk, straightens his arm, and extends a finger as he backpedals to a spot six feet or so in front of the body, eyeballing the angle of entry. "Right about here?"

I visually align the entrance wound with the hole in the back of the chair, to estimate the trajectory. "Yeah, I'll buy that."

"So." Silvestri begins scanning the carpet below him. "The game wraps up. What happens with the guests? One stays, one goes? They both stick around, and one distracts him while the other takes him out? Is it someone else altogether?"

"If the wife's telling the truth, that's a pretty tight timeline for a third party to get in the mix," I point out.

"True," he agrees. "Plus, it would have to be someone else he knew."

"Right." I pause. "Okay, let's hit it this way; what's *not* in the room?"

"Yes, sir," he says, tapping his middle finger against his palm. "Okay, there's a gunshot wound but no gun." He drops to his knees and lowers his face to the carpet like a bloodhound on the trail.

"And there's a card game but no cash. Any chance someone lost big and got sore over it?"

He pauses mid-crawl and looks up at me. "With a two-thousand-dollar bottle of bourbon sitting on the table? I don't think losing a little walking-around money was going to get any of these guys exactly homicidal."

"Two grand?!" I sputter. "Jesus. That why you gave up the sauce?"

"Yeah, *that* was the reason." He smirks and continues his hunt. He parks himself near the corner of the desk, where the carpet abuts the carved wooden foot. "Peekaboo," he says, pointing at an empty shell casing.

"What do you got?"

He squints to get a better look. "Nine mil," he concludes.

"So, we're thinking one of these two shot him and took off in a hurry?"

"Or the wife did it, and stashed the gun. From that range, the shooter wouldn't have caught the spatter."

"Right. Now, if she's *not* being straight about the timeline—"

I'm interrupted by the buzz of his phone. He stands up, retrieves it from his pocket, and answers. "Silvestri . . . uh-huh . . . Yeah, we're still in Kingsland." He cocks a brow and glances in my direction, a look of curiosity spreading across his face. "Wait, 22 Bayberry Lane?" He stretches each syllable to make sure I catch it, and I retrieve the pad, check the address against my notes, and nod to my partner, who speaks back into the phone. "You don't say . . . right . . . okay, thanks." He ends the call and pockets the cell.

"What was that?" I ask.

"Well, now." He tilts his head. "Looks like we may have confirmed ourselves a suspect."

⁂

We're on the walkway in front of the Barneses' home when I notice a nosy neighbor standing on the porch next door, arms crossed over her chest, craning her neck to get a better look at us. As I catch Silvestri's eye and nod in her direction, she waves a hand, descends the steps, and hurries across the lawn toward us.

"Officers," she chirps. "What's going on? How's Vicky?"

"Ma'am," I say, which causes her to wince. "Can I ask your name?"

"Millicent Addison-LeFleur," she answers pointedly. "My neighbors call me Milly. Vicky ran to my house earlier, after the incident." She corkscrews her mouth into an expression of distaste, but the gleam remains in her eye.

"Uh-huh," I respond. "Milly, did you see or hear anything out of the ordinary leading up to the *incident*?"

"I'm afraid I didn't," she says, frowning. "My husband and I had come in from the back porch, where we'd been watching the fireworks earlier with a glass of wine. People tend to light their own in their yards throughout the evening, so I might have heard the shot and not even realized it."

"Understandable," I say. "Can I ask how long you've lived next door to the Barneses?"

"Roger and I and our son, Bryce, have been here right from the start." She beams. "It's such a marvelous community that Terry's built."

"I see. And what's your impression been of your neighbors, as long as you've known them?"

"Well, Vicky and I have gotten very close over the last few years. Almost like sisters, you could say." She flutters her eyelids like she's caught a schoolgirl crush. "And Terry and Vicky are a wonderful couple."

I nod as I take notes. "And as far as you're aware, things have been normal with them as of late? Nothing unusual?"

"Oh my," she exclaims, clutching her fist to her chest. "You don't think . . ." She laughs off the idea, and as she pulls her hand away, I catch the sparkle of jewels encrusted in the crown-shaped keychain she's grasping. "Oh heavens no. Those two are the real deal. I mean, how many couples do you know who just run off on a spur-of-the-moment vacation, this many years into a marriage?" A forlorn look finds its way onto her face.

"A recent trip?" I ask.

"Oh yes," she chirps. "The lovebirds got back from Palm Springs only about a month ago."

"Nice," I acknowledge, jotting down the information.

"Right? Listen, I can't imagine what horrible thing led up to the tragedy of this evening, but I just can't think that Vicky . . . No, absolutely not."

"I see. Well, thank you for your time," I say, handing her my card. "And please don't hesitate to reach out if you think of anything else."

"I certainly will," she says. Before Silvestri and I turn to walk away, I again catch that curious glint in Milly's eye.

CHAPTER TWO

MONICA

THE PHONE SHAKES in my hand as I close the lid on Spencer's empty gun box. *"We are sending someone over as soon as possible, Mrs. Nichols. We actually have units nearby for another call. Do you want to stay on the phone with me until they arrive? It could be a little while."* The operator's kind voice has remained steady throughout the call. The polar opposite of mine.

"Oh, thank God," I say, my Texas twang coming out strong. I reach for a Kleenex. I am well aware that the police have been all over our neighborhood tonight, but I don't need to tell her that my phone has been lighting up with texts from neighbors on Victoria's street, two blocks away. Everyone was outside for the traditional Fourth of July eve fireworks in Kingsland, which have likely been damped by the unexpected police presence.

"This was the right thing to do," I reassure myself. I hold my Cartier keychain in my hand, running my fingers over the fourteen-karat-gold crown, stopping at the diamond inlay in the center of the charm. The luxury trinket was my welcome gift from Terry Barnes our first

day here in Kingsland. *"This is something only a few select people have the honor to ever be a part of. Always carry this with you as a reminder that you are one of the chosen ones."* The charm is heavy in my hand and symbolizes so much that has gone wrong since Spencer brought me here.

I run my hand through my white-blond hair as I pace in front of the mirror. In the low lighting, I'm a ghost. My face looks drawn and my first-northeastern-summer lack of tan makes me look older than my thirty-five years. Kingsland is aging me faster than I'm comfortable with.

Before I called 911, I tried Vicky and Laura, and they are both going straight to voicemail. I have a small paranoid twinge that they are together and talking about me, but I shrug it off. It would be hard for anyone not to feel like a third wheel to sisters, especially those two. Before I was introduced to them officially and observed them at my first Kingsland homeowners association meeting, I felt that old junior high school ache of being the new kid and the desperation of wanting to be accepted. I would quickly learn that I was far from the only woman in the neighborhood who felt the same awe and jealousy of them.

"Ma'am, are you still there?" The gentle voice pulls me.

"Yes. Still here."

"Did you need me to stay on the line?" she repeats.

"No, thank you. I'll be okay," I say into the phone. "Thank you so much for your help." I realize that I need to put on some presentable clothes and pull myself together before the police arrive.

"Of course. Help is on the way." The call disconnects and I sigh loudly.

The empty house feels like it exhales with me. Even though we've been here for nearly a year now, I still think of it as the "new" house.

It is a quarter of the size of our old one and feels like a starter home compared to our place in California. Former place.

In our bedroom, I apply some foundation and blush at my vanity. An onstage candid of Spencer doing his TED Talk on the dresser is over my shoulder in the reflection. In the ten years since the photo was taken, he's aged well. His hair has gone from black to salt-and-pepper, and his glasses have gotten markedly more stylish since his computer-geek look. I feel a ripple of deep dread looking at his face and stand up and start for the kitchen to avoid the feeling.

I pour a glass of wine with shaky hands and swipe through Instagram. I'm always trying to escape through my phone and catch ahold of the life we had to run from. The distraction turns my dark mood darker with each highly filtered photo of my supposed California friends and their shameless and absurdly posed yacht shots and private island vacations. "Stop looking," I scold myself, and put the phone facedown on the table.

I pick up the copy of our book club selection from the counter. *The Rule of Three* by Sawyer Selwyn. The massive bestseller has been in the hands of just about every wife in Kingsland. I open to a random page. *You are an energy magnet and hold the power to attract and repel anything in the Universe you want (or don't). Are you ready for happiness?*

I rise, stretch, and move through each room. The police don't care about how I feel; they need useful information. What are the facts? Spencer's not here. He was supposed to come straight home tonight but he didn't. He took the gun, apparently. He sent me a very cryptic text. He's been really unhappy. We were starting over. Things were supposed to be getting better.

But they weren't getting better, were they? "Worse" would be more honest. They'll want to know when he went missing. Technically, he's only been missing for hours. And possibly by their standards it is too early for me to report it, but his text is too worrying to keep silent. Truthfully, he's been missing for a lot longer than this evening, but I can't very well say, "Officers, my husband has been missing for the last year and a half and I've been so alone."

If only I could have seen where this all was going when he was released on bail when we were still on the West Coast. "I'm finished," he'd said before locking himself into his office for two months straight. He shifted from fully formed man to a barely there apparition haunting the long, dark hallways of our oceanfront compound in the middle of the night.

I call Laura's phone again and listen to it ring into her calming voice, inviting me to leave a message. I think about how effortlessly she and Vicky would be handling this situation.

I take a breath and rein in my twang. "Laur. It's Monica. Please call me back. Something's happened to Spence. He didn't come home from the game, but he sent me a really weird text. He's not answering his phone. I called the police . . ." I break down into fresh tears. "And something's going on at Vicky's. I can't get her on the phone and there's police at her house. Please call me as soon as you can."

I disconnect and dial Victoria's number again, and a robotic voice informs me that the voicemail I'm trying to reach is currently full.

An alert on my phone signals that the holiday tomorrow will be warm with clear skies, a harsh contrast to the choppy weather inside my head. The early warning signs of a panic attack make themselves known at the thought of talking to the police. This is a familiar nervousness, and unhappily I'm transported to the media training Spencer arranged for me a few years ago so that I would learn how to appear more "polished" no matter how anxious I felt on the inside. I was failing to impress when he and I were in the presence of important luminaries, billionaires, and tech scions. "You need to learn how to control your feelings better, Monica. You are embarrassing yourself, and me," Spencer informed me after a tongue-tied, red-faced night at a Gates Foundation gala.

The media coach, a former Hollywood something or other, was patronizing from the outset.

"You remind me of a less refined, shorter Daryl Hannah, Mrs. Nichols. Splash Daryl Hannah, not Steel Magnolias," he'd quipped. "Now, let's polish you up and tone that adorable backwoods accent down and prove those catty magazine writers wrong about you."

Humiliated, I worked hard to get polished and did my best Eliza Doolittle until I was no longer deemed a liability.

It was only a few months later that I got an opportunity to show that my husband had gotten his money's worth in my training—an interview with the San Francisco Chronicle Magazine about my new humanitarian foundation for the survivors of sexual assault and exploitation—when the news about Spencer broke.

The reporter's phone began buzzing five minutes after we'd started the interview, and when she paused her recording and said, "Excuse me, it's my boss," her eyes were wide and blinking fast as she listened intently. "I understand. Got it. Will do," she said calmly, and then put the phone down. "Sorry about that." I immediately felt the pressure in the room change.

"Monica, if we could switch gears for a moment," the reporter had said sweetly, my stomach dropping at her tone. "I've just gotten word that a few minutes ago your husband was arrested for alleged fraud. Can you comment on this?"

That was the first day and last day I allowed the press into my home, but every day after they'd shown up at our door and camped out on our street. Until after the trial, when we fled to Kingsland.

The doorbell chimes and I'm back in this new chaos. From that horrible beginning to this night, where Spencer Nichols, my fallen-from-grace husband, is gone. I take a few deep breaths and smooth my dress as I move through the house toward the door, thinking about a phrase I have taped to the inside of my medicine cabinet: "The present moment is yours to master or ruin."

CHAPTER THREE

LAURA

"HELLO?!" I RAP on the double-paned partition so hard that the laminated sign forbidding knocking dislodges and falls soundlessly to the floor. I try to keep my focus and balance despite the nausea I'm feeling, the flashbacks to the last time I was in an emergency room. The worst day of my life.

The ancient analog clock on the yellowing wall reads two A.M. My current surroundings harshly clash with those of a few hours ago, when I was drinking Pinot with my sister and Monica and debating the need for self-improvement books. My hands are trembling and I clasp them together to steady myself. I wish I was in my bed, blissfully asleep.

Frantically, I move to the closed "Hospital Personnel Only" double mechanical doors and catch sight of two police officers talking to a woman with a long braid down the back of her white coat. I rap hard on the plexiglass square and all three turn their faces to me. As one of the officers, a clean-cut man with a serious disposition, moves in my direction, a receptionist or nurse emerges from somewhere in the bowels of the hospital and returns to her post behind the intake window.

"Can I help you, ma'am?" she asks curtly. As I retrace my steps, she bends over to collect the sign I've knocked from its place and harpoons me with a sharp look before laying it faceup on the desk. She takes her seat in front of a computer monitor and barely acknowledges me.

"I got a call that my husband was brought here," I say breathlessly. She barely moves her glance from the screen.

"Name?"

"Laura Mathers."

Her indifference enrages me.

"Your *husband's* name."

"Gilbert Mathers," I choke out, steadying the growing frustration.

She hesitates for a nanosecond and I worry she's either a fan or a hater of my husband's. "How do you spell that?"

I spell out his name, relieved that he strikes her as insignificantly as I do.

"Insurance?" she asks mechanically. My irritation spikes.

"Can you tell me what is going on? Please," I say as I hand her my insurance card with quivering hands. It occurs to me that our insurance may not go through as she takes the laminated card. I have no idea if Gil has stayed current with it and I really can't remember the last time he or I have gone to a doctor.

The receptionist picks up a phone, pushes a few buttons, and says something into the receiver that I can't make out.

"Mrs. Mathers"—my name rolls drily off her tongue—"the police are going to speak with you shortly, and then a doctor will be with you as soon as possible."

My heart free-falls. "What is going on?" I plead.

"I don't have that information for you, but someone will be with you soon."

"Okay. All right." I stand in place.

"In the meantime, we need you to complete these digital forms with your husband's medical history, consent, and proxy info." She hands me an iPad, which I accept.

"There is a waiting room just over there." She indicates a door a few feet away, but I'm having major trouble getting the signals from my brain to my legs.

I clasp the iPad hard and head to the family waiting area. My phone is dead, so I'm not able to call anyone to tell them what has happened. We were using it to run Spotify through the speakers and I didn't realize how low my battery was until I'd already gotten into the car following the call from the police. I think about asking the icy receptionist for a charger but lose the will, and then try to click through the fine print on the iPad screen but am unable to focus. I half watch the TV screen bolted to the wall across the way, but it is placed way too high for anyone to view comfortably. I realize how similar this waiting room is to the last one. We were surrounded by a handful of other terrified parents. Gil was pacing so aggressively that one of the other fathers asked him to leave the room, and Gil had to be removed from the hospital for nearly starting a fistfight with the poor man.

The monitor is unreachable unless I stand on a chair, so I'm stuck on one channel with an endless cycle of biotin supplement infomercials and no volume control.

Then I hear the whoosh of the automatic doors and jump to my feet. The stone-faced officer makes his way toward me and a small smile crosses his face as I meet him halfway. He's followed by an equally serious-faced officer, who homes in on me when she sees that I'm the only person in the room.

"Mrs. Mathers?"

I am dizzy from standing too quickly and I sway on my feet. "Is he dead?" I practically scream.

"Are you Gilbert Mathers's wife, Laura?" she asks gently.

I nod.

She leads me back to my chair. "Your husband is alive. Dr. Mitali is going to be with you just as soon as possible to walk you through what is going on with him."

I am floored. The male officer stays standing while we sit but interjects, "He's extremely lucky. If two motorists hadn't stopped and called us, he might not be here right now."

The tone of his "here" tells me that he's referring to not the hospital but something more existential.

"I'm Officer Davis," says the striking female officer with blond chin-length hair and kindly eyes. "And this is my partner, Officer Pedone."

"I'm Laura," I barely get out, as my thoughts spin out of control from the news about Gil. "He's really alive?"

I don't mean to phrase it quite this way, but coherency is challenging.

"He is. We'll get the doctor to come out just as soon as she can to give you the details," Officer Pedone echoes.

"What happened?" I ask, rubbing my hands together as though keeping them warm over a fire.

"We responded to a 911 call around quarter after eleven tonight. A motorist spotted someone staggering along the shoulder of Route 572. She didn't pull over initially because she wasn't sure if it was safe and she was alone, but she slowed down, and when the person walked into the traffic lane and collapsed, she stopped to call for help," Officer Pedone recounts.

Davis speaks. "In the time that it took us to respond, another motorist stopped. Miraculously, she is a pediatrician from Manhattan who was on her way home from visiting relatives, and she knew how to slow your husband's bleeding significantly before the paramedics arrived. By the time we got to the scene, they were able to stabilize him enough to safely transport him here."

A doctor. I marvel at the odds. I'm racked with a hundred competing emotions. This feels like a nightmare, but I've never felt so awake.

"Bleeding? Jesus. Had he been in an accident? I don't understand."

"That's what we are hoping you can help us with, Laura. Your husband was walking alone on the side of the road with a very significant gunshot wound to his head. We haven't yet located a car or any witnesses to when and how he sustained his injury, but we are working on it," he says confidently.

"Gunshot?!" I squeak, and begin to cry.

"Do you know where he was this evening and who might have done this to him?" Officer Davis asks me.

I am speechless as the question wraps itself around my throat like a boa constrictor. With each passing second it gets harder to pull in a full breath. I'm about to pass out when a woman in a white coat makes her way over to us.

"Mrs. Mathers?" She stands erect, her dark French braid tangled with her ID lanyard, which hangs facing inward on her white coat.

"Yes?" I stand and feel the dizziness hit even harder this time.

She sees my legs buckle and guides me back to my seat and sits upright in the seat next to mine. "I'm Dr. Mitali. I've been handling your husband's case," she says. Officers Davis and Pedone take a few steps away to give us space but remain in earshot. I still feel utterly exposed.

"How is he?" I gasp, tears flowing freely.

"He's stable but critical. Because of the early intervention, his blood pressure and oxygenation were maintained and we were able to get him in for a brain CT very quickly. Luckily it has been a very quiet night. If it had happened tomorrow on the holiday, it might have been a different story."

I keep hearing the word "lucky" as it applies to my current crisis, and I am struggling to see how any of what has happened is lucky.

"Your husband's level of brain consciousness was higher than normal in a head injury of this nature, but we did find a hematoma on his scan and did a craniotomy to remove it and reduce the swelling."

"You did brain surgery on him without talking to me first?" I ask forcefully. The officers look at each other.

A look of concern dawns on Dr. Mitali's face. "Mrs. Mathers, your husband was going to die."

"I'm sorry." I take a leveling breath. "I'm just processing all of this." I resist telling her that this isn't the first time that someone close to me has been shot.

"I understand," she says.

"Is Gil going to survive?" I taste the salt from the tears in the corners of my mouth. My heart is aching as I think about our daughter.

"The trajectory of the bullet was really important to your husband's condition. Luckily, it didn't hit his spinal column, so he hasn't been paralyzed or had his motor skills compromised, as far as we can tell. And both are a good indication of survivability." She pauses.

"But?" I can tell the news is only "good" by comparison.

"The bullet's path was more superficial than most and only

affected one lobe, but it was the area that governs speech and memory, primarily."

"What does that mean, exactly?" My skin feels hot and I realize I've scratched the skin on my forearm red.

"Well, your husband will remain in the coma until we determine the extent of his injuries. His speech and memory could be greatly affected. The next week is the critical-care stage. Everything that happens in that time will determine the extent and speed of his recovery. Once we know how much swelling and pressure remain inside of his head following the surgery, we'll have a better sense of the functional consequences of his damage. It may be a long road, but I believe there's a chance of survival," she says.

"Thank you, Doctor," is the extent of what I can muster before I fold myself into a ball and moan quietly into my hands. I feel a tentative hand pat my back twice.

"I know this is an incredibly stressful time. We are doing everything that we can for him right now. The fact that a doctor happened to be on the road and was able to intervene before the paramedics arrived was critical tonight. I don't believe he would have survived otherwise. Your husband is a very lucky man."

There's that word again. Gil Mathers is the luckiest man *nearly* alive. I'm stupefied by the turn of events. I staunch my tears and sit up to face the three waiting faces.

"Can I see him?" I muster. "Please?"

"Let's give him a few more hours to stabilize. I'll allow you as soon as I feel confident that he can handle it."

"Did he say anything? Before he went into the coma?" I ask through my tears.

The officers look at the doctor and back at me. My heart lurches.

"He wasn't coherent when we arrived at the scene," Officer Davis says.

"By the time he reached us, he was unconscious," Dr. Mitali says.

"What do I do?" I ask them all, pleadingly.

"We have some questions for you," Officer Pedone says.

What a surreal, unbelievable night this has become.

Dr. Mitali stands and steps closer to the officers and says something that is inaudible to me. They nod. Mitali turns to me and then back to them.

"I need to process all of this," I say meekly.

Officer Davis responds, "We can revisit this in a few hours. We'll need to finalize the incident report and talk to the detectives assigned to your husband's case. They'll be in touch with you early tomorrow."

"Thank you," I say. I look at the doctor. "Do you really think he is going to make it?"

"I am cautiously optimistic. It is early to tell at the moment, but whoever shot him did it in the best possible way," she says oddly.

I am jolted by the sound of her phone ringing. "I have to get back," she says. "I'll be in touch." She waves at me and the officers as she sweeps out of the room.

I stand with the police, unsure of what to do next. Officer Pedone leads the way out of the waiting room and toward the exit.

"We can drive you home," he offers.

"I'm okay. I'll need my car tomorrow to get back," I protest.

"We'll escort you, then. Just to make sure you make it safely. You are in shock," Officer Davis says kindly.

"Sure. Okay," I relent.

I let them guide me past the intake desk, where I'm relieved to see the nurse on duty is absent again, allowing me to avoid a possible confrontation about insurance or the abandoned iPad I've left in the waiting room. I'll deal with it when I return to the hospital. *When I return to the hospital.* I marvel at how radically different this day ended from what I'd imagined when it started.

As we walk into the crisp air I point to my car. Officer Pedone leaves us to wait while he gets their squad car.

Officer Davis puts a steadying hand on my arm and gives me a warm smile. She has that look of someone trying to process the horror of what I'm going through and having no idea what to say. It is a look I've become all too familiar with in the last five years.

"Get some sleep, if you can. Then call family, friends, anyone who can give you support right now."

Victoria's face flashes in my mind and my stomach somersaults. I need my sister.

"Do you have someone you would normally call?" Officer Davis studies me.

"Yeah. My husband."

CHAPTER FOUR

SILVESTRI

"Mrs. Nichols," my partner says. "Whenever you're ready."

Normally, they wouldn't have bothered involving us with a missing persons report this soon, but aware of the action in Kingsland tonight, the station saw fit to reach out. The criminal activity in this upscale section of town tends toward the white-collar variety, making the earlier homicide decidedly unusual. As a result, Wolcott and I find ourselves in Spencer Nichols's study, trying our best to calm and comfort his obviously rattled wife. She gives the appearance of having just rolled off the set of a Hawaiian Tropic commercial, all tanned limbs and sun-bleached hair, making the distressed expression on her face seem wholly out of place.

The room we're standing in isn't quite as ostentatiously put together as at Terry Barnes's place, but it ain't far behind. I'm also not confident that I fully grasp the difference between a den and a study—apart from the wives' choice of noun—and while that's the kind of thought that can pop in when we're looking at a long night ahead, it's hard to complain when the arrows are materializing in front of us as fluidly as they seem to be.

"Just walk us through the evening," I say, holding my notepad at the ready. "One step at a time."

"The girls were over earlier," she begins, and I find myself caught off guard by the remnants of the Texas accent she's clearly worked to tamp down: the echo of the twang and the intentional softening of the vowel sounds. "Vicky and Laura. Sorry, that's Victoria Barnes and Laura Mathers. They're sisters. They come over once a week for book club while our husbands get together for their poker night."

"And what are you ladies reading at the moment?" asks my partner.

"Um, *The Rule of Three*, it's called." She seems thrown by the question.

"Just wondering," he explains. "My wife's in a book club as well, so I'm always curious."

"Okay," I say, redirecting the conversation. "And the evening unfolded normally, Mrs. Nichols?"

"Yeah," she answers. "We did our usual thing over here. Had a nice time. Terry always texts Vicky to let her know when the men are wrapping up their game. At some point, the girls left, and I finished my wine, just enjoying a quiet moment before Spence got home. Except it got later and later, and he still hadn't returned."

"Just to get us on the same page," I say. "Around what time did the ladies take off?"

She looks up and to the side, recalling. "Little after eleven? Something like that. I'd noticed earlier that Spence had taken the car."

"And what does your husband drive, Mrs. Nichols?"

"It's a classic Mustang. Hunter green. He bought it because it's the same one from that Steve McQueen movie."

"The '68 Fastback, from *Bullitt*?" .

"That's right. He sometimes likes to go for drives at night, to clear his head, so I figured he'd left the game and was just taking some time before he came home. But then it was getting late, and I heard from the neighbors that there was some commotion over at Vicky's, so I got worried. I came down, just to make sure he hadn't snuck back in and been hiding out in here." A brittle chill slips into her tone. "That's when I found this," she says, recoiling slightly as she regards the hard plastic gun case lying open atop the desk.

"Mmm." I nod. "And would you happen to know what kind of gun your husband owned?"

She lets out a burst of nervous laughter before chastising herself for the slip. "I'm so sorry. This is hardly the time to be . . . I'm sorry."

"Quite all right," I assure her. "People deal with these things in different ways."

"No, it's just . . . Well, it's funny, really."

"What's that, Mrs. Nichols?"

"This is actually kind of embarrassing. Spence would kill me if he knew I were telling you."

"It'll stay between us," chimes in Wolcott, with the perfect hint of levity. "Go on."

The comment has the effect of loosening her up, and I watch her shoulders drop. "Okay," she begins, blushing. "Do you remember that song 'Ice Ice Baby'?"

"Sure." My partner smiles. "That one really got things open at my junior high dance."

"Right?! So, there's that line where it's something-something-something, and then Vanilla Ice has the nine?"

"A nine millimeter?" I clarify, glancing at my partner.

"I guess so, yeah." She's temporarily lost in the moment. "I just know because when he first got that gun, he rapped the lyrics while he was holding it." She cringes slightly as she recalls the memory.

"Pardon me for a moment," Wolcott interjects casually, catching my eye before he ducks out of the room. I realize he's excusing himself to go call in the make and model of Nichols's Mustang for the purpose of issuing an APB, and I continue the interview with Mrs. Nichols.

"I need to ask," I say. "How would you describe your husband's state of mind lately? Any noticeable changes emotionally? Anything like that?"

Her eyelids flutter, and she sets herself as if she's been bracing for this question all along. She takes a deep breath and exhales as she focuses on me pointedly. "I'm sure you've heard about the controversy surrounding my husband? Read about him in the papers?"

"I have, yes," I respond, keeping a neutral tone.

"It's been really hard on him . . . on us, I should say." Her eyes shift to the door, and I catch Wolcott quietly reentering the room. "He's always been an intense man, Spence. Very focused. But he used to have a certain spark to him. There was a vibrancy that's just . . . gone."

"And how long would you say this has been going on?" I ask.

"Oh goodness. I mean, since before we moved out here. This was supposed to be a fresh start," she explains, looking around the space. "But I don't know that he's been happy for a moment since we got here." She uses her thumb to flick a tear from her eye as the tremor in her voice threatens to open into a full emotional flood. "It's like everything is a daily struggle with him. And if I'm really being honest, I would use the term 'unstable' to describe my husband."

"I see," says Wolcott as he produces a handkerchief from his pocket and hands it to her. There's the hint of a smile as she accepts the offering from my partner and blots her eyes.

"You know, I knew I should have sought help for him. But Spence is so proud. I knew he'd be furious if I betrayed his trust and took our problems outside the home." She frowns as she balls the handkerchief in her fist and pounds it against her thigh, reprimanding herself. "And I just never thought . . . well, it just didn't occur to me that he was that type of person."

"I'm sorry, what type of person is that?" I ask.

She looks from me to my partner with an expression of annoyed confusion, as if we've just joined the conversation she's been engaged in all along. "The kind of person that would, you know . . ." Her eyes go wide as her voice drops to a strained whisper. She nods toward the gun case. "Harm themselves?" She catches the glance between Wolcott and me and shakes her head. "Detectives," she says, in a tone usually reserved for explaining fresh concepts to wide-eyed children. "My husband sent me *this* text earlier tonight." She plucks her phone from the desk, wincing at its proximity to the hard plastic case, and taps the screen. She frowns as she turns the phone toward my partner and me, and inhales sharply as she holds in her palm for our perusal the last message she received from Spencer Nichols:

There's something I need to take care of. Don't wait up.

CHAPTER FIVE

VICTORIA

"Right this way, ma'am."

I hold my tongue as the young officer steps aside and lets me pass through the front door. There's something uniquely disorienting about being allowed admittance into my own home, and in this case the feeling is compounded by the fact that the authority figure appears young enough to be my child. Being referred to as "ma'am" is a dependably unpleasant reality check, but I take some solace in realizing that at this kid's age, most anyone out of college likely qualifies for the title.

Unable to reach either Mon or Laura on the phone last night after leaving the police station, I ended up crashing at the neighbors' house for what amounted to a very fitful few hours of sleep. I woke up feeling as exhausted as I'd been before bed, but with a sense of relief at my close proximity to our home, and I couldn't help but laugh at the odd paradox that is Kingsland; life in a tony enclave like this can bring on feelings of stifling homogeneousness one moment and comforting familiarity the next.

I'm on my way upstairs when I hear noise coming from down the hallway on the first floor. I pause on the step and lean my head over the banister for a better listen, then double back when I hear sound again. I make my way down the hall and realize that what I'm hearing are voices coming from inside the den. I open the door quickly, taking the men by surprise. I recognize the detectives from last night and slowly relax.

"Mrs. Barnes," says the scruffier of the two—Sylvester, if I'm remembering right. "Victoria." He saves me the trouble of correcting him. "Sorry, we didn't mean to startle you." They've both turned to face me, and I notice they're looking about as worse for wear as I feel.

"Not at all, Detectives." Before I can form my next thought, my eye is drawn to the empty chair behind the desk, and the image of the last time I saw my husband—the last time I'll ever see him alive—flashes through my head. The detectives must notice me staring, because they step toward each other in an effort to block the view, and I'm hit with a surge of gratitude. I shake off the sight and return my attention to the men. "Is it okay that I'm here right now?"

"Not a problem," responds the well-dressed one. "How are you feeling this morning? Were you able to get any sleep last night?"

"Is it that obvious?" I reply, stifling a yawn. His expression softens, and he reveals the suggestion of a grin.

"We're in that same boat with you, paddling upstream," he says kindly, shrugging as he does. "Believe me."

I feel myself smile. "I have a few things I need to attend to," I say. "But I'm happy to put on a pot of coffee, if there are any takers?"

"My partner here is the virtuous sort." He nods to Sylvester. "But I'd love a cup . . . *only* if you're going to the trouble, that is."

"No trouble at all," I assure him. "Is there anything else I can be of help with, Detective . . ."

"Wolcott," he says, sensing my hesitation. "And this is my partner, Detective Silvestri." *Oops. Close.*

"That's right," I say. "Sorry."

"Not at all," Wolcott continues. "We just wanted to have another look in here. See if we missed anything the first time around."

I sense Silvestri sizing me up and turn my attention to him. He seems to be gauging my level of discomfort at being in this room, and I make a point of holding his gaze steadily.

"If it's not too much to ask," he ventures, "it might be helpful to get your impression of things. See if anything looks amiss to you. Out of the . . . ordinary." He realizes the grim absurdity of his statement and shifts uncomfortably.

Wolcott clears his throat. "Just, you know, you're more familiar with the space than we are."

"Sure," I say, tacitly agreeing to join them in this game where we all pussyfoot around the fact that my murdered husband was wheeled out of here on a stretcher mere hours ago.

I rest my hands on my hips and scan the room. The only thing that's different from the scene last night is the absence of Terry's corpse, and everything about that absence shouts its very presence; the impression in the leather where his body had gradually molded its shape into the chair; the remnants of blood on the desk, and on the edges of the chair and the armrests, which now look as if they were caused by some vanished apparition.

I'm suddenly reminded of the Wonder Woman cartoon from my childhood, in which she's shown flying in the invisible plane and appears to be hovering in midair in a seated position. This scene resembles the reverse of that—some sort of eerie photonegative version. I feel a prickle on the back of my neck and stifle the shiver that follows it.

I reset my stare and let it move across the surfaces in the room. The poker setup on the tabletop looks the same. The bookshelf, the mantel, and the filing cabinets all seem undisturbed. The room is more or less as I remember Terry keeping it. He was well organized, I must say—a combination of *his* capacity for singular focus and *my* influence in directing that focus. We really did make quite a team.

I'm continuing to visually sweep the room when my eyes come to rest on the old maritime oil painting on the back wall to the left of the desk, now hanging just a bit crookedly. The pause draws their attention, and they look back and forth between the cockeyed canvas and my furrowed brow. I catch them in the corner of my eye, exchanging glances and nods.

Finally, Wolcott breaks the silence. "Well, I'll be," he says, shaking his head. "Nearly missed that entirely." He pulls a pair of rubber gloves out of his pocket and puts them on, then approaches the painting and carefully removes it from the hook, revealing the wall safe behind it. He lays the painting to the side and turns to his partner.

"Victoria," says Silvestri. "Were you aware that your husband had a safe hidden in here?"

"Well, sure," I answer. "Terry had that installed right after we moved in. Hadn't thought of it in years, though."

Wolcott tugs the steel door, which opens freely. He turns to look at me. "Any idea who might have had access to the combination?"

"It was oh-five-oh-five," I say. "Terry's birthday. So, anyone who knew him had a shot at it, I suppose. He used that configuration for every four-digit code in his life." I sigh. "I would always tell him to change it up, but my husband had his routines."

Silvestri and I step forward to get a look inside. There's a file folder sitting atop a manila envelope. Wolcott removes both, then turns back to me. "Victoria, do you happen to know what your husband normally kept in here?"

"Well, the important documents should be in the envelope; birth certificates, Social Security cards, passports. All the stuff he kept in there in case of a fire." He opens the envelope, glances inside, and nods. "And Terry maintained files on a number of his associates," I say, narrowing my eyes to make out the name on the tab attached to the folder. "Something he picked up during his time in Congress."

"Hmm," he says, turning the file toward me. "Does the name Randall Hemmings mean anything to you?" he asks.

"Not offhand," I answer. "But there's a whole drawer full of those." I slide open the lower section of the filing cabinet to illustrate my point. "I can hardly be expected to keep track of everyone."

Silvestri stares at the sea of folders. "I don't think I even *know* that many people."

"We'll look into it," Wolcott assures me. "Anything else missing?"

"Just the cash, as far as I can tell."

"Your husband normally kept cash in the safe?"

"He did. Terry always liked having some on hand. It was something he learned as a kid, from his grandfather," I explain. "The old man had lived through the Great Depression, and he was always a bit distrustful of banks after that. He would keep a quantity of cash in the home, you see. It was a lesson that Terry really took to heart. He always insisted on having a hundred thousand dollars readily available, for emergencies. It struck him as a nice round number."

I watch as Detective Wolcott places the envelope back in the safe before studying the folder in his hand. He pulls a plastic sleeve from inside his jacket, slips the folder into the sleeve, and seals it shut. "Yeah, plenty of zeros in a hundred grand." He glances at Silvestri, then at me, a look of curiosity brightening his eyes. "A nice round number indeed."

CHAPTER SIX

LAURA

THE TRAIL FEELS good under my feet.

For someone else in my circumstances, going for a run would be the last thing on their list, but without my daily five miles, I am unbearable. This run is for the sake of every living person I will encounter today.

The dappled light through the trees creates a slideshow effect as I move fluidly along the pathway. I put my hand up above my eyes in place of my forgotten sunglasses while my feet pound over the packed dirt.

The trails connecting our houses were one of Terry's many ideas for his Kingsland, his post-scandal-inspired utopia. When he scoped out the land, he purposely selected a plot inclusive of woods that he could put at the center of the development. He claimed that it was because of his affinity for the great outdoors, but he told Vicky that it was really because he wanted an inconspicuous way for residents of Kingsland to easily flee anyone unwanted who showed up on their doorstep. For the storied members of the community, that could include the paparazzi, the FBI, the IRS, or the INS, among others.

Thus far it hasn't been necessary as an escape route, but instead has become a commonly used place for the husbands of Kingsland to smoke pot away from their wives and kids.

Happily, today I'm alone on the main pathway.

Even though my chest is pounding with the exertion, I feel like I can breathe fully for the first time in twenty-four hours. I crank up the M.I.A. track and let the hard bass carry my feet forward. The repetitive motion sends charges of adrenaline and achiness through my body. I know that I can't run away from this forever, but I can at least eke out a few more forward-motion miles before I confront what will be lying in front of me, motionless.

The collective events of last night haven't exactly permeated my consciousness; instead they are circling about six feet above me like vultures that periodically swoop down to take a chunk out of me. When I finally connected by text with Monica, our exchange was jarring. Spencer is missing and she's waiting for the police to locate him. We've all tried to get one another on the phone, but our unimaginable circumstances have thrown all previous availability into a shitstorm of missed calls and straight to voicemails. Vicky was unrecognizable in her emotionally wrecked voicemail left for me when my phone was dead. Hearing it after returning from the hospital leveled me. This morning, she was barely audible when she told me that she needed me, and I nearly lost it on the phone. My sister's never "needed" anyone, no matter how bad things have gotten.

After the completely sleepless night, I called Dr. Mitali and she reported that Gil's vitals are still stable and nothing has changed, which she deems a good thing for the time being.

*"Because he's been medically induced, he won't be waking with-
out warning and you'll only be allowed in the room for short periods
of time. It is critical that you stay calm and positive in the presence
of your husband. Even though he is unconscious, his subconscious
is very active and sensitive. Assume that he can hear and sense everything."*

I promptly put on my running shoes to work out some of these
awful feelings rising in me and visit Vicky without drawing any attention to either of us. The neighborhood is alive with outdoor
events; the cul-de-sac turns into a barbecue crawl, kids are running
free, and the day drinking will no doubt embolden people to be more
invasive than normal. And beyond our neighbors, running the back
trail between our houses is more inconspicuous than pulling up in
front of her house, where I expect the press has begun to gather. If
not, it is only a matter of time. Now more than ever, I am thankful
for the wooded trail interconnecting the houses of Kingsland to pro-
tect me from prying eyes or wagging tongues.

I think about the closing sentiment of Dr. Mitali's update: *"We are
far from being out of the woods, but it is quite amazing that your husband
survived. That gunshot should have killed him."*

It is pretty amazing how he was able to cheat death. Especially
when his general attitude before being publicly canceled was that he
was immune to the fates of mere mortals. Even when far worse happened to us, he refused to admit defeat, publicly or privately.

I push off my heels and launch away from the thoughts as a sharp
cramp takes hold. I stop and double over, then catch sight of something gleaming in a sunny spot of the trail a few feet away. I look
around to make sure I'm still alone on the path and move quickly to
the object. As I catch a clearer view of it, a sick feeling passes through

me as I scoop up the object and shove it into the small zipper compartment on my wrist with my house keys.

I slow my pace as I move close to the back of an expensive property, owned by Vicky's next-door neighbor and the resident busybody, Milly, who has given refuge to my sister in my absence last night. She is on the phone, pacing the dramatic sweeping back deck. The sight of Milly irritates me, but I need to put aside my deep dislike for her and make my way to my sister, no matter what or who stands between us.

My Apple Watch notifies me that I've missed a call from a number that I don't recognize. I emerge from the trees, making a sprint across Milly's enormous backyard. I'm shielded from Vicky and Terry's property next door by six-foot topiary enclosures and an impressive collection of elm and willow trees spanning the perimeter of the yard. I pass the pool area and ascend the stone stairs leading to the deck. My throat tightens when I see Milly, who pulls the phone from her ear and opens her arms to me and guides me inside.

"Laura. Honey. You poor thing. I just heard about Gil. You must be a wreck," she says mournfully while giving me a judgmental once-over.

"Oh. You are sweaty, aren't you?" She hands me a hand towel from a drawer in her enormous kitchen island.

"I needed a quick run to clear my head." I feel defensive as I move the soft towel over my head, neck, and face.

"Completely understandable. This is all so overwhelming. And with everything that you've been through already." She tut-tuts.

Keep it together.

"You and Vicky have been through way too much already, and now this?" She shakes her head solemnly. I've never made my business even remotely hers. But it doesn't matter to Milly whether someone opens their life to her; she'll appropriate everyone's bad news shamelessly and become a self-appointed expert. She revels in being the authority on everyone in Kingsland, with plenty of artistic license and creative interpretations about details. She's liberal with nicknames and likening people in our community to famous people in place of any imagination. Vicky tolerates her much better than I do: I think she's a complete shrew who lives every day like she's auditioning for a *Real Housewives of Long Island* spin-off.

"Milly, I need to see my sister," I say emotionally.

She takes an overly pregnant pause to revel in the drama of the moment. "You just never know when life is going to happen," she says gravely while shaking her head from side to side dramatically.

What an absolute idiot.

"Vicky?" I call out to the cavernous house beyond the kitchen.

Milly isn't listening to me even a little bit; she's been refining her monologue for any willing listener all morning, no doubt.

"Oh, it is just awful. So unbelievable. I can't believe it. Terry is gone. And killed right in their house? I always said he was just like our very own JFK, and now . . . well, Roger always said I was psychic." I stare at her in disbelief as she shudders dramatically.

Milly's casting of Terry as Kingsland's JFK and my sister as Jacqueline Onassis is every bit as unoriginal and boring as she is, but she has persisted in her assumption that this is an amazing compliment.

Undeterred by my apparent disgust with her, she prattles on. "What is the world coming to? Who would do this? If we aren't safe here, where are we safe?" She wrings her hands.

"Milly, *my sister*?" I ask again, this time with an undeniable edge. I see her finally register my impatience.

"She's in the living room. I made her sit down and breathe."

I know Vicky does not need help breathing from anyone, least of all this silly bitch.

"Thanks," I force out as I walk to the front of the house, which is about a football field's distance from the kitchen. Vicky is sitting on the couch rigidly. She looks up and her eyes say everything.

"Laur," she says weakly but stays put. I move to her, sit down next to her, and pull her close to me.

"What the fuck happened?" I cry.

"Terry's dead," she says flatly, and then begins to cry harder and louder than I've ever heard.

I hold her and we sit and cry.

"What is going on with Gil?" she squeaks out.

"He's in a coma," I finally say.

"I can't make sense of any of this," she says quietly.

"Me neither."

"Is he going to pull through?" She squeezes my hand.

"They don't know yet. It's touch-and-go," I tell her.

"Well, if anyone can, it will be that tenacious asshole," she dead-pans through her tears.

I release a tense laugh and immediately regret it when I hear Milly move in the next room.

"I should have been here for you last night," I say, louder than intended.

"It's okay." Quietly she says, "I couldn't reach you."

"I'm here now. What are the police saying about Terry?" I ask her.

"Not much." She sniffles. "I don't think they know anything right now. They asked a lot of questions and my house has been crawling with police. They just left a few minutes ago. Have you spoken to them?"

"Just in the ER last night about Gil. But they want to question me today."

Vicky nods, her face in an expression of utter shock.

"He was just stumbling along the road, bleeding, until he collapsed."

"They found Gil by the side of the road?" she asks, horrified.

"Yes. I'm shocked."

"It doesn't make any sense. Have you spoken to Monica?" Her eyes meet mine.

"Just over text. But I'd really like to talk to her," I say seriously.

"Me too. All I know is that they haven't found Spencer yet."

We hear Milly moving around in the kitchen, noisily opening and closing cabinets followed by complete silence every few minutes.

"Who would do this?" Vicky yells.

I place a heavy hand on her leg and squeeze. "I hate that you had to come here," I whisper. "You should have been at my house."

"She was the closest, and when I couldn't reach you . . ." She trails off and looks at her hands. "Laur, it was so horrible. Blood everywhere."

"I'm so sorry you had to see that."

We hear Milly humming to herself and doing something in the hallway closet, a few feet from us on the other side of the wall.

"Who do you think did this?" I look at my sister.

"I don't know. Terry had some enemies."

"Not as many as Gil." We lean into each other, and the weight of my sister on me takes away some of the horrible feeling in my head.

"Do you think *he* did this?" I ask her.

"Spencer?".

"It seems like it," I say. "Who else would it be?"

"But why?" she says. "Terry has been helping him. And why Gil?"

"I don't know. You know they've been acting really weird. Something has been going on," I say.

"Poor Monica. I hope she's okay." She stands and catches my eye. "You should get to Gil." I stand up and accept her hug.

"I want to be here, to help you. I hate that I have to go to the hospital."

"Don't worry about me. I can handle this," she says stoically.

"You should be at my house. We need to stay close right now. Please come over as soon as you can." We both glance at each other, expecting Milly might pop in and object.

"I will. I just want to stay close to the house for a little longer. God knows how long it will be a crime scene, but I want to see if I can grab some more of my things first."

I take hold of her hand again. "I have anything and everything you could possibly need at my house, sis. Just come with me now." I feel a sense of desperation overtake me.

She hugs me hard. "Soon. I'll come to the house or the hospital, wherever you are, as soon as I can. Promise."

"Okay."

Vicky whispers into my ear, "I love you."

I squeeze her hard. "Love you more."

⫶

Once I leave Milly's property, I sprint through the woods, my mind wild. When I near my house, I see a car that I don't recognize pulling into the driveway and my heart two-steps. I watched the serious-faced pair emerge from their car and approach them from behind as they make their way to my front door. I muster a smile and brace myself for the worst.

CHAPTER SEVEN

WOLCOTT

THE SMILE'S NOT quite right.

In our line of work, this happens more often than not. People shellac all sorts of expressions onto their faces, hoping to lead our assumptions in one direction or another. And smiles come in countless varieties, on all manner of people.

There's the husband greeting us at the front door, trying to convince us that the bruise on his wife's cheek is from that same pesky cabinet she keeps walking into. There's the woman who has no clue how the floodlights on her neighbor's garage—the same ones she'd filed a formal complaint with our department about only weeks before—came to have their electrical cords severed.

There are the smiles born of nervousness, on the faces of those just waiting to get caught. And there are the smiles born of arrogance, on the faces of those who assume they never will be. Occasionally, there's even genuine relief behind the smile; the person is glad to see us. But this isn't one of those occasions.

"Mrs. Mathers," I begin. "Did we catch you at an okay time?" She keeps the expression in place as she fidgets, hands moving from her hair to smooth the front of her jogging shorts. She shares the same sinewy frame and chestnut hair as her sister, and while her hazel eyes lack the brilliance of Victoria's, they suggest a similarly vigilant intelligence. The most glaring difference, at least at the moment, is Laura's open display of nervous energy.

"Um, yeah," she says. "Sorry, I just got back from a run." She checks her smartwatch, then looks between Silvestri and me. She appears flummoxed. "I assumed the hospital would phone me if anything changed. Is Gil okay?"

"Oh, I'm sorry," I clarify. "I'm Detective Wolcott, and this is my partner, Detective Silvestri. We're following up on the conversation you had with Officers Davis and Pedone. My partner and I are here to ask you a few questions."

"Oh." She shakes off her previous thought and reconsiders us. "Please, call me Laura. How can I help you, Detectives?"

"We were sorry to hear about the incident involving your husband," I say. "Do you have any idea what could have led to him being shot?"

"I wish I did." She takes a deliberate breath. "Gil had his poker game last night. He and a couple of the guys get together every week to play while my sister, our girlfriend, and I hold our book club. I knew they were wrapping up, because my sister's husband texts when they're finishing. Gil hadn't come home, and I was tired, so I texted him to tell him I was going to bed. I was lying there, annoyed, because I thought he was off getting drunk with the boys." She rolls her eyes unconsciously. "It felt like I had just gotten to sleep when I received the call about my husband." Her mouth tightens. "It was a blur after that. I rushed to the hospital, where I was with him all night, and just came home to take care of a few things before I go back today." She drops her head, appraising her outfit. "I know this probably seems strange, with what's happened." She self-consciously crosses her arms over her torso.

"Everyone has their own way of coping," says Silvestri. "Now, Laura, can you think of anyone who would want to harm your husband?"

"Not off the top of my head," she says, seemingly baffled. "I mean, the death threats had subsided. All of that was in the past. At least, I thought it was." Her tone is more question than answer, until she realizes the lack of context she's offered us. "Oh, I should explain, about the threats."

"We're familiar with your husband's situation," I say, before switching gears. "What was your sense of the dynamic between the poker partners? Had your husband discussed any issues he'd had with Mr. Barnes or Mr. Nichols as of late?"

She considers the question, her arms tensing across her abdomen. "Not that Gil mentioned to me," she answers.

"And are you familiar with a Randall Hemmings? Does that name ring any bells?"

The corners of her eyes crinkle as she considers the question. "I don't think so, no."

"Okay. Had you noticed anything strange with your husband's behavior recently?" asks Silvestri. "Maybe over the course of this past week, or yesterday in particular?"

"No more than usual," says Laura, a nervous laugh accompanying the comment.

"And there's no one you can think of that might have wished your husband dead?" I ask. "Anyone at all?"

"Detectives," she answers, her jaw tightening. "I can think of a million people who would have liked to see my husband dead. He wasn't very well liked. But no one in particular, who actually knew him in real life, comes to mind." Her voice quivers on the last sentence, and before I know it, tears are streaking her cheeks. I offer up a handkerchief, but she waves it away, opting instead to dry her eyes with the back of her wrist.

"I see." As I reach into my vest pocket, Silvestri pulls out his phone, excuses himself, and steps away to answer the incoming call. I produce my business card and hand it to her. "We'll leave you to take care of what you need to take care of, Laura. We may need you to come down to the station to speak with us some more. In the meantime, if there's anything we can do for you, or if you hear anything, please don't hesitate to call, okay?"

"Thank you, Detective." She sniffles, then palms the card and takes a last look at my partner and me before turning up the walkway toward her front porch.

I catch up to Silvestri, standing near the unmarked, just as he's hanging up and pocketing the phone. "What's up?" I ask.

"That was the station," he says, raising his eyebrows. "We just got the location of Spencer Nichols's Mustang."

CHAPTER EIGHT

VICTORIA

"VICKY, I'M FREAKING the fuck out." I catch Monica as she approaches me on the front porch of my neighbor's house, where I'm hiding out until I can escape to my sister's. I can always measure Mon's level of distress by how much of her accent is slipping out, and this current display strikes me as cause for concern. I put a finger to my lips before I wrap her in a tight hug. "What?" she whispers into my ear, a fissure in her voice.

"Milly," I say softly, hiking my thumb toward the door behind me. "She's got ears like a bat." I lend a comically ghoulish tone to my voice in an attempt to ease my friend's anxiety as well as my own. "She can hear you through the walls."

"You're not kidding." She half laughs.

Milly's a lady of leisure, with a husband who's a high-powered attorney, providing her with plenty of alone time to poke around in any old thing that might pique her curiosity. In this case, that thing happens to be a violent homicide on the other side of her fence. She's also not the type to be easily deterred, and if it's occurred to her that

I might be grappling with some ugly mixture of grief, anger, and angst, it certainly hasn't stopped her from sticking her surgically enhanced nose directly into my business.

She *has* been kind enough to let me weather the storm here—more grist for her self-generated rumor mill, I'm sure—and I've spent the last hour or so marveling at just how much space this wisp of a thing can take up once she gets going. In an almost awe-inspiring display of passive-aggressive territory marking that began the moment I'd entered the house, she pried the overnight bag I'd brought along out of my grasp before physically parking me on the sofa, commandeering my phone, and beginning to field the barrage of incoming calls.

Truthfully, I'm relieved to have her running interference. I'm having a hard enough time keeping it all together and can't imagine getting on the phone with any of the neighbors right now. I dread the very thought of the endless circle of verbal reassurances that would entail, never mind the news outlets that are trying to chase down the story of last night's disturbance. But missed calls will simply lead to more missed calls, so I'm happy to provide the busybody with somewhere to focus her energy.

I give Mon a squeeze before slipping out of the embrace, then take her hand and lead her into the house. We walk in on the end of a phone call, as Milly is saying, "We have no comment right now," curtly into the phone. She hangs up, sighs, and rolls her eyes. "These people," she huffs, in the tone of someone who hasn't expressly signed up for the job she's now complaining about having to perform. She takes notice of Mon and quickly shifts to a compassionate expression. "Oh, here to check in on our Vic?" she asks cloyingly. "How sweet."

"Hi, Milly." I can hear Mon strain to keep her tone pleasant and neutral. "Nice to see you again."

"You too, honey." Milly makes a big show of waving her off. "But don't mind me. Just here to help. Can I get you anything?"

"Um, water would be great," says Mon flatly. "Thanks."

"No problem," Milly says, crossing to the cabinet and retrieving three glasses. As she begins filling them from a pitcher, the phone in her pocket—my phone—rings, and she abandons the hydration station to answer the call. She sets off on a lap around the room, and I seize the opportunity to catch Mon's eye and nod toward the door to the back porch. With my neighbor absorbed in the phone call, we dart outside unnoticed.

As soon as I close the door behind me, she lets loose. "Good God." She muffles a scream. "I swear I was going to strangle her."

"I know," I say, rolling my eyes in commiseration. "But she's helping me out. I really can't face all of that right now."

"Oh, babe." Her tone softens, and she puts her arms around me again. "I know, I know." She pulls back and studies my face. "You holding it together okay?"

I nearly balk at the question but keep my expression steady. If anything, this line of inquiry should be happening the other way around. Of the three of us, Mon is the one who makes me the most nervous in terms of her ability to keep a level head through all this. Laura and I have discussed our concern for her privately.

Monica's always lacked confidence and a clear sense of how to assert herself, which has a history of manifesting itself in her relationships. It's how she came to marry that overbearing asshole husband of hers, and how she ultimately came to be standing here, on Milly's back porch, wondering over that missing husband as she consoles me over my murdered one.

She's way too deferential. Spencer's always walked all over her, simply because he could. He's made a show of encouraging her to speak up for herself, but I've always wondered if his fragile ego could handle it if she ever truly did. And I'm afraid she's going to default to the same dynamic with Laura and me. Ultimately, if we're going to make it through this, she'll have to learn to stand on her own.

"I'm okay," I say, as eager to believe the sentiment myself as I am to assure her. "How about you? Have you heard anything about Spence yet? Anything from the police?"

"No." I can feel her body vibrating. "The uncertainty is driving me nuts. I just need to know that they found him."

"I get it." I clasp her hands in mine and nod reassuringly. "There should be news any time now. I'm sure of it."

"I know." She mirrors my nodding. "I know you're right, Vic."

"Hey," I say, gently pivoting the conversation. "Any word from Laura?"

"Just texts. I know she's back and forth from the hospital, trying to take care of everything with Gil." She shakes her head. "I'm sure she'll be by when she can."

"Of course," I say. "I get it." And I feel that I do. I'm realizing the powerlessness and desperation involved in having to speculate over one's own fate. Of having to wonder if a man might wake up or not, and how either outcome can affect you in dramatically different ways. As tragic as my situation might be, at least it comes with the modest gift of certainty attached. I let go of her hands and set mine on her shoulders. "We're going to be okay," I promise her with a firm squeeze.

"We're going to be okay," she echoes back, nodding and summoning a tentative smile. "I love you, Vic."

"Love you too," I say.

CHAPTER NINE

SILVESTRI

"WHAT DO YOU make of this?" I ask.

We've pulled up to the spot where Spencer Nichols's Fastback sits, parked in front of the Porsche Cayenne that's just been ID'd as belonging to Gil Mathers. Both vehicles are tucked into a narrow clearance on the edge of a stretch of woods no more than half a mile outside Kingsland, set back from the highway and obscured from sight by a row of scraggly bushes. A trail runner passing through earlier spotted the vehicles and called the station to report them.

We cross the grass to the back of the Cayenne and come around to the driver's side, where I find the door set slightly open. I push it the rest of the way with my elbow and look in to find a zipped duffel bag sitting on the passenger-side floor. A couple of file folders identical to the one we found in Terry Barnes's safe lie on the passenger seat. As I lean in closer, I can make out the names "Spencer Nichols" and "Gil Mathers" on the tabs attached to the folders.

"Silvestri," I hear my partner say with some urgency. I snake my way back out of the Porsche and walk to the front of the Mustang, where Wolcott is standing over the corpse of Spencer Nichols. A Beretta nine millimeter lies a few feet from the dead man's hand. The body is rag-dolled across the dirt, the side of the neck messily punctured with a bullet hole. "Shit," says Wolcott, shaking his head as he pulls out his cell to call in the second homicide of our current shift.

⁂

By the time the team arrives, Wolcott and I have the core area of the scene secured. We've blocked off a space around the vicinity of the vehicles, where the photographer is busily snapping away. An examiner is making a cast of a shoeprint we found near the Mustang that appears to have been left by a smaller-size men's driving loafer. We've recovered a Smith & Wesson pistol that was flung under the Porsche near the left rear tire, as well as a corresponding .40-caliber shell casing from a spot in the brush several feet away and a nine-millimeter casing found in close proximity to the Mustang. I make a mental note to check the registration on the Smith & Wesson, suspecting that Gil Mathers will come up as the gun's owner.

Fisk, the ME, is standing near Nichols's body when she waves us over, the familiar neutral expression plastered on her face.

"Fiskers," I say, approaching her. "What sort of magic you conjuring today?"

"Prepare to be dazzled," she deadpans, adding abracadabra hands for good measure. "Gunshot wound."

"Yeah, we got that far, wiseass," I say. "Can you give us any idea how long the victim's not been with us?"

"Well," she begins. "Based on core temp and degree of rigor, I'd put time of death somewhere around eleven last night. Looks like he was killed right where he's lying, hit from the side."

"Okay," says Wolcott, jotting something down before pocketing his notepad. "Fisk, you're class all the way."

"Thanks, doll," she says, and turns to assess me. "Silvestri, you're looking very relaxed lately. It's making me nervous."

"Oh yeah," I say. "I've been seeing a dynamite acupuncturist. She's really getting me straightened out."

"Huh," she says. "So, you're paying money to get stabbed repeatedly. Okay." She shrugs and turns back to the corpse.

"Stay golden, Fisk," I say in parting.

My partner and I duck off to the side. "Silvestri," he says, "I gotta eat something. I'm operating on fumes over here."

"I'm with you on that. Let's get this shit checked into evidence and sent off for ballistics. Then we can run Barnes's and Nichols's cells over to Clarence," I say, referring to the phones we retrieved from the dead men. "Let him crack those open while we hit Gus's for some chow."

"That's the move, my guy."

⫴

"You sure you got enough microgreens on that salad, Jack LaLanne?"

We're sitting in the unmarked, in the lot outside our go-to deli with the dependably surly service we've come to know and expect. I've just finished texting my neighbor to ask her to look in on the dogs and have barely gotten the fork out of the bag by the time Wolcott starts giving me the business. "Look, pal," I respond. "Just because my idea of fine dining doesn't involve yelling into a clown's mouth to order . . ."

"Yeah, yeah," he says, unwrapping a sandwich and setting it on his lap. "So, let's get to spitballing. Thoughts?" he asks, before digging in.

"Okay," I start, taking a long swig of tea. We've been plowing straight through since responding to the call that brought us to Kingsland last night, and this blessed well of caffeine in my hand is proving to be clutch. "These guys made off with a hundred large in cash and a couple of files that Barnes was keeping on them. Was the whole thing premeditated, or did it turn sour in the moment?"

"Well," he says. "Seems they knew where Barnes kept the files, which makes me think they had it mapped out ahead of time."

"Makes sense," I say. "Okay, Nichols's time of death lines up pretty closely with Barnes's. And we're going to assume the slug they pulled out of Gil Mathers will match Nichols's nine mil. So, after the poker game, Nichols and Mathers kill Barnes, grab the money and the files from the safe, and drive to the rendezvous spot to divvy it up before going their separate ways?" I take a bite of salad.

"Right," he says. "Except something goes wrong. Do they turn on each other then and there, or was one of them planning to double-cross the other all along?"

"Good question," I say. "Once we get a look at those files, we may find ourselves some answers."

"That's right," he says, swallowing a bite of sandwich. "Now, here's what I'm curious about. Is taking the cash just, 'It's there, so why not'? These guys are planning to make a run for it, so the dough helps them move around without leaving a trail? Or was there legitimate money trouble somewhere along the way?"

"Nah, I don't see it," I reason. "I mean, I know these guys both got ousted from their gigs and all, but even so, people in that tax bracket have a tendency to land on their feet. I remember reading in the paper about the severance package that Galapagos gave Nichols when they booted him. A parachute that size catches plenty of air, know what I'm saying?"

"No doubt. I'm just throwing ideas around. Maybe one of 'em's got a mistress? A drug problem? Degenerate gambler? He's gotten himself in over his head and he's desperate?"

"Always a possibility," I say, closing the salad container and stashing it under the seat. "Whatever it is, I have a feeling the key to this whole riddle is going to be somewhere in those files. And let's not forget about this Hemmings character. He could figure into the mix somehow."

"Right," says Wolcott, shaking his head. "Let's just hope we don't have to dig any deeper into that drawer. I don't think the station's got enough manpower to work through the contents of that filing cabinet any time this year."

"You're not lying," I say, digging a fingernail between my teeth. "So, feelin' better, pal?"

"Like a new man," he says, keying the ignition. "Now, let's go break some bad news."

CHAPTER TEN

LAURA

I FEEL SHAKY from my conversation with the detectives. They apologized for bothering me while my husband was in a coma, and so quickly after Terry's murder, but I am skeptical of how genuine their sentiments really were. Their cavalier detachment reminded me of when the police spoke to Gil and me after the shooting. The contrast between the devastation of violence and tragedy and the mundane act of "doing their job" has left me deeply unsettled in both of my encounters with law enforcement. I can't ever help feeling like I've done something wrong.

Today, when I was having the initial conversation with Wolcott and Silvestri, the Beechers were uncharacteristically active on their front lawn for the conversation, those assholes. I glared at them until they ambled back into their house, where I'm sure they were watching through their curtains.

Through a haze of shock and exhaustion, I told the detectives what I could, which wasn't much, and that I needed to get to Gil in the ICU. When I thought they were satisfied with my recounting of the evening with Monica and Vicky, they kept digging. Asking the same sort of question but phrasing it differently. It was insulting, but they finally relented when I burst into frustrated tears. Thankfully, one of them got a call and they had to be somewhere else quickly.

I numbly floated from the detective ambush to the second check-in of the day with Dr. Mitali, which wasn't great. The swelling in Gil's brain is going down, but things are still very critical. I mentally strap myself into my life now. Hospitals and police stations and, very soon, the funeral home with Vicky.

The privacy curtain next to Gil's bed on the opposite side of where I'm sitting flutters with movement from the family who've just become our neighbors. An elderly man was wheeled in a few hours earlier and I've been listening to the sounds of his grown daughter getting settled in her new environment and her phone calls to her family members letting them know he is on death watch. Every time a nurse or doctor enters the space, she's up on her feet with questions. It has been only half a day for me, but I've already grown used to the sound of the machines keeping my husband and his suite mate alive and the various noises of the hospital around us.

I catch a glimpse of white Crocs, belonging to one of the ICU nurses, and a pair of patent leather women's loafers standing nearby. Their disembodied voices are speaking in hushed tones and I'm overcome with a feeling of indignation. We should be in a private room and no one is listening to me. Apparently, concierge medicine isn't an option at this hospital, but we can't move him to Manhattan, where private rooms are easier to secure on short notice.

"I didn't exactly have any notice that my husband was going to be shot in the head," I said angrily this morning to Amanda, the head of the hospital, who was unmoved by my mentioning my maiden name and the contributions to the cancer wing of the sister hospital on the Upper East Side.

"We'll do the best we can," Amanda informed me with little sympathy.

Gil's respirator brings me back to earth. I hit the call button just as the machine stops beeping.

"Hello?" a deep voice from beyond says.

"My husband's machine was beeping, but it stopped."

"We'll send someone in," the voice replies.

I hold his hand and apply pressure. "Gil, give me a sign that you can hear me." I lighten my grip to give him a chance to make any small gesture of acknowledgment, but there is no response. The only sign of life in him is the rise and fall of his chest in step with the respirator.

Gil is too tall for the standard hospital bed they've got him in. His six-five frame and size-fourteen feet are practically hanging off the end of the bed, and he looks even bigger than usual in spite of his weakened condition. His head is bandaged and his hair has been shaved and the dark stitches look crude against his exposed scalp. His skin, usually glowing from monthly facials, is sallow, and his straight perma-white teeth are concealed by his slack mouth. Without animation he is so much dimmer. I feel sick seeing him like this.

"Remember when we first met?" I say in his ear, hoping Dr. Mitali's urging that I talk to him about happier times will be effective. I laugh. I close my eyes and feel the warmth of Gil's enormous hand in mine, his steady pulse lulling me into the memory.

I was on a date with Dan Marxton, of the Birmingham megastore Marxtons. He was trying to impress me with front-row seats to see the hugely popular motivational speaker and bestselling author Gil Mathers. "I've never heard of him," I'd told Dan.

He'd been disappointed. "The tickets were five grand."

I'd shrugged, which incensed him.

The guy on the other side of me had leaned in close and offered, "This guy makes Tony Robbins look like a pussy."

I was ready to leave before the first strains of "The Final Countdown" blasted through speakers, but we were front and center and the exits became miles away as the smoke machines at the base of the stage turned from dramatic to blinding. Before I could get my bearings to make a move, two thousand people were on their feet dancing, fist pumping, and high-fiving. It was my fucking nightmare.

Surprisingly, Gil's opening monologue was entertaining, something like a TED Talk given by a fully grown high school bully. This was followed by a lot of foreplay for the next portion of the surreal evening, endlessly teased with footage of past performances shown on a dozen loud 360-degree screens while Gil occasionally disappeared offstage. I watched clip after emotional clip of Gil summoning a complete stranger right from the audience and getting them to reveal something terrible and secretive about themselves in front of thousands of spectators in what seemed to be a series of mash-up interrogative tactics learned from TV detectives and psychologists. The technique as explained in the four-color sheet on my chair was Gil's trademarked "vulnerability demolition" and was required to get to the next level of **YOU 4.0**. This, apparently, was where money, power, and underwear models looking for boyfriends waited.

From the impatient foot stomping and hooting the longer we were made to wait, it was clear that some audience members' public humiliation was the intended main event. I would eventually become well versed in Gil's fans' sycophantic love for the emotional breakdown of someone from the audience, reducing them to nothing more than a pile of tears and sweat. But that night, as a "Gil Mathers Experience" virgin, I had no idea what I was in for.

I had absolutely no interest in watching a perfect stranger being broken down and/or revived. And I was perfectly happy with who I was, aside from my choice in date. So, when the name Gil called to the stage was mine and Dan Marxton leaned over to me and said, "I pulled some strings. I know you've been through a lot and could really use this," I glared at him before jumping out of my chair and beelining for the closest exit at warp speed.

A strong hand on my arm rerouted me up the side stairs of the stage and I couldn't understand how I'd gotten from the terrible Point A to the even worse Point B. I was under a spotlight, surrounded by applause and six angles of myself on the jumbotron. Gil excitedly paced up and down the periphery of the stage like a caged animal waiting for its dinner.

I'm sure some of the people in the audience recognized me when I surrendered into the chair across from his. Vicky's and my pictures had been everywhere because of the massive speculation following our father's death under "mysterious circumstances" (a more salable headline than death by jumping). We were trying to live outside the vortex of tabloid journalism and rampant online conspiracy theories, each one more absurd than the one before it. It all stoked the fire of unending lawsuits against my father's financial firm, which would dog our family for years after he was dead and buried, making it impossible to step outside our front doors without cameras and invasive questions in our faces.

Gil's whole demeanor from the start of this circus softened. As this giant of a man sat across from me, his ruggedly handsome and open face urging me to thaw, I let go. In the presence of each other, neither of us could keep a grip on our self-protective masks. Inexplicably,

I lost all ability to hide my feelings. It was as terrifying as it was exhilarating. Under hot, glaring lights, Gil took my hand and, uncharacteristically, I accepted it. There was a shocking electrical current surging between us. Gil asked me if I was ready to stop saying no. And to my great surprise, my defensiveness began to release. The opposite effect of what I expected from being in front of hundreds of strangers was happening. I was exhausted and couldn't think of any more reasons to fight. I'd been teetering on the edge of losing control of my emotions for months and living in an icy limbo between "no comment" and "go fuck yourself."

Gil later told me that he'd also lost all grasp on his earlier ringmaster persona and couldn't muster anything beyond his actual self. I disarmed him, and he did the same for me.

The room was transfixed as we launched into a heartfelt conversation. I finally opened up about the death of our father and I was able to set the record straight; he had not been murdered by political enemies or a shadowy terrorist organization, or faked his own death to evade prosecution, or been pressured to kill himself by the families of his clients who'd met similar fates. He'd taken his own life in a moment of fearful weakness after a life of scandal and meteoric highs and lows of financial success and loss. The constant media glare had slowly worn away Vicky's and my quality of life. I wasn't asking for sympathy, just some privacy to grieve and rebuild.

Gil listened. He didn't break me down or build me up; he let me open up and supported everything I was saying, but he let the audience hear me, not him. The video footage from the event went viral and pushed Gil into the tens-of-millions-of-views club. It remains his most successful marketing footage and gained him his biggest untapped audience, and the most coveted customer base, women between the ages of thirty-five and sixty-five.

Turned out, Gil did his best work unscripted and gentler. Ever the shrewd businessman, Gil made sure not to let me go when he saw what a great team we made. We wouldn't be apart after that night, for a long time.

He could blame everyone else but himself until he was blue in the face, but his authentic self was digitally etched for anyone with a search engine.

∿

"How are you holding up?" a sweet-faced nurse asks as she enters the room.

"His machine made some noises I haven't heard before," I say coolly.

"I'll take a look. It could be an increase in heart rate. He's probably dreaming," she muses.

I don't respond, but this sounds medically suspect to me. I make a note to complain about the folklore-based medical care here.

"I'm going to freshen his IV."

I let go of his hand and fish out a Kleenex from the box next to his bed. The nurse inspects the medical tape secured to the top of his palm and swaps out the hanging bag of dwindling fluid.

I smile appreciatively and stand to stretch my legs.

She looks at his face for a minute. "I keep trying to place him . . . Is he an actor?" She cocks her head. I clock her name tag. Lila.

"No," I reply, not anywhere near ready to enter into a conversation about why my husband looks familiar. Lila looks young enough to not be able to place him from the height of his career and downfall, but definitely old enough that she has read *In Touch* in a nail salon.

"Huh. He looks so familiar. Maybe he just has one of those faces."

"Yeah. He gets that a lot," I mutter.

"Okay, he's all set. I changed out his catheter earlier, so he should be good to go for a few hours."

"Thank you so much," I muster.

"Everything okay here otherwise?" she asks, slightly solicitously, and I wonder if my complaining this morning has trickled down.

"We still need a larger bed," I say without any concealment of frustration.

"Oh. That could be tough; I don't know if we have anything bigger." She laughs nervously.

"Just, please let me know if you hear anything about the private room becoming available," I say, exasperated with the conversation.

"Sure. That really isn't my department, but I'll ask." She heads out of the room.

I stew in my anger and check my phone for any new messages and see that I've missed a call from Monica. My chest tightens. Before I can key in my code, she's calling me.

"Monica," I say abruptly. "I'm a little busy right now."

"I'm here at the hospital, Laur, but they said that no non–family members are allowed into the ICU."

"You're here?" I ask her.

She pauses for a half beat. "I-I-I'm sorry. I didn't think it through. I just got into my car and drove. I thought you might need some moral support."

"You really didn't need to do that," I say.

"How is he?"

"He's alive." I leave that hanging. "Have they found Spencer yet?" I ask.

"Not yet." She's quiet and I hear her sniffle. "I'm just really freaked out. Everything is so fucked up."

"Where are you?" I ask.

"The family pavilion. I'm sitting outside."

"I'll be down in a few minutes." I disconnect.

I take Gil's hand in mine and sigh heavily. "Don't you go anywhere."

CHAPTER ELEVEN

MONICA

As I wait for Laura, I shakily sip iced green tea and try to read my book. *Control what consumes you, or become consumed.* My heart races with the worry and dread persisting inside me.

My mind lands on Laura's husband lying in intensive care. The image is hard to conjure given how larger than life he is. Years before I became his neighbor and a member of his inner circle, I used to watch his YouTube videos daily and attend every one of his events that I could afford. Gil is as physically oversize as his personality is, but you can't really get the full effect of how tall and intimidating he is until you see him in real life. On-screen he has the looks of someone who'd probably been told that they should go into Hollywood, right down to a beauty mark and a dimpled chin. I wasn't prepared for what a powerful presence he was. I had no idea just how much influence he would have on the course of my life until I met him in person.

"Monica." Laura's voice snaps me into the present. She takes a seat and looks at me miserably. Even in this bleak setting, Laura is glowing and head-turning with her perfectly appointed clothing and hair. Like her sister, Vicky, Laura is ageless, with an utterly symmetrical face populated by huge light eyes, perfectly pouty lips, gleaming skin, and the kind of hair that seems possible only in shampoo commercials. If she is nipped or tucked, her money has assured that you'd never be able to prove it.

Laura places her Birkin bag on the table and begins to absently drum her perfectly polished cantaloupe fingernails on the table, her enormous emerald-cut diamond ring catching the sun with every round of ring finger rising and falling on the tabletop.

"I was worried about you." I swallow hard. "And Gil. I wanted to see how you were both doing,"

"He's alive," she says quietly.

"Laura. I'm so sorry. I don't know what to say."

She says nothing and I feel my anxiety kicking in.

"Tell me what I can do to help," I offer.

"There's nothing that can be done," she whispers, defeated.

"I know things are horribly out of control right now, and whatever our husbands' issues with each other are—"

"Monica. Don't," she says sternly.

I look down at the ground.

She leans in so close that I can smell the coffee on her breath. "You promised you were going to end things with him," Laura says carefully.

"I know, I really tried." I put my face in my hands.

"People are watching us."

"Sorry."

"I need you to keep it together, so that I can keep it together. And we both really need to be strong for Vicky."

"Yes. You are absolutely right."

She stands and adjusts her clothes and hair. "Monica."

I look up at her. "What?"

"When Spencer turns up, things are going to get ugly. Are you ready for that?"

"Yes," I say. People at other tables have started to look over at us.

"If it turns out that Spencer did this, you are going to have to pick a side," Laura says, more loudly than I'm comfortable with. "I have to get back to Gil." She pecks my cheek and turns to leave.

I feel stung as I watch her make it halfway across the courtyard before doubling back.

"I almost forgot. You dropped this," she says cryptically as she pulls something out of her bag. My stomach lurches as she hands me a small white square.

I unwrap the package under the table and reveal a familiar dangly earring. I reflexively reach up to my right ear, which holds an identical earring, and then my left, which is naked of its mate.

My eyes meet hers and I shiver at the darkness in them.

"You need to be more careful."

CHAPTER TWELVE

WOLCOTT

"You know that show *Prognosis?*"

Silvestri and I are sitting in the unmarked, parked on the street out front of the Nicholses' residence. There's no sign of Monica Nichols, and her phone has gone straight to voicemail. We're waiting on a call from our IT guy, as well as the Nest doorbell footage from around the time of the murders that the Nicholses' across-the-street neighbor has promised to email us after our conversation minutes ago. My partner and I hang tight in the meantime in the hopes that Monica returns home soon. Silvestri's thumbing away on his phone, getting a jump on some research relevant to our case.

"Oh yeah." I nod. "That's the medical drama that always cleans up at the Emmys, right? I've caught a couple episodes when Abby's been watching."

"Well." He reads his phone screen. "Our man Randall Hemmings is a producer on the show."

"That right?" I say. "What else you got on this guy?"

"Uh, he has a few smaller credits. Couple indie films, a series that ran one season. *Prognosis* is his biggest project by far."

"I mean, that thing's been running forever. He's gotta be set up pretty nicely at this point."

"Sure." Silvestri nods.

"Any personal background?" I ask.

"Hmm." He squints as he pulls up text on the screen. "Looks like he grew up on the North Shore. Local boy made good."

"Well, *stayed* good." I chuckle. "A Gold Coaster, then. Maybe he came up with Barnes. Family friends and so forth."

"Right." He scrolls a bit, following the stream of information. "Here's a bunch of red-carpet shots. Couple photos of him at some lawn party, probably raising money for endangered ocelots or something. He's dressed like the Man with the Yellow Hat, from the Curious George books." Silvestri gives the screen a series of taps. "When I type in his name along with Terry Barnes's, nothing comes up."

"Hmm," I say, thumbing through my own phone. "We'll poke around and see what else we can find." I pull up Laura Mathers's Instagram account and begin to scroll through her feed. Every second or third post is a shot from the ladies' weekly book club meeting and features the three women in an elegant grouping, holding up a copy of that week's selection. As promised, *The Rule of Three* is the latest featured title.

"What do you got there?" asks Silvestri, leaning toward me to peek at the screen.

"Book club," I explain, angling my phone toward him. "One photo every week, consistently, posted sometime between ten thirty and eleven P.M. that night, with a thumbs-up or thumbs-down emoji from each of the women for that particular book. This last one was posted right at eleven P.M." I close the app and replace the phone in my pocket.

"Right around the time these guys were getting plugged."

"Looks like that part of the story checks out," I agree.

My partner's phone dings, and his eyes brighten as he consults the screen. "Here we go," he says, and opens the incoming email from the neighbor. We'd been sitting out here a short while ago, Silvestri trying and failing to get Monica Nichols on the phone, when I noticed the doorbell camera on the house across the street. We approached the home and ventured a knock on the door, and were greeted by a very enthusiastic armchair detective who was more than happy to help when we mentioned our investigation. She's forwarded us three clips from the night before.

He clicks on the first link in the email, and a video pops up; time coded 10:21 P.M., the sequence shows a man walking tipsily past the front yard of the home, prompting the motion-activated software to record the footage. He clutches an open bottle of beer in one hand and a bunch of bottle rockets in the other. In the background, Monica Nichols's Jaguar sits in the driveway of her home while light illuminates the front porch and emanates from a handful of windows on the first floor.

"And this is about ten minutes before Barnes texted his wife?" asks Silvestri.

I check my notes to confirm. "Uh-huh." We watch as the drunk fellow wanders out of the frame and the video cuts off. My partner clicks on the next link, and a second clip begins playing. This one is time coded 10:37 P.M. and shows a group of kids boisterously shoving one another as they pass in front of the house. In the background, the Jaguar remains parked in the driveway, and the same lights are on as in the previous video.

As that clip ends, we click on the final link. This one—at 10:52 P.M.—shows an older couple walking hand in hand in front of the home. The details as they pertain to the Nicholses' residence remain unchanged. As the footage cuts off, Silvestri turns to me.

"Looks pretty tame to me," he says. I'm nodding in agreement when I catch sight of the familiar Jaguar in our rearview, pulling into the driveway. Silvestri notices and swivels his head.

"Ah shit," he says, returning the phone to his pocket. He gives me a look. "You ready, pal?"

I feel sourness ooze through my stomach. "Let's get this over with," I say, climbing out of the car and approaching the driveway.

Monica Nichols steps from the Jag and freezes as she sees us. "Detectives," she says in a strangled voice as she sets both hands atop the open door and leans into it for support. A look of panic crosses her face, and she seems desperate in her unease. As we approach, she appears to buckle, and we hurry to help steady her. She looks at my partner, then me, and falls back into the car seat.

"Mrs. Nichols," I begin, but she beats me to it.

"You found Spence, didn't you?"

I take a breath, making sure to maintain steady eye contact. "I'm sorry to have to tell you that we found your husband earlier today. He'd been shot dead last night."

Her body appears to uncoil as my words sink in. "God, I knew it. I just *knew* it." There's a trace of relief in her voice as she speaks out loud the thoughts that she must have been sitting on, wrestling with, and dreading since her husband's disappearance. Just as quickly, her eyes well up, and her voice cracks. "He killed himself?" Her lips quiver as she has to push out the next thought. "*Shot* himself?"

"Mrs. Nichols," offers Silvestri. "We're looking into that as we speak. But we have reason to believe that he was killed by another individual."

"What?" she spits, shaking her head. "By who? Where did you find him?"

"Your husband's body was discovered out near Hopewell's Woods," I explain. "We're investigating—"

"Wait, what?!" She squeezes tears through a face crumpled in angry disbelief. "Isn't that . . . that's where they found Gil wandering around in the road." She stares at the ground, her expression showing confusion, dread, and rage.

"We're looking into Mr. Mathers's involvement in the events of the evening," I assure her.

She hits me with an icy glare. "Gil. Fucking. Mathers." The volume and intensity of her voice climb as she punches each word. She looks from me to my partner and back again, her eyes narrowing. "If that son of a bitch ever wakes up, he's going to answer for what he's done."

CHAPTER THIRTEEN

VICTORIA

THE CIRCUS IS officially in town.

Fuck.

Members of the press have begun camping out in front of my house, drawn to the recently confirmed tragedy like hyenas to the carcass of a felled antelope. News vans line the street, and reporters mill around, eyes glued to my front door, eager to pounce on any sign of the grieving widow. I've given them nothing to slake their thirst, which has served to work them up into even more of a lather. They still haven't figured out that I'm not at home.

As if that weren't enough, I just got a call from a deeply shaken Monica letting me know that those detectives showed up at her house to inform her that they'd discovered Spencer, shot dead on the side of the road, presumably by Gil. What an ugly, senseless tragedy this whole mess is turning out to be.

And don't even get me going on Milly. When I'd endured as much of her performative empathy as I could stomach without decking her, I managed to coax my cell from her grasp and convinced her to let me escape to her spare room to get the hell away from the fray and give myself a minute to breathe.

My plea served only to speed her in the direction of her own phone. I can hear her now through the closed door, squawking away to the neighbors, using her proximity to me as social currency while humblebragging about her deep well of altruism. Once I've had a minute to get my head together, I'll sneak out the back and head to Laura's place to lie low until mine is no longer a reporter-infested crime scene.

Sadly, this is not my first fiasco. One of the things about growing up in a prominent, recognizable family is that you get plenty of practice deflecting the accompanying attention, criticism, and gossip—both founded and otherwise. Enduring that particular way of life imbues you with a very specific resilience—a suit of armor, if you will. A big part of the bond that Laura and I share comes from having grown up in such a family—and having managed to survive the experience reasonably intact.

It's a double-edged sword, of course. The price one pays for becoming inured to the outside world is a certain desensitization; a hardening; a conditioned coldness. It becomes just a part of the cycle. And while it made our childhoods that much more challenging, it allowed the scandal involving our father that came later on to feel much less earth-shattering. By the time the horrific accusations—and speculations of suicide—began dogging our family, my sister and I had developed a very tough shell and had each other to lean on.

Years later, when my niece, Libby, was killed so senselessly, Laura and I turned to each other once again. I imagine the pain of losing a child has the potential to break anyone—losing my *niece* nearly broke me, Lord knows—and I've tried my best to be a rock for my sister. Terry and I were able to convince her and Gil to stay here with us in Kingsland despite a strong pull on her part to start over away from this place, and I take a small measure of comfort in knowing that the close proximity has at least helped with the healing that she continues to experience.

Most of the heat that my husband caught during his days in Congress came from the anti-gun crowd, who were incensed that he'd taken a position backing the Second Amendment. The lion's share of vitriol that's come his way over the years has tended to be tied to that issue above all others. I don't concern myself with the Twitters and the Instagrams, but social media being what it is, I can only guess at the comments coming out of the faceless, anonymous army of thumbs right now.

Apparently, I haven't escaped the virtual conversation unscathed either. Milly, who spends much of her days mindlessly scrolling, couldn't resist dropping this hot coal in my lap earlier; when the news of Terry's murder first hit online, some commenter referred to me as a "black widow," bringing up my father's tragic death to reinforce the label. Which doesn't even make any fucking sense. As if I'd had anything to do with his demise. Or that there was some component of incest at play. Jesus. Idiots. I'm reminded again of why I've attempted to live my life free of that toxicity.

With the police having turned up Spencer, I'm trying desperately to steel myself against this whole mess by remembering that there will be a way out for us. I have to believe that the detectives investigating the case will be able to make sense of it all; will be able to put the details together in a way that explains the violence, the ugliness, the loss. They'll map out the greed and outsize egos and come up with an explanation of how it led these men to turn on one another, to betray one another in the name of self-interest. It will allow us, the wives and families of these men, to achieve some semblance of closure after such a harrowing ordeal.

I can't say I envy Monica at the moment. Once news breaks of Spencer's murder, speculation will fly far and wide, stirring up a whole new round of pain for my friend. Selfishly, I'm relieved to be on the more forgiving end of all this. Spencer Nichols was an almost universally reviled figure not that long ago, and while I believe that people tend to have short memories, I can't imagine that she'll get through this unscathed.

Mon's already had to contend with some sizable trauma in her life, but she doesn't come from the world that Laura and I do. She hasn't had that same toughness hammered into her. If anything, her shitbag husband has been tearing her down under the guise of building her up throughout their marriage. I need to be there for Mon, and I need to bring Laura back around. I can sense the tension fraying the bond between the two of them, and it won't do any good for me to keep my own house in order if my friend's is burning to the ground right in front of me.

These coming days are going to be a real test. And if I know anything from personal experience, it's that Monica Nichols's life is about to be turned upside down.

She has no idea what she's in for.

CHAPTER FOURTEEN

SILVESTRI

"LOOK AT THESE smooth criminals."

Wolcott and I have returned to the station, and as we approach our desks we find Clarence, our IT guy, leaning casually against mine. He's holding the phones we recovered from the dead men, and as he hands them to me, I surprise him with a brown paper bag.

"What's this?" he asks, intrigued.

"We hit Gus's for lunch," I explain. "Grabbed you the Rosemary Tun-ey."

"Ah, you guys are legends," he says, snapping his fingers with a flourish. "Thank you."

"Think nothing of it," offers Wolcott. "Silvestri and I appreciate your particular artistic flair."

"You flatter me," he says, waving off the compliment. "And I got you covered. Phones are both open. Turned off password protection, so you can check texts, emails, whatever. Good to go."

"Right on," I say.

"Couple things jumped out at me," he says, nodding first toward

Nichols's phone. "When I got into that one, there was a GPS tracking app pulled up." His face has taken on a look of amused curiosity.

I hit the button on the side and consult the screen. "What the fuck?" I say as I stare at the icon on the map.

Wolcott leans in to get a look. "Wait, is that the impound lot?" he asks incredulously.

"Bingo," answers Clarence. "I went over there to check it out. The GPS is tracking that gorgeous old Mustang that got hauled in earlier today."

I look from Clarence to my partner. "What the hell was Nichols doing tracking his own car?" I ponder.

"Right," he follows, stroking his chin. "And if Nichols didn't drive it to that clearing last night, then who did?"

"Good question." I return my attention to Clarence. "You mentioned a *couple* of things that jumped out at you?"

"Yeah," he answers. "So, that other phone you got?" He eyes the one we collected off Terry Barnes. "There's a tracking app on there as well."

"Hmm," I say, turning it over in my hand. "Same type?"

"Nah." Clarence shakes his head. "It's a more sophisticated setup. And whoever that phone belonged to? Looks like they were keeping themselves *very* busy."

⊹⊹⊹

"Think I got something," announces Wolcott.

Following a brief tutorial on how to navigate the tracking apps on the phones, Clarence took off, leaving my partner and me to examine both devices. I'm actively thumbing through Nichols's as my partner handles Barnes's.

"What is it?" I ask, noticing Wolcott's expression brighten.

"Well, it seems like Terry was keeping tabs on half the neighborhood. And he uses some sort of code or abbreviation for each individual. But I think I've isolated the wives."

"Oh yeah?" I drag my seat around the side of my desk and set it next to his, to get a better look at what he's studying.

"Check this out. I've got 'V,' 'SIL,' and 'Cowgirl.' Those sounding about right to you?"

"'SIL'?" I ask.

"Sister-in-law, no?"

"Right. So, you figure he's tracking the cars, same as Nichols?"

"That's the odd part," he says, brow creasing. "I'm looking at Victoria's right now." He points to the dot on the screen. "This has her inside the neighbor's house currently."

"Weird."

"I know, man." He gives the screen a series of taps, and a line tracing a route on a map appears. "Okay, so here's Laura Mathers earlier today. You see how the path cuts behind the house, then over here through a backyard? Must have been when she was out running." He shakes his head, a sour look on his face. "This is definitely not a tracker on a vehicle."

"What the . . . ?" I'm hit with a queasy feeling. "Jesus. Was he microchipping them?!"

"Or he's got trackers in their clothing or something," he offers with a shrug.

"Pretty ghoulish, any way you slice it." I'm attempting to shake off the unease when a thought occurs to me. "Wait, though. If we can go back and check their movements—"

"We can check their alibis," he says, already digging around in the app.

He brings up the trackers one at a time on all three of the women and checks their whereabouts around the time of the murders. The tech confirms their stories, with Monica Nichols staying put in her home the entire night, and the sisters leaving to head to their respective homes right around the time they initially claimed.

"Well, worth a shot." He sighs before dropping the phone on his desk. He cracks his knuckles, then grabs the stack of files from Terry's safe that we've checked out of evidence and begins scouring the contents as I pick up Spencer Nichols's phone and search his text history. "Maybe *you'll* have better luck," he says.

"Nothing jumpin' so far," I answer. "Last text was the one he sent off to the wife. Makes more sense now, with the missing car."

"Right." He nods absently, perusing the contents of Randall Hemmings's file. "So, you figure Mathers had an accomplice? Someone stole the car to lure Nichols out to the woods, knowing he'd be able to track it with the GPS? Planned to ambush him, and it went south?"

"Yeah." I consider. "Sounds feasible. Turning anything up in those files?"

"The one on Nichols reads like a greatest hits collection. Defrauding investors, getting ousted from his own company. There's something in there that alludes to insider trading as well. And it looks like Barnes was a thorough fellow. Went to the trouble of putting together a bio on the wife while he was at it."

"Huh. She an aspiring criminal too?"

"No." He chuckles. "Seems like a solid citizen. Even ran a charitable organization for a time."

"Well," I say. "Glad there are *some* upstanding folks around that place." I nod to the collection of documents in front of my partner. "What about the Hemmings folder?"

"Just finishing up. Looks like he and Barnes did come up together. There's some copies of court records from Hemmings's juvie file.

Destruction of property, a DUI. There's also a record of a bank transfer between the two. Recently."

"Hmm," I say. "Hemmings hasn't returned your call yet, has he?"

Wolcott shakes his head.

"Let me give him a nudge." I set down Nichols's cell phone, then pick up mine and dial it. After a few rings, I hear a voice on the other end.

"Hello?"

"Randall Hemmings?" I say.

"Who's this?" The voice is thick with impatience.

"Mr. Hemmings, this is Detective Dennis Silvestri of the Stony Brook Police Department. I'm following up on a call my partner made to you earlier today."

"Oh, right. Yeah, been a bear of a day."

"I hear you on that. Listen, I'm reaching out to ask you a couple of questions about Terry Barnes."

There's a significant pause before he speaks again. *"Yeah, I just heard about Terry on the news. I grew up with the guy. It's a real shame."*

"Sure is," I say, motioning to Wolcott to slide the folder my way. "Say, Mr. Hemmings. Were you aware that Mr. Barnes kept a file on you?"

I hear a sharp exhale, followed by a snort. *"Yeah, Terry would keep a file on his own mother. And, in fact, might. What's mine say?"*

"You don't seem very surprised by this," I observe.

"Look," he says. *"I've known Terry for a long time. He's always operated a certain way, and as far as I can tell, his congressional run did nothing to quell either his paranoia or his opportunistic streak. If anything, it may have served to put an even finer point on both."*

"I see. Well, the file I'm looking at here lists some of your youthful transgressions, but the thing that's piquing my interest is a payment of fifty grand. Money you transferred to Mr. Barnes's account, dated just a few weeks ago."

"Oh that," he says, sounding relieved. *"Terry was a silent investor on a small picture I was producing. I told him I could double his money, and I did."*

"I see. And what was the name of this project?"

"The Egret, it's called. A little indie I had a piece of. Picked it up at Sundance."

"Uh-huh." I stall as I check IMDb to confirm the story. "Yeah, the title sounds familiar. I'll have to check it out."

"Detective." I hear irritation seeping back into his tone. *"I'm terribly sorry about Terry, and I don't mean to be rude, but I need to run to a meeting. Is there anything else I can help you with?"*

"There sure is," I say. "Can you account for your whereabouts around eleven P.M. last night?"

"Yeah." Now he just sounds bored. *"I was in New York, for a film festival. I was winding down afterward, enjoying some adult entertainment."* He pauses for dramatic effect. *"Things went late."*

"Right. And is there anyone who can confirm that?"

"I, uh, don't usually bother with names." He chuckles. *"Know what I mean, slick?"*

"I see," I mutter, making no attempt to hide my distaste. "Oh, one more thing, Mr. Hemmings: What size shoe do you wear?"

There's a stretch of dead air before he answers in a decidedly unamused tone. *"Nine,"* he grumbles. *"Why do you ask?"*

"Devil's in the details. We'll be in touch," I say before ending the call.

Wolcott's begun digging through the file on Gil Mathers, and he continues reading as he addresses me. "What was the story there?"

"Hemmings says Terry Barnes invested in a picture he produced.

He also claims to have been in the city last night, hanging out after a film screening. He did, however, cop to wearing a size-nine shoe."

"Hmm," he says, looking up from the paperwork in front of him. "Same size as that print from the crime scene. That's interesting."

"Could be something." I shrug.

"Could be," he agrees, then returns his attention to the contents of the file. He begins reading again before suddenly flinching, his face tightening up.

"What'd you find?" I ask.

"Oh man. You remember that school shooting that happened out here a few years back?"

"Windstone Elementary. Of course." The story had made national news at the time and had led to a push for stricter gun-control laws before eventually cycling out of the headlines and largely fading from public consciousness. "What about it?"

He looks at me gravely. "Gil and Laura Mathers lost their daughter in the shooting."

"Oh man." I feel my stomach turn in on itself. "Jesus."

He flips over the sheet of paper and begins reading the document underneath it. "Oh shit," he says, shaking his head. "This just gets worse."

"What is it now?"

He makes a face as if he's just caught a whiff of something foul. "Seems our man Gil has an unnatural taste for young women."

"Oh yeah," I say. "That's what brought him down. That and the drugs." I angle my head to get a better look at what my partner's reading. "You've seen the video, right?"

"No, no, no," he says. "I'm not talking about that." He removes the sheet of paper from the file, sets it on the desk, and turns it toward me, tapping on the spot he's referring to. As I read, a chill trills along the length of my vertebrae. The document details an out-of-court settlement that Gil Mathers's legal team negotiated with a young woman—sixteen at the time the complaint was filed—who accused Gil of sexual assault. The whole thing seems to have been handled discreetly and swept under the rug, yet Terry Barnes managed to dig up the evidence.

"Damn," I say. "Looks as if Barnes was trying to put the squeeze on his pal here. No wonder this thing went the wrong way."

Wolcott leans across his desk, staring at me intently. "As soon as Mr. Mathers wakes up, I want to be in his ear." His eyes narrow as he raps the surface of the desk with his knuckles. "Let's see if we can't find out just how hard this guy squeezed back."

CHAPTER FIFTEEN

LAURA

THE SOUND OF pained moaning wakes me.

"Mawwww."

I am disoriented and take a minute to place my body in space. The only lights in the room are emanating from the heart monitor, casting an eerie red pall over Gil's face. He appears to have moved while I was sleeping, which feels like progress. I lean across him to straighten the oxygen mask.

He is warm to the touch and completely still. He looks peaceful, and I wonder if the moan I heard was just the remnant of a dream I was trapped in. I hit my phone screen to check the time and see that it is exactly 3:33 A.M. and squint away from the burst of light punching through the blackness. My head has been pounding at a constant assaultive beat for twenty-four hours.

My body feels jacked from sleeping in the uneasy chair after watching him all day. Endless hours of waiting and willing my husband to open his eyes and speak to me have been met with no more than a face twitch.

Vicky has come and gone with food and headed back to my house for sleep and supplies. There is so much wreckage between us right now, it feels hard to know which thing we should focus on first. The passiveness of sitting and waiting is both anxiety provoking in my lack of control and a morbid respite from anything else outside this hospital room.

I'm desperate to hear Gil speak. It is very disconcerting to be in his presence for so long without the sound of his voice; he is a man who can't go more than a minute before pontificating on any given situation. I'm sure he'd have plenty to say about this quagmire we've found ourselves in. My need to know what happened and what he remembers about who did this to him has become obsessive, but the only progress he's made is to display some movement in his hand and feet, and a slightly improved brain scan.

I take the plastic pitcher from his bedside and refill it in the bathroom, at a sink under a mirror. A dour, sallow-faced woman stares back at me while the water runs. I splash a handful of frigid water on my face to wash away the sleep and perk myself up. When I kill the tap, I flinch when I hear the sound again.

"Mawwwwn."

I dart to his bedside and see that he's moving his head from side to side slowly and his eyes are scrunched in an expression of pain or fear.

"Gil, I'm here."

I put my hand on his and am alarmed by the swift rate of his pulse. His chapped lips part and he exhales with a soft groan.

"Gil? Can you hear me?" I am inches away from pressing the nurse call button when his body becomes still again. His chest movement is so slight, I'm not sure if he's still breathing until I see movement again. I freeze in place, afraid that one small move might send him back into the twilight realm for good. A few long minutes pass with the two of us in the dark breathing shallowly together.

"Honey? Can you hear me?" I say carefully. Surprisingly, he responds immediately, murmuring as though I've just woken him on any given night in bed. My chest begins to pound.

I see his mouth moving with painful effort. "Mawn . . . i . . . ca," he manages to strain out.

I fight the rage cascading at the sound of her name. This isn't the time to get angry; my energy will affect him. He's communicating; that is the most important thing right now.

"Gil, I'm Laura," I say lovingly. "I've been by your side this whole time."

He squeezes my hand back very faintly and then with more pressure.

"Gil, you are in a hospital. You were shot in the head."

I see rapid movement under his eyelids and the growing agitation in his limbs and neck.

"Honey, I've been so worried." I dampen the washcloth next to the pitcher and run it across his cracked lips.

His breathing is labored, but he pushes a word through in a hoarse whisper. "Monica," he strains.

My heart plummets and I feel ice shoot through my veins.

"I am *Laura*. Your *wife*," I say through gritted teeth.

I release his hand and face away from him and see the vague outline of myself in the darkened window. Behind me, he is coughing softly and I turn to face him. I recoil when I see that his eyes have opened and are locked on me.

"Gil!" I manage through my shock.

His mouth is twisted into a small O that I can't quite decipher. All the air has left the room. I put my hand on the chair back to steady myself.

"Honey?" I edge closer to him tentatively, afraid I'll spook him.

He keeps his eyes locked on me. They are filled with fear.

"Gil? What happened to you? Do you remember anything?" I plead as I grasp his hands in mine, realizing my shortsightedness. "Let me call a doctor." Help is more important than getting information out of him.

As I reach for the call button I see his eyes rolling back into his head while small sounds of gurgling escape. I lean in close to him, moving my ear to his mouth.

"What is it, honey?" I say.

"Spencer," he whispers painfully.

It feels like I'm pushing through wet concrete to reach my finger to the button. My hand lands heavily on his chest as an excruciating ringing in my ears pierces through the quiet.

It takes me a second to comprehend that the sound is the alarm from his heart monitor.

"Help. Somebody. Please," I cry out into the night, knowing in my heart that I am calling out for someone to help not him but me.

PART TWO

ONE WEEK EARLIER

Whatever energy a person puts out to the
universe will come back to them threefold.

The Rule of Three, Sawyer Selwyn

CHAPTER SIXTEEN

MONICA

"WE NEED TO talk," Spencer announces as he walks into the kitchen where I've been sipping my coffee and highlighting passages. I finish with *When you don't treat yourself the way you want to be treated, everyone will follow your example*, before closing the book and putting it out of sight.

"Morning, dear." I rise to kiss him and he turns his head just before my lips meet his. I catch the roughness of his three-day stubble.

"Coffee breath," he grumbles.

"Sorry." I clap a hand over my mouth and take my mug over to the sink, drain the rest of the liquid, and retrieve an Altoid from a drawer. He takes the seat farthest away from where I was sitting. He pulls at the skin on his neck, which has noticeably begun to sag with age and stress-induced weight loss. Between leaving the house at dawn and cycling for hours before returning to take calls on his stationary bike, he's clocked hundreds of miles on both bikes. It seems as though he can't function or focus unless he's moving his legs in circles.

"How's your morning so far?" I palm his shoulder as I pass him.

He isn't making eye contact with me; instead he's intently examining something on the screen of his iPhone. Spencer's never been a big "look me in the eye" kind of guy, but I'm used to it after a decade around computer nerds.

"Fine, fine," he mutters.

"I have to talk to you too," I inform him.

"Hmm?" he says distractedly.

"You said you needed to talk. Well, I have some things I'd like to say too," I say firmly.

He raises his head from his phone and looks at my face. "You do?" I see a flicker of worry pass over him. It is unusual for me to be confrontational, and when I am, he doesn't like it at all.

"Yes." I'm happy that I've gotten his attention. "But you go first." I sit across from him and mirror his posture. The midmorning sun casts a lovely slice of yellow light on the table between us. If I were a cat, it would be a perfect place to sun myself. I smile at the thought and Spence smiles back at me, mistaking my warmth as directed at him. Relief enters his face, and I let him hold on to it for the time being. Still, he doesn't say anything and looks at me peculiarly after a few seconds of expectant silence.

"What's on your mind?" I say neutrally.

"I'm concerned about the amount of time you are spending at the Matherses' house." He is looking at something on the ceiling and then at the wall behind me. In an article after charges were first brought against Spencer, a former employee referred to him as "shifty," and I haven't been able to shake that description since.

I let the statement resonate before I ask a question that I already know the answer to. "How do you know how much time I'm spending at Laura's house?"

He responds with a disapproving expression. I have a choice before me; I can reengage Spencer in our years-long debate about his
tracking software on all our devices and vehicles, or I can forge
ahead.

I pick happiness over being right.

"Of course," I say. He looks surprised that I've rejected the bait.

"I'm just not sure why this is such an issue; you never monitored
my social activities in California. I want friends, Spencer. I know these
aren't your favorite people, but I need to make an effort to be part of
the community, no? Terry is the reason we moved here, right?"

I think back to when Spence was pitching the move from Santa
Clara to Kingsland, as if I had a choice in the matter. I couldn't bear
the thought of any more upheaval in our life, but Spencer had been
acquitted of criminal charges on a handful of technicalities that I still
haven't completely untangled in my understanding, and his career
was over for the foreseeable future. We'd all but been run out of
Northern California with pitchforks.

"We can start over," he'd promised. *"We can have the experiences that
we didn't get to have in the beginning of our marriage because I was working
so much."* I'd felt some resentment at his singular self-reference, as I
too had worked plenty hard to put our life together and make a home
that was worthy of a tech giant when he was building Galapagos.

A new start sounded like exactly what we needed. I'd never lived
east of Texas and always loved New York City when we'd visited
many times for Spencer's work. But it wasn't Manhattan he'd had in
mind.

He'd given me the hard sell about a very exclusive, private community of people who wanted to be out of the spotlight, away from
the city but close enough to take advantage of its amenities. Kingsland was a community for discerning VIPs who wanted to live their

lives quietly and without drama, and it was invite only. When I saw the images of the house Terry Barnes was offering, a stately home surrounded by grand-looking arborvitaes, protecting its occupants from the prying eyes of the world, I agreed to the move. Though I was sad and defeated to be leaving our home, my desperation to escape the press and our icy neighbors was greater.

Of course there was no mention of Gil Mathers being one of the illustrious residents of Kingsland. Spencer had no reason to think that I would have any opinion either way about a disgraced motivational speaker that he'd never even heard of. I do still wonder how that information might have changed the course of things. It is doubtful that I'd have been able to sway Spencer from the move without telling him the whole story of how I knew Gil in the first place, and that would have been another world of pain. And I never would have gotten to meet Vicky and Laura.

"Spence, they are my friends."

"What exactly do you do all day?"

"We hang out by the pool and talk."

"Why there? Why not Victoria's?"

"Would you prefer that?" He shakes his head from side to side. "We go to Laura's because Terry is always home. He's annoying," I say.

"That asshole is in constant need of an audience," he cracks. "Anyway, we have a pool. You can sit out there unbothered all day long."

"Unbothered and alone. I don't want to be alone, Spencer."

It isn't lost on me that this conversation could as easily be between a father and his teenage daughter. The present feelings between us are probably closer to that dynamic.

"I'm here," he says.

"But you aren't really *here*. You are always someplace else in your head even when we're sitting in the same room together. We barely talk anymore."

"We talk all the time. We are talking right now."

I sigh. "You know what I mean."

He sighs louder. "This is what I'm talking about, Monica. Before we moved here and you started spending all of your time at Gil Mathers's house—"

"Laura's house," I correct.

"Tomato, tomahto."

I put my hand over my face.

"Before you spent all of your time at the Matherses', you never complained about how much we talked or how much time we spent together. This is because you've been absorbed into this unnecessary self-made drama factory that this neighborhood perpetuates. Every last one of them has too much time and money and nothing useful to do with either."

"Why is it okay for you to have a weekly poker game with two men who you claim to despise, but I can't spend time with their wives?"

"That is completely different. That's business."

I laugh and pick at my cuticles. "Whatever, Spencer. So am I grounded from going to the pool with my friends?" I snap.

"This isn't about the pool. This is about me not wanting you to get too close to those women. I don't want you talking about our business with anyone."

"What is it exactly that you're afraid of?" I try not to cry.

"That they'll take advantage of you. That they'll get something out of you that you don't realize you are giving up."

"Give me a little more credit than that, Spence. Besides, there isn't anything that we have that they could possibly need," I say calmly.

"Don't be so sure of that," he says cryptically, then releases his other heavy hand from my shoulder and comes to sit in the chair catty-corner to mine.

"You don't exactly tell me the details about what's going on anyway."

"I tell you what you need to know," he says darkly.

"I don't like this side of you, Spence." I frown. He is already back to his phone screen.

"And steer clear of Gil Mathers," he mutters.

My throat tightens.

"You realize how incredibly controlling this is all sounding, right?"

"You are not seeing the bigger picture, Monica." He emphasizes every syllable of my name as a warning. "We just need to finish out our time here and then we can move on." He takes off his glasses and begins cleaning them with a special microfiber cloth that costs more than my cell phone. "And yes, Terry Barnes is the reason we are here, but that reason is entirely business."

"I thought we were here for a new beginning." I catch his eye before it darts away.

"This is a means to an end. We are not required to socialize with them, no matter how hard Barnes bullies us to," he counters.

"I want to socialize. Vicky and Laura have been good to me."

"Mon, you can't ignore the fact that your *friends* are questionably trustworthy and undeniably married to two liabilities. And they are sisters. And if you think that Laura and Victoria don't tell their husbands everything, the way you do with me, you are being naive."

An urge to correct Spencer on this matter knocks at me, but my pride is right sized by common sense.

"I just wish you, Terry, and Gil would get along. The three of you are like teenage girls."

"Excuse me?"

"You are all talking shit about each other and then acting like everything is fine."

"What have you heard?" He watches me closely.

"Nothing. Just that Terry's been stressed about some deal and Gil's been over at their house a lot this month behind closed doors," I tell him.

"Do you know what about?" he presses.

"No. We don't really talk about you all as much as you'd like to think."

Spencer scowls.

"Would you prefer that I have Vicky and Laura come here during the day?" I ask, knowing full well that he doesn't want anyone in our house.

"No. I don't think that's the answer."

"Then what is the answer, darling? That I spend all of my time alone with nothing to do or no one to talk to?" I say bitterly.

"You're making it sound like you're a prisoner." He sniffs. "You know you can come and go as you please."

"I know." I stand and move my chair close to his. He seems surprised by the counterintuitiveness of the gesture, especially when I put my palm lovingly on his cheek.

"What is it you're afraid of, Spence?"

"I only agreed to move here because of Barnes's help with the case. I thought we'd have more privacy here, but it is the opposite." He catches himself.

"What do you mean?" I ask.

"It doesn't matter since we are moving. You haven't said anything to them, right?" His eyes narrow.

"Of course not. I promised that I wouldn't," I lie. "I already told you that I'm not going anywhere, so there's no reason to even bring it up with Vicky and Laura."

"Monica. Be reasonable. There is no good reason to stay here. I've already found some places in Colorado that could be perfect."

"Colorado? Spencer, you think going even further away from society is going to solve our problems?" I struggle to keep my cool.

"I can't work here, Monica. I need space and quiet. You know I'm right at the threshold of something really big. I can get us back to where we were. Back into Santa Clara into our old house or an even better one. This neighborhood is just a chessboard for Terry Barnes to play with when he's got nothing else to do." Bitterness oozes.

"Okay," I concede. "As long as we're together, Spence. That's all that matters."

"Really?" He regards my face skeptically. "You're okay about the move?"

"Yes." I yield. "And I will not say another word against the move on two conditions."

He raises his eyebrows. It isn't like me to bargain with Spence; he has been known to trash billion-dollar deals over power plays.

"What are your conditions?" he asks, vaguely amused.

"In the time left here, I can spend as much time as I want with Laura and Vicky."

He furrows his brow. "Maybe. And the other?"

"You go with me to the Barneses' Fourth of July barbecue this weekend."

He groans and shifts in his seat. "Is that really necessary?"

"It is if you want me to accept my being uprooted for the second time in a year and leaving behind my friends."

"You didn't have any friends left in California," he says.

I'm stung, but I don't let on. "Think of it as a going-away party for both of us, one only we know about. It might be fun." I hold his hand and look up at him with the most loving expression that I can muster.

"Fine. I'll go to the barbecue, but only for a little while, and I'm not going to enjoy myself," he says finally.

"You never know, Spence. Stranger things have happened."

CHAPTER SEVENTEEN

VICTORIA

"THEY'RE FOR THE upside-down cake, honey." I add a little sugar to my tone as Terry scrunches his nose in disgust at the sight of the pineapples standing atop the counter of the kitchen island that separates us. "Don't worry," I continue. "I won't let them anywhere near the fruit salad. Promise."

"What about me?" he whines, half smiling. "Where's my sweet treat?" Buried beneath the teasing comment is an actual petulance bordering on the infantile. It's one of my husband's least attractive qualities, and the one I relish pushing back against the most.

"Well, sweetheart." I've fully taken on the voice of an adult addressing a toddler. "Your doctor said that's no good for your blood pressure, remember?" Apparently, my inner sadist has decided to come out and go a few rounds with the guy. "So, only fruit for you." I tap my finger to the air as if I'm booping him on the nose.

"Fine," he says, the suggestion of a smile having left his face. His irritation is only encouraging my feeling of glee in the moment.

"My hands are tied," I say with a shrug, in a comically haughty tone. "Our guests have come to expect certain traditions when attending the Barnes Annual Fourth of July Barbecue. I'm afraid they'll revolt if there's no cake."

"Yeah, 'revolt' is the word for it." He mimes sticking his finger down his throat and gagging.

"Oh, chin up, Terry. It'll be a fun time." He glares at me, unconvinced, and I have to tamp down a grin. As much as I'm enjoying this personally, the real reason for taking him down a peg is to provide a service to both my husband and the guests at our upcoming party. In years past, he's gotten into the habit of turning insufferable over the course of the festivities, doing his whole cock-of-the-grill routine and getting a little too alpha with the men and flirty with their wives. By the time he's been a few beers in, I've found myself fantasizing about grabbing the garden hose and spraying down the fucker with it. So, really, my infantilization of him is just a proactive service, letting some of the bluster out, like the air from the tires of a Jeep you're about to drive onto the beach. It simply wouldn't do to have my husband getting stuck in the rut of his own arrogance in front of our friends and neighbors. Again.

"Sure," he grumbles. "Speaking of which, have our illustrious guests done us the courtesy of RSVPing?"

"Well." I stretch out the word as I retrieve the sheet of paper from between the pineapples and unfold it. "Milly and Roger have confirmed."

"Terrific." He rolls his eyes. "Just who I was hoping for."

"Oh, you can play nice for a few hours," I chastise.

"The guy's a total drip," he complains.

"I know," I say. "But take pity on him. The poor thing's been browbeaten into submission. Plus, he *does* work for you, Ter."

"Yeah," he huffs. "I'm nice enough to give the guy a job, and in return I'm treated to him coming over once a year, standing around my yard yammering away and eating all my food."

"Well, he's never really home. The man spends all of his time in the city. It's not his fault he's still working." I can feel the air cool around me as soon as the words leave my mouth. Terry clears his throat and raises his eyebrows, his glare equal parts wounded and angry. I've located the line. "Not what I meant," I say, showing him my palms.

"Uh-huh," he grumbles.

"Listen, you're welcome to entertain Milly, if you'd rather." He flinches at the suggestion, and I laugh in spite of myself.

"Well, now. I wouldn't want to ruin all *your* fun," he counters.

"You're a real doll," I deadpan, glad for the break in tension.

He slips his phone out of his pocket and begins tapping the screen. "So, who else's company do I have to look forward to?"

"Laura and Gil will be in attendance," I respond.

He sighs. "This just keeps getting better."

"Ter," I say tightly. "Watch it."

"Not her," he clarifies. "I'm talking about her egotistical asshole of a husband."

I nearly scoff at *my* husband's pot-kettle description of his supposed friend but manage to keep my expression neutral. "You're just mad because he took all your money at poker last week."

His eyes widen. "Who told you that?" he demands.

"What, you don't think us ladies talk? Come on."

The look of embarrassment on his face quickly morphs back to one of annoyance. "Fucking guy. He's got no table manners at all."

"What does that mean?" I ask.

"He's a cowboy."

"Huh?"

"He bets recklessly," says Terry by way of clarification.

"It *is* gambling, right?"

"Yes, Vicky. But there's an etiquette to it." His tone has taken on the quality of a figurative pat on the head. "You wouldn't understand."

I feel the heat climbing through my collar and up my throat as I return to the list in my hand. I tamp it down and turn up the cheer. "Diana Porter will be there. And the Prestons, from over on Juniper. They're bringing the coleslaw."

"Uh-huh," he responds absently.

"Oh, and Spencer and Monica just confirmed."

This gets his eyes away from his screen and back to me. "Mmm-hmm," he answers, an indecipherable expression on his face.

"What's wrong, Ter? Did he take your money too?"

He lets out a snort and smacks a hand against his thigh. "That's rich." My husband laughs, a little too heartily. "He wishes."

"Oh yeah?" I encourage him.

"Babe, I've got that guy's number all day." He smirks, pleased with himself. "He's nothing but tells. It's embarrassing, frankly."

"Good for you," I say. "Glad to hear you're getting along with one of your friends, at least."

He answers that with a derisive grimace. "Meh," is all he bothers to muster.

"Oh, come on. What's your problem with Spence now?"

"Ask him," says Terry. "Guy's been acting weird lately. Squirrelly." He drifts off, lost in whatever set of considerations is spinning through his brain. "Just trying to figure him out." He trails off for a long pause before snapping back into the moment and looking at me self-consciously. "Never mind," he says, waving off his previous musings. "I'm just talking my shit."

"Okay, honey." I refold the list and tuck it back between the pine-apples. "You know, you should really try and enjoy this time with Spence before those two pull up stakes and take off."

"What?" He abruptly shoves his phone back into his pocket, approaches the island, and slaps his hands down on the countertop across from me. It feels like the molecules in the air around us have been reconfigured. "What the hell are you talking about?"

"He hasn't mentioned anything to you?" I study my husband's face carefully and catch the telltale twitch of his eyelid. "About moving out of Kingsland?"

"Honey." He stares at me intently, his voice thin, the anger barely suppressed. I catch the tremor in his forearms from the pressure he's exerting against the countertop. "I need you to tell me exactly what you're referring to."

"Don't bite my head off," I protest, taking a reflexive step backward. "I assumed it would have come up at your card game."

"You assume *what* would have come up, Vic?" He's putting a great deal of effort into speaking evenly.

"I don't know the details," I say. "Mon just mentioned that the idea of a move had come up recently. They've been discussing it, I guess."

"Was this her idea?" he asks. "Some notion she's gotten into that silly little head of hers?"

"C'mon," I say. "You think she's calling the shots in that relationship?"

"Right." He nods.

"She was bitching to Laura and me about it. Saying that she'd finally found a place where she belonged after they had to leave Cali, and now he wanted to uproot them all over again. I don't think that woman's ever had a lot of friends." I watch Terry consider the implications. "She's really come to look at Laura and me as sisters. It's sweet."

He looks past me, sucking air greedily into his nostrils. "That ungrateful son of a bitch," he says.

"You're taking this awfully personally, honey."

"Does he not remember who gave him a lifeline when he was drowning?" He's speaking more to himself than to me. "Does he not realize who the fuck I am?"

"Terry, Jesus." I cross my arms over my chest. "Maybe he's just ready for a change. Give the guy a break."

"Guy thinks he can just pick up and go." He's fully in his own head now, disconnected from the world around him.

"What's your problem?" I ask pointedly. The edge on the question snaps him back into our kitchen.

"We had an understanding, Vic. He knew what the move here entailed."

"What's with you, anyway?" I shake my head in frustration. "You've done nothing but complain about this guy lately. Him and Gil, the two guys you spend most of your time with these days, the two guys who one might go so far as to mistake for your actual *friends*, and all you can manage to do is whine about them constantly. It's a little boring, frankly."

"Look," he says. "I get that you're tight with his wife, and you want her hanging around, but there are just some things that you don't understand."

"What's there to understand?" I ask. "The guy's life isn't tied to Kingsland. Just because he doesn't revere this place that you were kind enough to help him move to doesn't make it a personal affront to you, Terry."

"It's not—"

I'm hitting a nice stride, and I won't have him nip it short. "I hate to break it to you, but not everything in this world, or even in this community, revolves around the whims of the almighty Terry Barnes."

"Vic," he growls, his lower jaw jutting forward. "You're out of your depth here."

"Right." I feel my own jawbone tense. "Really glad we had this chat," I say, my tone bathed in sarcasm, before I step out of the room, leaving my husband to stew in his suspicions.

CHAPTER EIGHTEEN

LAURA

As I shut the front door and kick off my running shoes, the house is quiet around me. The air-conditioning is on full blast and my skin quickly prickles with goose bumps from the polarity of the ninety degrees I've just run seven miles in and the arctic temperature of our house.

"Gil?" I call out, and my shoulders relax at the lack of response. I expect he is holed up in his office, since his car is in the driveway, but I don't make a move to hunt him down. Not yet.

I pull off my sweaty tank top as I move to the laundry room and toss it into the washing machine before doing the same with my saturated sports bra, underwear, and running shorts. Naked, I stand in the window and take in the vivid colors of the summer backyard. I scan the carefully landscaped scene for Gil and don't see him lying by the pool or pacing around the fire pit on his phone, the two most predictable locations after his office.

I pull a clean beach towel from the top of the recently stocked linen closet and wrap it around my body as I step out into the sunlight. Barefoot, I walk over the freshly mowed grass onto the smooth stone walkway leading to the bamboo changing hut and open-air shower stall. I hang my towel on the hook and turn the handles, stepping between the two showerheads on either side of me, the warm water washing the sweat down the drain.

I look upward when I get a whiff of skunky pot and see a smoke cloud drifting out of Gil's office window and into the otherwise cloudless blue sky above. I see him standing in the window looking down at me and I give him an acknowledging wave, which is returned with a vexed smile and the pull of the curtain across the window. The gesture is a perfect expression of my husband's attitude toward me for the last few months.

I'm conflicted about how his evasive behavior makes me feel lately. We've been strained for the past few years to varying degrees, sometimes indifferently, sometimes resentfully, but we've stayed stuck together, somehow. We aren't a heroic story of a marriage plagued with scandal and tragedy that has emerged stronger and better. The less dramatic truth is that we were a problematic marriage from the outset, compounded by tragedy and scandal, resulting in utter emotional exhaustion and motivational defeat.

I shut off the water and stand for a few moments feeling the warm sun drying the moisture from my body. I run my hand across my belly and down over the mottled cesarean scar, ropy under my fingers. It is a reminder of what once was. The few inches of skin incite oppositional emotions simultaneously: the happiest I've ever been in my life, and the most devastated.

The shower has energized me and rinsed away any doubt of what I need to do. I wrap the warm towel around my body and tuck one corner into my cleavage to hold it secure before pulling a smaller towel flung over the stall and wrapping it around my hair in a turban before heading upstairs to get dressed and face my husband.

On the way to our bedroom, I hear Gil groaning loudly behind the closed door of his office. I backstep and lean my ear against the door and hear him moan again, and I'm unsure of whether the sounds are pain or pleasure induced. Knowing Gil, it could be a little of both. I pause in my irritation at him before knocking and hear him clear his throat and move around in the room quickly.

"Gil? Can I come in?"

"Gimme a minute." He strains and I turn the knob lightly, confirming my suspicion that he's locked the door. I step back from my lean and wait for him to gather himself.

"I can come back," I say through the door, and take a few steps in the direction of our room. He doesn't answer and I hear more shuffling. I take more steps away before he responds or comes to the door, wishing I'd restrained myself from knocking in the first place.

As I pad down the carpeted hallway, I hear the door open.

"I was doing push-ups," he says to my back, and I stop and turn to face him from the door of our bedroom. His face is flushed and I can see sweat lightly beading his forehead.

I nod. "Sorry to interrupt. I just wanted to give you a heads-up that Vicky and Monica are coming over this afternoon." I clock his face for any tell when I drop Monica's name. His expression stays the same.

"Okay." He shrugs.

"I thought you'd like to know," I say.

I can see his irritation slide into confusion about why I've intruded on his personal time with innocuous information. It isn't standard practice for me to inform him about anything going on in my daily life, and he does me the same courtesy.

"I'll steer clear of the pool, then." He gives me a quick once-over in my towel, and his evident detachment scratches my emotional surface, only slightly.

I wish I could be straightforward and just ask him what has really been burning me from the inside out, but I'm scared of what I might do if he confirms what Monica has told me, or what he'll do when confronted about it. I didn't think it was possible for Gil's secrets to hurt me more than they already have. But the cascading disappointments in my marriage have been like a never-ending game of Whac-A-Mole.

"I just wanted to make sure you were comfortable with my friends coming over."

"Why wouldn't I be?"

"Well, I know you've been working on something 'top secret.' I thought it was respectful to make sure that we aren't disturbing you."

He raises his eyebrow. Gil knows when he's being baited, but knowing it and resisting it aren't mutually exclusive.

"Top secret? Where'd you get that from?"

"Didn't you say that?" I ask.

He looks perturbed. "No, I definitely didn't."

"Oh, I guess not." I laugh nervously. "Terry said something to Vicky about a project he had you working on, but that was as much as she could suss out. He was uncharacteristically tight-lipped, for Terry."

I see his face flush. "And I'm not doing shit *for* Terry. I only do work for myself, you know that," he says defensively.

"Okay. I just thought it tracked."

"How so?" He looks pissed.

I match my tone to his face. "Well, the locked door and secretive phone calls, your leaving the house at all hours of the night with no explanation, the new computer equipment and other mysterious charges on the emergency Amex. It all seemed like you were making sure I didn't know what you were up to." I feel my face getting hot. "Or maybe the simplest answer is that you are having an affair."

He pales and I see his gears turning, and quickly. "Don't be ridiculous."

"Am I?"

"Since when do you care about what I'm working on?" He cocks his head.

"Gil, I've always cared." I push out this half-truth with a heavy sigh.

I actually did care about his work before everything fell apart. I cherished when he shared ideas with me and valued my input, when he couldn't go onstage without rehearsing in front of me. But those feelings dissipated after Libby was killed. At present, I'm way more interested in whether he will lie to my face right now.

It is looking more likely by the minute.

"I know you've been unhappy being in between books and gigs, and I'm glad to see that you are inspired again." I smile at him, trying to defuse the growing tension, pulling my arms around myself.

"What's your angle, Laur?"

"I'm just trying to have a conversation with you. You are getting awfully confrontational."

I can see him assessing which mindfuck tactic to employ right now. I am hoping for something good and dirty; I am looking for a fight.

"You are right, sweetie. I apologize." His eyes are steely. "Thanks for checking in. I'm going to get back to it, then."

I'm incensed by his refusal to even make an effort. "I have to say, Gil. The push-ups and whatever else you are doing are really working. You haven't looked this good in a while."

He can't help himself from relishing a compliment, even if it is soaked in subtext. His stance changes; he leans against the doorway of his office facing me and smiles widely.

"Thank you, I appreciate that." I suppress a smirk when I catch his biceps flex.

"Do you want to run anything past me? Maybe I can help with what you are working on. Like I used to?" I offer.

He tenses. "I'm still working out the kinks on some new material," he says evasively. "Maybe later."

"Sure," I say sweetly. "If you need an audience, you can come down and share what you've been working on with Vicky, Monica, and me. I know you and Vicky don't always agree, but I think Monica is very bright, don't you?"

His face remains effortlessly unchanged and he crosses his arms over his chest. This pisses me off. I step into our bedroom and flip on the light since the curtains are still drawn and the room is dim. Gil follows me, evidently unmoved by the Monica comment.

"What else has Terry been saying about me?" His serenity from earlier has devolved quickly and he looks like he might put his fist through the wall.

I casually pull a pair of panties and a bra out of my dresser and a sundress from the closet and drop my towel onto the bed. I pull on my underwear and clasp the closure on my bra in two quick moves before sliding the dress over my head.

"You know Terry, Gil. He just loves to feel superior. Like he's in control of everyone around here."

Gil frowns. "Right."

I walk closer to him and hold the question in my mouth that keeps trying to get out, and all the questions queued up behind that one. I see Gil scan the room and land on my copy of *The Rule of Three* on my nightstand.

"You are actually reading that crap?" he says disparagingly.

"For our book club. It isn't bad." I smile as he frowns.

"It is a stupid title. Sounds like a book about advertising. The author is a hack. Everything in there is just recycled from other books."

"Sounds like you've read it, then?" I say.

He shoots me a look of death and slams the door behind him.

I walk to the closed door and rest my head on it and ask very quietly, if only to hear the words out loud for my own sake.

"Is it true about Monica?"

I already know the answer.

CHAPTER NINETEEN

MONICA

WHEN I CROSS the threshold of the Hot Shakti yoga studio, I am hit with the wall of heat and the smell, which remains rank no matter how much essential oil they diffuse.

I am never, ever going to get used to sweating this much on purpose. In every class, I keep hoping for the transcendent moment of bliss but can't seem to get past the nausea and headaches. It is hard not to feel like a failure compared to all the other lithe, limber bodies of my neighbors flowing through each posture as though the environment is perfect. But with every class I survive, it does seem to get easier, and it is a guaranteed sixty minutes of complete mental diversion from everything outside these doors.

It is the subtle peer pressure that has me re-upping my class package, compounded by the fear of missing out. Hot yoga in Kingsland isn't just the exercise fad du jour; it is more like a test of worthiness than of fitness. Every class I get through without puking on myself feels like a major accomplishment. And being there with Vicky and Laura every week makes it all worthwhile.

I step through the check-in point and deposit my belongings in a locker. I see a class regular reading a copy of *The Rule of Three*. "I'm totally obsessed," she says when she meets my eyes.

"Me too," I say brightly. "I'm reading it for the second time." I smile.

When I enter the swampy studio, the few topknotted heads in the room turn my way as I survey the mats for Vicky and Laura, who are nowhere to be seen. Most of the women smile at me and return to setting up their areas, their perfectly manicured hands and pricey jewelry gleaming in the afternoon sun coming through the skylights. The woman from the dressing room comes in behind me, spots her friend, and hands her the copy she was holding.

Her friends gushes. "Did you see her on *Super Soul*?" she says in a heavily accented croon. She looks and sounds South American.

"Sawyer was amazing. This book has completely changed me."

They are engrossed as I move past them.

I've made a point of getting here early so that I can hold three spaces for us. Happily, I see plenty of space, and then I am nearly bowled over by Milly Addison-LeFleur, who is beelining for her usual spot in the front row. No one with any sense takes the front-row right-corner mat, and on the rare occasion that it has happened, I've seen Milly ask them to move without any shame.

Our collision morphs into an awkward and sticky one-sided hug. "Monica!" Milly crows. My late mother would have said Milly has a ten-gallon mouth. She is as talkative as she is botoxed, which is to say excessively. The decibels of her voice draw looks from a few of the women setting up blocks and straps alongside their mats. I already feel the sweat forming on both of our bodies even though the heat in the room hasn't reached its max yet. Soon we'll be slick with perspiration and touching each other will be unthinkable.

I release myself from her grip, which is surprisingly strong for her five-foot frame. We generally aren't "hugging" friends, but Milly has become extra-friendly toward me since I've become inseparable with Vicky and Laura in the last few months.

In the few interactions that she and I have had one-on-one, the saccharine demeanor that Milly exhibits in the company of the sisters is noticeably less sweet without them. I've come to learn that Milly's been gunning for a regular spot in their circle of two since she moved in, which explains her apparent iciness around me in certain situations. The book club is a particularly sore spot.

"You are looking very healthy," Milly says as she tracks my body with her dark eyes. She's an attractive woman who is as garish in her workout ensemble as she is in every other social occasion. She's head to toe in Alo, her hair is flawlessly plaited into two boxer braids, and she has a dramatic smoky-eye and red-lipstick combination. She will still be flawless by the end of the class, while the rest of us will be runny, sloppy, sweaty messes. Although it is entirely unsubstantiated, I have a theory she may have undergone a cosmetic procedure that prevents her entire body from sweating. I'm not sure that it even exists, but if it does, Milly has done it.

"Hi, Milly. Great outfit," is as much as I can summon.

"I didn't expect to see you here," she says as she eyes her still empty spot near the front of class.

"I'm here every week," I say.

"Since Vicky and Laura aren't coming today, I thought you might be skipping it too."

"Oh, they aren't coming?" I casually unroll my mat where we're standing and try to hide the sharp sinking feeling brought on by this news.

"I saw Vicky this morning. I offered to carpool to class, but she told me she was on her way to meet Laura, and they weren't coming today." She reads my face when I meet her eyes.

"Oh. I didn't know." A sour feeling blooms.

Milly looks ecstatic that she's in a loop that I'm not.

"Why don't you sit next to me today?" she suggests brightly.

At a loss for a nonawkward excuse, I fold my mat in half under my arm and follow her to the front row, where I lay it next to hers. I feel like an outsider in this room without the sisters.

A few more women from the area filter in and I nod at them and half wave and I am relieved that they warmly return the greeting. Everyone in Kingsland has been friendly and welcoming from the beginning, but I keep expecting that people will change their minds about me or shun Spencer and me.

Vicky often reminds me that things are different here. Neither Vicky nor Laura has laid it out explicitly, but I've come to understand why no one is going to run us out of town. Most of the residents of Kingsland Estates have dark splotches on their own reputations, which keep them safely ensconced in their own glass houses, rock-free. We've all been "canceled" for our transgressions in some form, or more accurately, looking around at the roomful of younger, exotically beautiful women, our husbands have.

I hate that I know the second-most common search term after "Spencer Nichols" is "Who is Spencer Nichols wife," yet there is comfort in now knowing that I am not alone in this invasive experience. Many if not all of the women on these mats have that same unique identification with one another. Not one of them is defeated by this, and in many cases they met their husbands after the men experienced their downfalls and married them anyway. It became apparent that in addition to being a man of many talents in the areas of politics, business, law, and real estate developing, Terry Barnes is quite the prolific matchmaker. He unabashedly takes pride in pairing up multiple couples in Kingsland, making it chock-full of many May-December romances, and enough foreign countries represented among the Kingsland wives to rival the United Nations.

One of the first things Terry Barnes said to me when I met him in person: *"Kingsland is one of the most richly diverse American communities you'll ever find."* Which made me feel a little better about living in such a blatantly exclusive enclave.

I look at my watch and see that class won't start for five more minutes, which feels like an eternity with the rising temperature and the lack of the sisters here. I sit with my legs tucked underneath me and gather my hair into a ponytail holder before reconsidering and releasing my mass of curls. Milly says hello to the women seated in the row behind us and introduces me, even though they are neighbors whom I've met multiple times. I say hello and try to keep a smile on my face, with diminishing success.

"So, how are things going?" Milly has perched herself in lotus pose atop two cork blocks and sweeps her arms while she speaks. Her enormous four-carat diamond stunner catches the light from the giant window, and it sparkles with each swoop of her hand. The class is a starfield of sparkly high-carated fingers.

"Great."

"How does Kingsland compare to Silicon Valley?"

"It is really great and totally different from California."

"It is a special community, isn't it?" she says, her veneers gleaming.

"It is like no place I've ever lived," I answer just as enthusiastically.

"We've been here from the beginning, you know. We had the second house built, after Terry and Vicky's, of course."

It would be virtually impossible not to know this info, since Milly had told me every time we've spoken that she and her husband, the insufferably dull Roger LeFleur, were Kingland's third and fourth residents. Roger is one of Terry's many lawyers on call, who always seems to be working on a landmark case. While he was not one of the lawyers who worked on Spencer's team, he knows Spencer's counsel "extremely well," something he reminds us of every time we interact with him. This infuriates Spencer to no end. *"I didn't move here to have my court case brought up by that imbecile at every goddamn Kingsland soiree."*

Terry seems to collect powerful lawyers the way some wealthy people collect boats or cars. My few exchanges with Roger LeFleur have been predictably annoying and unforgettable aside from the consistent impression of Roger's being enamored of himself and sliding his and Terry's alma mater, Harvard, into virtually every conversation.

"I heard you mention that your son got into Harvard. That must be exciting," I say. Milly brightens by sixty watts.

"It was such a relief. We knew Bryce was going to be admitted, but there is always that little seed of doubt with the way college admissions are going now. People practically get *penalized* for being legacy."

I look her over the way she's been doing to me for the past five minutes. Every statement she makes has an outsize physical flourish, like she's a former silent film star who's adjusting to being heard.

I pull my hair out of my face and into a ponytail because the heat has gotten unbearable. When I do, I hear the woman behind me, Ramona Salton, gasp. I catch her motioning to her friend Harmony that she's caught sight of the bruise that I was concealing and I see Harmony's frozen face make a microreaction of horror in the mirror. I see Milly looking at Ramona and then craning her neck to see what has prompted her friend's reactions. Her eyes return to the front of the room, but the distinct energy of a cat ready to pounce is coming off Milly in waves.

The class has begun to reach its maximum capacity now and it seems to have fallen eerily silent. I feel many eyes on me, but I don't dare turn around. Let them talk; I don't care what people think about my marriage or my husband any longer. All I can think about is what I've done to make Laura and Vicky exclude me. I'm burning with worry now and can barely focus on the opening remarks from the teacher about the light in all of us.

As the teacher lowers the lights and increases the heat, she turns to face her eagerly awaiting students, and I prepare myself for hell.

CHAPTER TWENTY

VICTORIA

"You've always had a good instinct for these things."

I'm sitting across the table from Laura at Halliard, the nautically themed bayside dining experience that's been a regular fixture of ours since moving to Kingsland. I use the term "dining experience"—as opposed to the more conventional "restaurant"—to mirror the level of pretension that the establishment traffics in.

The humidity is thick today, so we've opted away from a table on the outdoor deck in favor of the aggressively air-conditioned main room. The space is outfitted in gleaming white tile with steel accents—the height of austere minimalism. Peppered around the room are a couple of lobster traps perched high in the corners, as well as a few errant mooring buoys hung along the wall and a length of fishing net affixed to the ceiling above the bar area.

On offer below is a carefully curated menu of craft cocktails, each named after references to maritime literature; there's the Coyotito's Pearl, the Sargasso Weed, and the Pequod, among others. The food is predictably sea-centric, unusually refined and dependably excellent. They don't offer any sort of fried monstrosity with a name like "The Angler's Net," nor some half-assed kids' menu with fish sticks and tartar sauce and a paper place mat where the child colors in a pirate ship using a cardboard cup's worth of half-gnawed crayons. For these merciful gestures I'm eternally grateful. The service is crisp and efficient, the amenable staff dressed as if they've recently disembarked from a catamaran after sunset cocktails. Not a single one of the fishermen who supply the restaurant would ever be caught dead patronizing the place.

Lunch at Halliard is normally a table-for-three affair, but we've strategically neglected to inform Monica of our absence from hot yoga today in order for my sister and me to have some alone time with the aim of getting to the bottom of the situation with Gil. After all, it simply wouldn't do to have the object of the upheaval on hand while we're trying to tamp down the fallout resulting from it.

"A good instinct?!" Laura nearly spits sparkling water all over the tablecloth. "What single part of this entire mess would lead you to believe that I've ever had 'a good instinct' about anything, Vic?"

I've seen this one too many times before. My sister will flash a particular look before a hard truth sets in, when she's still wrestling with whether or not to allow herself to believe something that she innately knows to be the case. It's the expression of her emotional self grappling with her intellectual self, in a fight that's often spirited but inevitably resolves with her brain getting the better of her heart. Accompanying all this is a feeling of deep self-consciousness born of vulnerability; her sense that you're already aware of the thing she's just coming around to. The embarrassment brings an almost animal ferocity out of her. Having watched it over the years has not made it any easier to bear, and I've realized that the further I skirt around the turmoil's epicenter, the better for all involved.

My first memory of traipsing across the minefield came in the wake of a nasty breakup between Laura and a serious college boyfriend. She'd found out rather unceremoniously about his *other* girlfriend after he'd bailed on a date with my sister, claiming that he felt under the weather. She'd offered to come over and check on him, only to be told that it would make him feel worse knowing that he'd ruined a perfectly good Saturday night by asking her to come play nursemaid. He'd promised to call in the morning with an update, and they'd agreed to leave the matter at that.

Later that evening, despite their agreement, Laura had stopped by his room to leave off some chicken soup and crackers. From behind his door, she'd heard an unmistakable series of noises. She proceeded to let herself in using the spare key he'd gifted her, only to find some freshman she vaguely recognized from around campus riding her boyfriend while moaning all manner of unholy sounds. If his dorm had been a shorter walk from the dining hall or the outside temperature hadn't cooled the soup as much as it had, that poor girl might have been chased out of the room with third-degree burns setting in.

It had been the weekend before winter break, which meant that the sting from the incident was still fresh when both Laura and I arrived home from our respective schools. I could tell something was eating at her, but she seemed especially reticent to discuss whatever was going on. Finally, after a couple of drinks and not a little prodding, she opened up about what had happened.

My sister had never been particularly demonstrative with her emotions, so it was surprising when she broke down in a heap of tears, but what caught me equally off guard was the level of self-recrimination laced through her words, as if she'd been angrier with herself than with him. It seemed as if she were bearing the brunt of the blame.

I listened patiently as she seesawed between the roles of victim and enabler, and when she paused long enough to take a breath, I'd asked her whether it was possible that she'd expected the betrayal on some level and had stopped by with the soup as an excuse to catch him in the act. The look she gave me in response—a piercing blend of accusation, anger, humiliation, and acknowledgment—rattled me to the marrow.

In that moment, a fact I'd been subconsciously smothering leapt to the forefront of my brain. A hard truth about our very own family was thrown into sharp focus. I was suddenly faced with the reality of the way we were raised and the damage that had resulted. A terrible knowledge finally dawned on me, and it was this: Our father was an unscrupulous man. And the problem, I realized, with being raised by an unscrupulous adult is that you're made to feel foolish for simply wanting to have faith in a parent you love and depend on. It's an excruciating feeling, akin to a taunt, a sneer, a sucker punch.

I stare at my sister across the table and again recognize that pained expression on her face. I know that I need to approach the situation gingerly, and I allow myself a breath to regroup. "Laura," I begin, meeting her glance with soft eyes. "I just meant that your intuition is generally pretty spot-on, you see."

Her shoulders relax a touch as her mouth softens. She lets out a sigh. "I guess you're right," she says. "I just . . ." Her eyes narrow. "I dropped Monica's name right in his lap, and there was . . . nothing. No change on his face. Not a glimmer of recognition. Zilch." She shakes her head. "It's kind of fucking with me now."

"Well, keep in mind that Gil made a career out of turning manure into magic." I see the cords in her neck tighten. "Your words," I remind her, plucking the white linen napkin from my lap and waving it in mock surrender. She snorts at the gesture, and I feel my chest relax.

"That's just it," she says. "I've been with him long enough to be able to spot his tells. He can bullshit most people, but there's always something, some little flinch or tic that I've seen before, that gives him away." She picks up her fork and halfheartedly pushes a poached shrimp around her plate of Cobb salad. "But today? Nada. No emotion whatsoever. It was like I'd asked him what he thought of the mailman." She sighs and gives up on the dish.

"Do you think he's maybe just gotten better at compartmentalizing?" I offer. "The stakes are very high in this case. Could he just be playing the whole thing extra-cool?"

"I don't know." She shrugs in frustration. "He sure got all red in the face when I mentioned his big secret project with Terry. That one threw him all sorts of ways." She snorts. "So, what the hell does that tell you, Vic?"

I take a sip of water, as much to buy time as to slake my thirst. As I drink, our server appears at the table, all smiles and overly solicitous cheer. "Ladies," he says, surveying the table, a subtle look of concern forming on his face at our barely touched meals. "Is everything tasting okay over here?"

"It's fine," Laura responds curtly.

"Everything is great," I say in a warm voice, attempting to sand the rough edges off of my sister's response. "Thank you so much." He grins and retreats from our table. I set down my glass, shift my body back toward Laura, and focus my stare on her as I offer a compassionate smile. "Look," I begin. "You know Gil Mathers better than anyone in this world. You've been along for the ride, from the highs to the depths and everything in between. In spite of all of his bluster and bravado and bullshit, you know him down to the core. So, what I think you need to ask yourself is whether Gil is capable of this. Whether this is something that he would do. That he *could* do. Whether your husband is really this person."

She holds my look defiantly, her lips puckering. "I don't know, Vic. I just . . . I'm just not sure."

I reach a hand across the table and set it firmly atop her own. "Honey," I say steadily. "Who is this man you married?"

I feel her fingers squeeze mine, and it seems as if she's grasping at a life preserver. Her face screws up, and I see that primal, wounded look in her eyes, the one I know so well, the look that eats away a piece of me each time I receive it. She stares at me with that adolescent indignation, daring me, before her expression morphs into something more raw, less guarded. Finally, she lets herself blink, slowly and deliberately, as if her lids are relieving themselves of a burdensome weight. When her eyes open, she's looking at me sheepishly, timidly. I study my sister, and without her speaking a word I realize that she's known who her husband's been all this time.

CHAPTER TWENTY-ONE

LAURA

MOST OF THE drive home is a stormy blur of flashbacks until I throw on Lizzo and sing along to "Good as Hell" at the top of my lungs.

As I ease the Lexus around the bend and up our long driveway, my vision goes from normal to red as I see stacks of boxes in the open garage come into focus. They weren't there when I left this morning, and I'm shocked at how apparently busy my husband has been in my absence. My daughter's name is written in Gil's sloppy hand over and over. At the sight, my ears begin to ring with an excruciatingly painful frequency, prompting me to reach for the buttons to turn off the music that has already stopped playing.

I am going to kill him.

There are about thirty cardboard moving boxes with *Libby* emblazoned across the sides in black marker. I feel the air in my lungs completely empty, leaving me behind the wheel of my car heaving with rage. The sight of our daughter's name out in the open, waiting for me, has brought forth an old anger that I had forgotten.

He's taunting me.

There is no sign of Gil as I storm into the garage and tear off the tape from the top box of one of the neatly stacked towers. A monsoon of my tears cascades into the container holding her light pink security blanket, which is shoddily folded on top of the cache of stuffed animals, baby books, and fingerpainted artwork. I pull the box from its perch and place it on the ground and proceed to tear the strip of packing tape from the box below it. This one is filled with her baby clothes, piles of lush Laura Ashley dresses, and adorable miniature Ralph Lauren Christmas sweaters that are soft in my hands. I pull a BabyBjörn from the box and put it around me and begin to feverishly gather as much of the box contents into the sling as I can before bolting into the house.

"GILBERT!" I scream into the abyss, my voice reverberating throughout the open space.

I race through the kitchen into the vestibule, scanning for signs of him. I almost trip over more boxes on my way to check the backyard. I shakily call his phone from the house phone with no success as I clutch at Libby's belongings, shaking with rage, pulling her blanket to my nose, desperate to catch a long-faded scent of my daughter.

"GILBERT ANDREW MATHERS! Where the FUCK are you?" My bellows are answered by the sound of faint drilling coming from the direction of Libby's room. I bound up the stairs two steps at a time, dropping some of the baby clothes along the way and pausing to gather them, my vision clouded by tears. I bust through the closed door.

Gil is in the center of the room, on his knees on a drop cloth surrounded by cans of paint. He flinches as I barrel in and looks at me, startled. I eagle eye the room and feel immediately disoriented because the space I am now standing in is most definitely not the one I left intact yesterday morning, the last time I was dusting the surfaces of my daughter's treasured things.

"What did you do?" I wail.

Scattered about the space are stacks of gray foam squares, and in the corner of the room nearest to the en suite bathroom, there are boxes of video and audio equipment, microphones, lighting stands, and a number of computer and flat-screen TV boxes.

"Why? WHY?" I plead to a speechless Gil.

The room smells like fresh paint. Where the walls were once lavender with a border of fairies sitting on colorful flowers bifurcating the room, all of it has been stripped away and replaced by a light gray hue, appropriately giving the room a cold, empty, and somber feel. In front of one of the walls there is a plush leather chair and a pedestal table next to it.

I stand slack-jawed in the doorway, and I start to wobble. I put my hand on the wall nearest to me for support.

"Watch the walls—they aren't completely dry," Gil warns as he rises to his feet. I close my hands into fists and start pounding the wall hard. He flinches with each blow, which gives me fleeting satisfaction.

"WHOA!! Calm down, Laura! You're fucking up my paint job," he yells.

"WHAT THE FUCKING FUCK, GIL? YOUR *PAINT JOB*?! *What the fuck have you done to her room?*" I shriek through fresh tears into Libby's baby blanket, which is still in my hand. I swear to myself that I will never let it out of my sight again. I wrap it around my forearm like I'm about to be attacked by a dog. Then I reach for a paint-roller pole that is leaning against a large box and wield it in his direction.

"Whoa. Laur. Calm down." He puts up his hand defensively and I wish the pole in my hand had a sharp blade on the end of it.

I glare at him, speechless.

"I didn't think you would be this upset."

"Gil," I say slowly as I look around the room. "I need you to explain to me what is happening right now. What have you done?"

"I figured you'd be relieved to have this done. I know you didn't want to do it yourself, so I thought I'd take it off your plate," he says sanguinely.

"I shouldn't be surprised that you are turning this into something I should be thanking you for. You are fucking unbelievable." I kick at a closed paint can.

"Laura, let's go downstairs and talk this out," he says.

"Fuck you."

"I didn't want you to see this until it was done."

"What are you even doing here? How did you get so much done so quickly? You have barely done anything around this house in God knows how long," I yell.

"I didn't think you'd be home so early today. You're usually at Vicky's later on your yoga days. I was motivated."

He moves toward me as though to shepherd me out the door, but I don't budge.

"And what is *this* exactly, Gil?" I lean against the doorjamb and survey the space where he's emptied every last trace of Libby. "What would possess you to do this without talking to me first?"

"This isn't destruction. It's progression. I'm building something new."

"Why here? Why this room?"

"Because it is the biggest room after our bedroom and it has the bathroom and plenty of outlets and the acoustics are better," he lists as his head moves around the room, mentally gathering his rationale.

My jaw is sore from hanging open and alternately grinding my teeth.

"It was all that we had left of her."

"Laura, it wasn't healthy keeping it the way it was."

"You never came in here. You didn't even care," I say, incensed.

"How could you even say that? Of course I care. I'm her father."

"Oh, *now* you're her father? You didn't even acknowledge her birthday this year."

"Everyone mourns differently." He reddens.

"You are a monster," I cry.

"I'm sorry that's how you see me."

"Please God. Just stop. You barely reacted when Libby was killed. The only tears I saw were on your Piers Morgan interview, and I think those were more about you being bumped to the last segment of the show," I say icily.

"I'm not going to even engage in this conversation because it is hysterical," he says coldly.

"Go ahead, pull your misogynistic mindfuckery."

"Laura, sweetheart, I think you are rewriting history a bit. I poured my heart into the cause after Libby died."

"The cause?!" I spew.

"I spent nine months doing what I could on behalf of gun control! I raised millions of dollars for charity! I gave all of the parents of the kids who were killed those free seminars, and the survivors got the free therapy because of the calls I made—"

"Just stop. You're doing what you always do. You're making Libby's death and the shooting about *you* and what *you* did."

"What would you prefer I make this about, Laura?"

"About what you *didn't* do!" I yell with my entire body.

"I can't talk to you if you are going to throw a tantrum." He tries to move around me to get out of the room, but I block him with my body and by holding the paint-roller pole parallel to the floor in front of my chest.

"You've been doing this kind of shit for years, and I justified it as a habit because of your work, but now I see it for what it is."

"And what is it, Laura?" He cocks his head.

"Abuse. You are abusive, Gil."

"Abuse is a human construct. You are only construing my behavior as abusive because you've decided to label it as such," he says dismissively.

"Do you hear how crazy you sound?"

"You have always been a self-victimizer."

"Stop using your bullshit on me, Gil. I know what you're doing."

"Laura. You need to look hard at what it is you are really upset about. Is it really that I transitioned Libby's bedroom? The logical perspective is that it is simply a room in a house that looked one way yesterday and looks different today. Has anything essential really changed? Or is it really that you can't accept that life is moving forward and you aren't willing to make the decision to do that yourself?" He puts his hands on his hips.

"Do you hear yourself?"

He glowers at me. "Who are you really angry at right now? Your father?"

"OH. MY. GOD!" I scream. "Just talk to me like a real human being."

"Laura, you're hiding behind some melodramatic narrative because you can't face what is really going on here."

"What *is* really going on here, Gil? I mean other than you talking me into dizzy circles so that you don't have to take accountability for being a sociopath."

"And you are desperately waving the victim card so that you can dodge responsibility for your inability to move on and make your life about something other than the bad things that have happened to you."

"Some of those things happened to you too! And because of you!" I shout.

"I'm not doing anything to you, Laura. You are making a conscious decision to live in this state of drama and suffering."

"So I made the decision to snort lines of Adderall with a seventeen-year-old and disparage all of the 'whiny, weak pussies' who come to your seminars? And all on camera?"

He clenches his fists. "Jesus, Laura. Let it go. The rest of the world has moved on from the goddamn video, except my own wife."

"Maybe I could move on if I didn't keep learning about new, horrible ways that you abused your power and took advantage of your fans."

"I didn't take advantage of that woman. I took her on her word that she was twenty-two. That was completely consensual. And the drugs were prescribed to her. And technically I have an attention deficit diagnosis too."

"I'm not talking about the video. I'm talking about your VIP receptions and after-parties and the other women you were grooming."

I see a flicker of fear in Gil's eyes.

"You are disproving your own point by bringing up the video," he sidesteps. "You can't say that I lacked a response to our daughter's death and then throw the biggest personal and professional mistake in my face at the same time. I lost my daughter and my career. That event was a direct response to Libby's death. I was acting out. Pick a lane, Laura."

"Again!!" I throw up my hands and the pole goes flying behind me and into the hallway and he flinches. "You are fucking making Libby's death about you and your career!" I howl.

"Didn't we establish with Dr. Williams over many hundreds of hours of unendurable couples therapy that the video incident was my own coping mechanism in response to the tragedy? Which is what I was telling you before you forced me to go to that terribly basic psychotherapy situation. What we paid for those sessions and all that time, I could have explained to you in one night over dinner."

"Do you hear yourself? No wonder you got canceled."

"Let me put it plainly, then. You need to get the fuck over the past. You dig Libby up every day. Let her be. She's gone."

I feel like he's actually hit me with both of his clenched fists at the same time, one in the face and the other in my chest.

"I'm not the only one who's living in the past, Gil. If you think you are ever going to be relevant again, you are brain damaged."

"I wholeheartedly disagree, Laur. If Sawyer Selwyn can hit number one with that schlocky Law of Three crap, then it is only a matter of time before I can ride that wave."

I laugh in his face. "This was all we had left of her," I repeat. "And you just destroyed it for what? To become an Instagram influencer?" I scoff. "Start another podcast that nobody needs?"

His face reddens.

I laugh harder and see the whites of his knuckles pale another degree while his eyes narrow.

"Oh God. Gil, I was kidding. Are you really?" I say coldly.

"There is a lot of money in influencing. And if you think about it, I . . . I was one of the original influencers," he stammers.

"I think you are delusional."

"Back when people used to leave their houses to get motivated and influenced? I got them off their asses. I used to fill major venues, for chrissakes."

I look away from him and around the room at the soundproofing, A/V equipment, and umbrella lights. There's even a professional makeup kit.

"And how, pray tell, are you planning on getting any followers after belittling all of your 'pussy' followers? That footage is never going away, Gil."

"I know that. I've thought of nothing other than that fact for the past two years. But I was finally able to reframe it all and see this as the opportunity that it really is. I can own my mistakes and leverage them. I can use clips of that incident on my podcast in each episode and explain that what I was doing was turning the heat up on people's deepest insecurities to mobilize them, and things were taken out of context."

"But they weren't. You got caught red-handed talking shit and doing things that you had criticized so many people for publicly." I take a breath before plowing ahead, surprised that he isn't interrupting me more.

"Gil, what about all of your preaching about infidelity being for the weak, and how performance-enhancing drugs were shortcuts? How are you going to explain your way out of that?"

"By explaining that the grief I was experiencing due to our daughter's death led me down a dark path. I can talk about toxic masculinity as indoctrinated gender roles and then bring my ideas about men and vulnerability during crises into focus."

"Are you serious right now?"

"The only thing people seem to rally around more than canceling someone is supporting their comeback if they expose themselves vulnerably. I literally wrote the book on how to do that."

I hold my breath, waiting for him to point to one of the copies of his earlier book, *Men from the Boys*. But I realize he has yet to move those copies into this room.

"So, this is what you have been toiling away at in your office all this time?"

"Yes. And other things."

"Other things for Terry?" I needle.

His face tightens. "Terry is helping *me*, not the other way around."

I scoff. "Terry only helps Terry. You know that."

"Terry and I have mutual interests, and he sees my comeback as a sound investment. He has some connections in the influencer market, and a friend who produced three of the top podcasts in the last year. And there is a Hollywood producer interested in backing a documentary about my path back to the public eye. A redemption story post #MeToo, if you will."

"I won't." I stare at him. "The #MeToo movement isn't over, Gil, and it isn't going away. You are missing the whole point of it if you think that people are going to give you airtime after that shit—"

"I think you are wrong about what people will give their attention to."

I think hard about whether I want to wound to kill or just fuck him up for a while.

"Well, good luck to you, Gil," I say quietly.

He raises a wary eyebrow.

"Although I have to say that it's pretty ironic that you're getting help from Terry to rebuild your career."

"Ironic?" He smirks.

"Oh, I don't want to start anything, especially over something that's in the past. As you so eloquently put it, 'I need to move the fuck on.'"

"Laura," he warns. "Cough it up."

I stare at him and let the anticipation simmer.

"What do you know?" he pushes.

"I know plenty."

"Oh, bullshit, Laura. Now you're just playing games."

"I'm done with the games, Gil." And as it comes out of my mouth, I really want to believe it. "I think it is utterly moronic that you are letting the man who was responsible for tearing your career down in the first place 'help' you build it back up. Isn't that kind of like asking the person who just plunged a knife in your back to give you a ride to the hospital?"

Gil looks at me peculiarly as he processes. "I don't follow."

I leave him in silence and relish the building struggle in him.

"Terry didn't destroy my career; that video getting leaked did."

I let him mull a little longer.

"Gil, who the fuck do you think leaked the video in the first place, anyway?"

⑂

After Gil storms out of the house, I wait for the sound of his car before I swap my espadrilles out for my Nikes. Just as I am about to sprint out the door, I realize I've left my phone in Libby's bedroom. As I walk by Gil's office, I see that the door is slightly open, which is unusual. I step inside. His computer screen is facing away from the door, so I walk around and wake up the monitor. I'm prompted to enter a password and I take a chance and type "Libby" into the field, which doesn't work. I look around the room for a hint and see a few bogus awards generated by Gil's own organization, one of the plaques with the inscription "the Notorious G.I.L.," which prompts me to enter "Notorious," and the screen unlocks.

The last page he'd been looking at is a series of headshots, each rectangle showing a beautiful face or full-body shot. The pics have bookmarks at the upper right-hand corner, and I see that Gil has clicked on quite a few. According to the description of each woman, they span in age from eighteen to twenty-five, and their countries of origin range from South and Central American countries to countries in Southeast Asia and Africa.

The URL is numerical, so I'm unclear what the site is and I don't want to navigate away from the page and alert Gil that I've been poking around. I minimize the screen and see his Gmail is open on an email from Terry with the subject line "Hemmings New Crop," with the same numerical link in the body of the message. I click back to the page that was originally open, close the door partway, the way I found it, and fight against queasiness as I make my way downstairs.

I sprint out the back door and cut around the fence and straight to the running path. When the tears begin to come, I speed up to keep the emotions at bay. Dusk is settling in and the humidity has broken slightly. As I pound the ground hard, my sundress swooshes along my thighs and makes a sound like scissors cutting through paper.

I zip past Vicky's and Milly's houses and speed up. It is just a hunch, but an overwhelming one that I can't deny. A sharp cramp stabs my lower right ribs, but I keep my pace.

The sun is starting to fall below the tree line and swaths of orange and red light from the sunset are emerging in a halo effect through the spaces between the trees.

I round the final bend of the path just in time to hit the straight shot of visibility from a group of trees bordering Monica's backyard, right as Gil's car pulls into her driveway.

CHAPTER TWENTY-TWO

MONICA

"OH DEAR, YOU look like you've been up all night!" Milly exclaims when she opens the door to Vicky's house and grabs the stacked Tupperware out of my hands. Apparently, she's taken it upon herself to be the de facto host of the party.

"Hi, Milly." I force a smile.

"We were beginning to wonder what happened to you." She puts an arm on the doorframe, blocking the small space like a well-coiffed bridge troll.

I take in her silk Pucci caftan and matching scarf headband. She looks positively Sharon Tate in *Valley of the Dolls*. Love her or hate her, the woman knows how to put an outfit together.

But I don't have the energy. I have been up all night and I have Gil showing up at my house unannounced to blame for that.

"Just fashionably late." I shift my weight and regret my shoe choice. My platform clogs are pinching already and I haven't even made it inside the party. I'm eager to move along and not get caught in another heart-to-heart with her.

"And where is Spencer?" She cranes her neck to look over my shoulder. I'm tempted to let her keep craning until she pulls something.

"He's on his way," I tell her as I push past her into the house and to the kitchen.

Along the massive marble countertops is a huge array of food spread out alongside innumerable bottles of wine, pitchers of margaritas, and growlers of homemade beer. The windows are open and the ubiquitous summer barbecue music of Carlos Santana rings through the air alongside chatter, laughter, splashing, and squealing in the pool.

Outside the sliding glass doors I see that the cookout is in full swing, with Terry holding court at the enormous stainless steel grill surrounded by a number of recognizable men from the neighborhood who are dutifully engrossed while he dramatically gesticulates with tongs and a large burger flipper.

"I think it is so down-to-earth that Vicky and Terry don't professionally cater the barbecue. It would be so much easier, though, wouldn't it?" Milly says this to Stephanie Dryers, a drop-dead gorgeous South African woman who recently moved into Kingsland and whom I've only met a few times before. Stephanie is pushing a lime wedge into a bottle of Corona, and after she accomplishes this, she shifts the hemline of a translucent embroidered tunic, showcasing a metallic string bikini visible underneath.

She is easily thirty years younger than her husband, making her a good fifteen years younger than most of the wives, and an easy target. Rumor is that she was nearly a Victoria's Secret Angel, lore that quickly made her the focus of much shit talking among the threatened women of Kingsland and badly concealed ogling by their husbands.

Stephanie, who has been nothing but nice every time I've inter-acted with her, looks surprised that she's been included. "When Amar told me that it was a 'potluck,' I had to literally google what that meant. I didn't know what to bring, so I just got some potato salad from Whole Foods and put it in a nice bowl," she confesses.

"Monica, have you met Stephanie?" Milly drips sweetly.

"I have. Hi, Stephanie." I smile and move to hug her, and she air-kisses me on both cheeks.

"Hey!" she says warmly. "I've got to get this to hubby. He gets so possessive at these things, but I'd love to talk more later." She slides out the door.

"We'll see how long that one lasts. She's number four and I've heard that he's been spending a lot of time overnight at his place in the city. You know what that means," Milly says under her breath before Stephanie is fully three steps away from the open door. "I heard that Terry introduced them after Amar's last acquittal at her eighteenth birthday party."

"God, I hope that's not true." I cringe and grab a glass and help myself to a healthy pour of rosé. "I'm going to find Vicky and let her know I'm here."

"Mm-kay. See you out there," she says, already distracted by the sound of the doorbell.

I step out onto the deck and see Milly's husband, Roger, off to the side talking to Gil, and my stomach lurches. Roger's cartoonesque nasal carries over to where I'm standing: "In my Cambridge days, you couldn't get admitted unless you had at least two generations of direct blood-related alumni; now apparently *anyone* can get in," he laments.

I trip out the door and onto the deck, catching myself before any of my wine spills. I loudly curse my shoes and both men look in my direction, but Roger is the only one who acknowledges me, while Gil quickly looks away. I move into the rest of the party quickly.

I spy Vicky down near the pool looking stunning in a Tory Burch tunic dress and Isabel Marant sandals. Her hair is perfectly blown out and is pushed back from her glowing face with Prada sunglasses. As always, she is the most stunning woman at the party.

I catch Laura's eye a few feet from her sister, and she's also exquisitely put together with her hair pulled into a French twist and a formfitting BCBG tank dress. She looks away and resumes talking to someone I've never met, and I head toward Vicky, who is freshening some guests' glasses with a large pitcher of sangria that she's circulating with. She sees me over their shoulders and smiles broadly.

"Monica!" The guests turn, and it is the three women from yoga class, who acknowledge me and then conspicuously look at one another. Mercifully, they don't follow Vicky as she makes her way over to me and kisses my cheek. "You made it!"

"I'm so sorry I'm late." I squeeze her back. "This morning was rough."

"Don't be silly. The party is just getting going. Laura got here about ten minutes ago." She lowers her voice. "Milly's been here for hours. I think she was in my kitchen getting ready before Terry was even out of bed."

"She is relentless." I restrain myself, aware that we are surrounded by deft eavesdroppers. "Is she going to be this way until we let her into the book club?" I joke.

"How are you holding up?" she says, and puts her hand on my arm gently.

"I'm okay. I'm not sure if Spence is going to make it. I tried."

"Please don't worry. Terry is so preoccupied with his fanboys over there, he probably won't even notice."

And on cue, Terry's voice booms in our direction.

"Mrs. Nichols! Welcome! Fancy some filet? It's fresh from the grill. Or perhaps a swordfish steak?" He twirls his tongs and slings them into the pocket of his absurd bright-red apron with the words "Make Grilling Great Again" splashed across it. "Watch the fire for me," he orders the three men standing around him.

I feel anxious as Terry heads over to us. His energy is always overwhelming, and he engages me only if he wants something.

"Hi, Terry. This is great. I don't think I've been to a real barbecue since I was back home."

"Home for you is Texas, right?"

"That's right. Galveston."

"Hmm. You barely have a trace of an accent. How'd you manage that?"

"I was sent to boarding school pretty young; working the twang out of me was part of the deal."

"Sounds about right," he says knowingly.

I'm not sure what it is he thinks he knows about me or my past, since I've just flat-out lied. I mentally tally another bullshit flag confirming what I already know: Terry Barnes is a big, fat know-nothing instead of the know-it-all he presents as. I stay neutral in my expression and body language, giving him nothing to work with. Thankfully, his attention to me will be fleeting. I can see him scanning the crowd behind and around me to see who he'd rather be talking to.

"Spencer inside?" He sniffs.

"He got held up." My voice catches.

"What could be more important than the annual Barnes Fourth of July cookout? Doesn't he know that it's practically a legal Kingsland holiday?" He laughs obnoxiously while taking a swig of the bottle of beer in his hand. The label catches my attention.

"'Barnes's Brew'? What a coincidence," I say, and I see Vicky look at the ground and frown. I am well versed in Terry's homemade beer endeavors from hearing Vicky lament about them, but I feign ignorance for something to talk about.

"Actually, it isn't. This is my very own."

I widen my eyes because I know it's the reaction he wants.

"It's the first batch, actually, of the season. I've been saving it for this day," he brags. "Have a sip," he orders me, and shoves the bottle into my hand as Vicky mouths, "Sorry," out of Terry's sight line.

"I brewed it in my garage and I've already got it into the hands of the best beer connoisseurs in the business. You'll probably see this on the shelves of every gourmet grocery and liquor store in the country by next Fourth of July," he gloats.

I reluctantly take a small sip; my taste for beer is about as weak as it is for Terry. Vicky looks distracted by something near the house.

"Excuse me just a minute. Let me just go check on something."

"Let me help you," I say, trying to catch her before she bolts, but then feeling the weight of Terry's meaty palm on my arm holding me in place.

"She's fine," he says sternly. "What do you think about Barnes's Brew?" Terry looks at me expectantly as I smile and take another tiny sip, the foul liquid wending its way down my throat. I muster a pleasant smile as I swallow the nastiness down.

"Wow, Terry. This is really something."

This meets with his approval and he raises his bottle to the men by the grill. "Another fan!" He laughs loudly and everyone around us turns to look at him and nods or laughs along with him. An army of kiss-asses surround us.

"Well, I'll let you get back to your guests and your grill," I say as I attempt to move back to the house.

"Hold on there, Mrs. Nichols." He replaces his hand, this time with a stronger grip on my upper arm. He squeezes my biceps and a wolfish grin spreads. "Nice. Rock hard. I appreciate a woman who keeps it tight."

"What do you want, Terry?" I say, disgusted.

"A little birdie told me that you and the mister are thinking about leaving Kingsland."

My ears start ringing. "Oh?" I say weakly. "People love to talk in Kingsland. Worse than high school."

"So, this is just a nasty rumor?" His face has subtly morphed into an empty canvas, and I am painfully aware of how much my response in this moment will affect the course of the rest of this afternoon.

"Well, I mean, we've discussed returning to Santa Clara if we could get our old house back, but that isn't likely. You know how it is. Just talk. I doubt anything will come of it. I really love it here," I manage.

Terry stares me down as he takes a long, final swig from his bottle. The beer in his mouth obscures any readable expression and I hold my breath.

I look around the party, which feels as though it is also waiting for Terry's response, whether the ever-ticking bomb within him will explode or if we are all safe for another afternoon. Of course the crowd around us are in the midst of their own conversations, but I know that even then, everyone is aware of where Terry is and who he is talking to.

He takes the bottle away from his mouth and grins at me.

"You are a wild card, aren't you, Mrs. Nichols?"

"How do you mean?" I struggle to keep my voice even.

"I know more about you than you realize. I'm keeping a close watch on you," he says darkly. "And I'm glad to hear that the gossip isn't true. It would be a real shame for us to lose you both. Vicky is very fond of you, and I know she would be devastated."

"I adore Vicky," I manage, my shoulders tensing.

"And I've grown quite dependent on your husband. I might go as far as to say that I would do anything to keep him here in Kingsland. And people don't always like my methods for keeping my neighbors close." He does nothing to veil his threatening tone.

I'm stunned speechless until I feel another strong arm on my own. It isn't Terry's.

"Spence. You came," I say gratefully into my husband's steely face.

"Now, now, Terry. Let's save the bluffing for our game tomorrow night and leave our wives out of it," he warns.

Terry's brow creases and his eyes dim.

"Yeah, why don't we," he says to Spencer.

I feel Spence's hand pushing me away from him and Terry, and I turn my back and walk in the direction of the house, my heart pounding.

"We need to talk, Nichols" is the last thing I hear Terry say before their conversation is drowned out by the sounds of the party around me as I escape into the temporary safety of Vicky's house.

As I look over my shoulder, I see Spencer turn his back on Terry and stalk away from him, leaving our illustrious host in shock that he's been left alone at his own party.

CHAPTER TWENTY-THREE

VICTORIA

I STAND IN the oasis of my kitchen, the din of conversation outside muffled by the closed sliding glass door, assessing the array of gifted booze taking up real estate on my island countertop. Among the offerings is a magnum of Billecart-Salmon Brut Rosé, situated next to a budget bottle of Shiraz with enough dust settled into the foil around the cork to convince me it's a regift from last Christmas. I'm again reminded of the amusing dichotomy of wealth; for every person with money loudly announcing each comma in their portfolio, there's another who's astoundingly, cartoonishly cheap.

Monica's been here for all of twenty minutes and already looks shell-shocked, the poor thing. She's parked herself near the sink, arranging the vegetables and dip for the crudités platter as an excuse to escape the fray just a little longer. I offer her a knowing smile as I pluck a couple of still-cold bottles of Prosecco from the assortment, pop the tops, and head for the door. "Give a yell if you need anything, Mon," I call behind me as I exit onto the back deck.

Terry's holding court at the grill, sipping from a bottle of his silly home brew and regaling his company with stories of cookouts past at third-beer-in volume. Spencer's arrived and stands with the group, an irritated look on his face. I lay a kiss on Terry's cheek as I pass by and feel multiple sets of eyes subtly ogle me as I move on. I set one of the bottles of Prosecco in the ice chest on the corner of the deck before I step down onto the lawn and begin to circulate among our guests.

I offer warm smiles to a few neighbors as I move to refill their waning glasses. I hear a kid's voice roar loudly and turn my head just in time to catch him cannonballing into my pool, setting off a series of shrieks from splash victims in the vicinity. I pass by Roger LeFleur, who's pinned another hapless fellow to the spot with some inane anecdote from his "time in Cambridge." I could swear that the gladiolus have drooped since he's been standing here and quietly enjoy the image of ol' Rog literally boring my flowers into submission.

As I top off a few more glasses, I take note of Gil Mathers, off to the side of the yard, talking to a man I recognize as an associate of Terry's. I catch a snippet of conversation about soybean futures and pick up on a general air of distractedness on Gil's end. Earlier, when Monica first arrived, she'd made a point of sidestepping Gil, who was at the time standing on the deck talking with Roger. I wonder now if Gil noticed the slight, and if it has anything to do with his current look of preoccupation.

I catch Milly sitting in one of the pair of Adirondack chairs situated at the far end of the yard and find myself feeling relieved that she's abandoned sentry duty at my front door. She's balancing a plastic plate on her knees and eyeing me eagerly. I approach her, pour the remains of the Prosecco into her glass, and set the empty bottle on the ground as I take the seat beside her. The sight of her tiny frame being practically swallowed by the chair strikes me as comical, as does the daintiness with which she's attempting to gnaw on the rib she's holding tentatively between her manicured fingers.

"Vicky!" she coos. "The event of the season, as always."

"You're having a good time?" I ask.

"Of course. Roger and I look forward to this every summer. I think it's good for him to have some time with the neighbors. He really loves to chew the fat, once you get him going."

I do my best to stifle a snort, to little avail. Milly stares me down confusedly before I wave her off. "Sorry," I explain. "That expression just tickles me for some reason. Not even sure why."

"Oh," she says with a suspicious lilt, before pulling the last of the meat from the rib and setting the plate of stripped bones down on the patch of lawn next to her.

"I haven't seen Bryce yet," I say, mainly to shift the conversation. "Will he be able to stop by?"

"Oh, you know." She gives her eyes a good-natured roll. "Kids his age. I imagine he's off with his friends, getting up to some sort of trouble."

"Sure." I nod.

"Hey, I just noticed you don't have a drink in your hand. Everything okay?"

"Fine," I assure her. "Just busy playing hostess. Plus, these things tend to go long. Not a bad idea to pace myself."

"I see." She nods. "Well, anyway, yes. We're having a great time, as it seems everyone is." She holds eye contact through a pause so pregnant it's crowning, clearly savoring whatever scandalous barb she's about to drop on me. "Well, *almost* everyone," she clarifies.

I decide to do my good deed for the day and indulge Milly's insatiable appetite for gossip. "Oh," I say, feigning concern and performing a visual sweep of the crowd. "Did you notice something I haven't picked up on?"

"Well, honey," she begins. "I'm afraid there might be a little trouble in paradise, is all I'm saying."

I think I see where this one's going and decide to let it play out. "Who are you referring to, Milly?"

She looks around, for dramatic effect, before leaning closer. "Did you notice that Spencer Nichols arrived late, *separate* from his wife?"

"Oh, Spence?" I say casually. "I'm sure he just got caught up at home, tinkering away at something or other. You know how these tech guys are."

"I don't know," she singsongs, frowning. "Monica found you earlier, yes? She didn't seem a little, you know, *off*?"

"Hmm," I consider. "Gosh, I didn't pick up on anything there."

"I mean, far be it from me to start rumors, but she just seemed . . . preoccupied. And maybe a little distressed? And now *he's* over there with Terry, and *their* exchange looked a bit tense." I can see the muscles working to crease her forehead, but the amount of Botox in the equation is foiling the effort. I have more luck suppressing my amusement this time. "I just worry about our little longhorn," she says.

"I'll make a point of checking in on her on my next lap," I say. "Thanks for your concern. Though I'm sure everything between Mon and Spence is just fine." I pat Milly's hand to reassure her and catch her lips pulling into a tight smirk.

"If you say so." She nods. "After all, you know her better than I do." For once, Milly is underplaying it, and I can't help but notice how satisfied she appears, convinced she now knows something I don't.

I'm about to head back into circulation when Ramona and Harmony approach. Ramona is teetering on her wedge sandals, and some of the rosé sloshes from her glass as Harmony clamps a hand onto her friend's forearm in an effort to steady them both. The pair giggle before looking at us.

"Victoria!" they exclaim, in buzzed unison.

"Hi, ladies," I say. "Having a nice time?"

"The best," answers Harmony. "Hey, we were worried about you the other day. Not like you and Laura to skip class. Everything okay?"

"Oh, fine. Just had some errands that couldn't wait." I shrug as I offer a smile.

"Ramona," Milly cuts in. "So happy you made it. I heard the news this morning. How's your section of the neighborhood?"

Ramona stares at her, confused. "What do you mean?"

"Oh, the story's all over," explains Milly. "There was a carjacking a few blocks from you. I was hoping you and your family were okay."

The explanation does nothing to enlighten Ramona, but I'm aware of what Milly's referring to. There was an alert this morning about an Aston Martin having been stolen overnight out of a drive-way near the enclave where Ramona lives with her husband and his kids. The term "carjacking" has been egregiously misused for dra-matic effect, and what Milly's neglected to mention—whether as a result of ignorance or selective editing—is the fact that the car was retrieved shortly after it was reported stolen, dumped undamaged in a lot after an apparent joyride.

"Huh," says Ramona, before taking a sip of her drink. "Hadn't heard anything about it." She consults Harmony, who also seems blissfully unaware of the incident.

Milly frowns. "Haven't you ladies been following the news *at all*?" she chastises. "There have been a string of these carjackings recently. One last week in Stony Brook, another before that in Port Jeff. This is just the latest."

"But no one's been hurt, though, right?" I offer in an attempt to mitigate the damper my neighbor's line of conversation is putting on these women's good time.

"Well, not *yet*," she responds. "But these sorts of things have a way of escalating. I mean, that's just the nature of criminality." Milly's speaking animatedly even by her own standards, and I wonder how much of it can be attributed to the contents of the glass in her hand. The two women are politely nodding along, though they seem pretty well glazed over.

"I don't know," I say, trying to defuse the situation. "Seems like maybe just some kids acting out?"

"Isn't that how it starts, though?" she snaps. "The criminal element? We can't forget, ladies, that outside of our immediate neighborhood there's a rougher population. And we can't be naive about the class resentment at play. There are plenty of *these* people out there, who think they're entitled to the spoils of our success, even though they're not willing to work for them."

Ramona and Harmony have resigned themselves to sipping from their glasses, unsure of what else to do. I take their cue and mime a champagne flute in my hand.

"Well," I say. "Now that we've solved the problems of the world, I think it's time for a drink." I tip the invisible glass in a faux toast. The gesture elicits a relieved titter from the two ladies and a self-conscious reddening of the cheeks from Milly. She latches onto my hand desperately, to hold me in place.

"Oh, look at me going on." She makes too much of an effort at a casual laugh as she surveys the three of us. "Please don't misunderstand me, ladies. I mean, I'm not heartless." Ramona and Harmony nod mechanically, tight smiles fixed to their faces. I tilt my head sympathetically to mask the enjoyment I'm getting out of watching this ridiculous woman squirm.

"Of course not," I say.

"Right," she says, seemingly relieved that we haven't abandoned her here on the lawn. "I have a certain amount of compassion for some of the more, um, *disenfranchised* aspects of our society." She clears her throat in preparation for the big finish. "But that doesn't mean they can just come into our neighborhood and help themselves to the things we've rightfully earned."

"Mmm." I squeeze Milly's hand reassuringly before I slip my own loose of her grip. "Pardon me for just a moment, ladies. Going to go check on the rest of our guests." I flash a warm smile before I turn to walk back toward the kitchen, where I'll pour myself the tall, cold drink *I've* rightfully earned.

On my way to the house, I scan the crowd milling about the lawn, and my throat catches as I recognize that son of a bitch from the Palm Springs trip—the jaunt that Terry had billed as a spur-of-the-moment romantic getaway. Here he stands, in our backyard, engaging my husband in what looks to be a furtive exchange. With morbid curiosity, I skirt the edge of the yard in an attempt to drop in for an earful of their conversation. As I approach unnoticed, he leaves Terry to the grilling and heads toward the house. I follow at a distance, taking in his themed barbecue outfit—the red linen button-up, seersucker pants, and blue suede driving loafers on his diminutive feet.

I enter through the kitchen and trail him down the hallway, where he stops in front of the door to Terry's office and tries the knob.

"Excuse me," I say, eliciting a startled look. "May I help you?"

"Oh, terribly sorry," he says, his expression slipping into a leer as he gives me the subtle once-over. "I was looking for the bathroom."

"End of the hall on the left," I explain, overdoing the smile I offer up before turning and heading back to the kitchen. As he thanks me over my shoulder, I swear I feel the heat of those animal eyes taking me in.

CHAPTER TWENTY-FOUR

LAURA

M y sister's tolerance for the annual Fourth of July invasion borders on sainthood. I am awed by her grace as she circulates through the clusters of sycophants and wannabes, a huge smile spread across her beaming face, hiding any tell of resentment or disdain. She would never admit it, but I know that she dreads this event as much as Terry rejoices in it, and I feel her pain.

Summer after summer, Vicky shows up for this salute to Terry masked as an Independence Day celebration with as much enthusiasm and warmth as she did when he was still welcomed in the major political circles in DC, and center stage at charity events in New York. Those were the days when the demand for our presence at gatherings was so overwhelming, Vicky and I would sit down monthly and sift through our identical invites, playing each one like a hand of war.

After Terry was indicted, people were more or less tolerant of his presence, because he was by Vicky's side, and mostly, they stayed politely silent about the daily headlines of bribery, extortion, and political glad-handing leading up to his trial. Unless they'd had one too many scotches and would make a comment at Terry's expense within earshot of him, which happened with increasing frequency as time wore on.

Terry, being Terry, became obsessively preoccupied with retributional payback, which took away from things he actually needed to be doing, like working with his defense team, so Victoria put an embargo on socializing. After Terry made bail, he was placed under house arrest by his wife for his own good. But he was like a benched athlete and was already dreaming up Kingsland and a captive audience who would never turn on him even before he officially knew if he'd be acquitted.

Once Gil's professional implosion followed not too long after Terry's, and people were openly hostile toward us as a group, the endless invites ceased as swiftly as they'd piled up. After a lifetime of complaining about too many social obligations, we found ourselves blacklisted, with varying negative feelings about this new exclusion. I was of the mind that I wanted to be invited and have the choice not to attend, Gil and Terry couldn't bear the thought of any high-society fabric remaining intact without their participation, and even Vicky, who was more prone to small-group quality time, became wistful about being shut out.

We'd barely gotten settled into our post-Manhattan life in Kingsland before the shooting at the elementary school. After Libby was killed, Vicky and I just wanted to go someplace far away and never have to talk to people again. Everything felt hopeless and I didn't think I would ever not feel that terrible pain in my heart. Vicky said that she couldn't truly know how I was feeling, but losing Libby was the worst pain she had ever felt, so she knew I was feeling twice as badly. I was so grateful—I needed the acknowledgment that losing my child was in fact the worst thing that could have happened.

Our husbands weren't affected in quite the same way. They seemed to crave more time in a spotlight, any spotlight, in fact, and Terry was insistent that they go ahead with the inaugural Fourth of July fete that first year, even though it was only eight weeks after the shooting. Five years later, we've managed to find our way back to some version of being normal, whatever that is. But the barbecue always brings up complicated feelings that none of us will ever really talk about.

Terry lives for this annual performance and has engineered every aspect of it to fulfill his need to bask in unabashed adulation and lord over his people. The whole event is an exercise in reminding every-one that they owe him for their semblance of a normal life while we marvel at his house and his wife, drink his terrible home-brewed beer, and eat his undercooked meat. This is our yearly aide-mémoire that we wouldn't be able to exist in a group environment without swift cancellation and shunning if it weren't for Terry Barnes. In Kingsland, no one is ostracized for their bad decisions or murky pasts. As long as you are hand-selected by Terry, of course.

I've found refuge by the shady corner of the pool and watch the party reaching its peak as I sip my third glass of sangria. I'm happy for the buzz and the lift of persistent feelings of anger and frustra-tion, if only temporarily. Even so, I am finding it hard to mirror Vicky's geniality. I keep thinking about pushing various guests into the pool to amuse myself, which helps keep the frown off my face from yesterday's blowup with Gil and subsequent events. After I caught him going to Monica's house, I ran home and moved Libby's things into the guest room and fell asleep holding her blanket and favorite stuffed animals, exhausted from crying so much.

Gil didn't come home until after midnight, and he was gone before I came downstairs this morning. I was surprised to see he'd already arrived at the party when I got here, looking completely unbothered by yesterday's blowup and chatting up the neighbors without a care in the world. It was yet another reminder of how easily Gil can shrug off the difficult things, especially when he has a platform to promote himself as a distraction.

I see a group of women standing in a circle not far from where I am edging closer, so I decide to move before I'm lassoed into their conversation.

"I heard that the TV anchor sold his house in the Hamptons and has been talking to Terry about getting one of the new houses on Pine Street," Ramona tells the group as I glide by.

"Please tell me that isn't true," someone responds.

"I would rather get that comedian; at least he's funny."

"Eww. Are you serious?"

I dart past the hen circle before they can drag me into the ridiculous chatter. I spot an open chair by the pool under an umbrella and head for it. On my way, Spencer Nichols, who is standing awkwardly by himself on the periphery, meets my eyes. I've gotten too close to where he is planted to not acknowledge him or change my course, so I make my way over to him.

"Hello, Spencer."

"Laura." He nods.

Spencer Nichols always seems to have a look of being recently startled.

"Having fun?" I ask lightly.

"Not really." He fidgets.

I laugh. "I appreciate your honesty."

"Parties are a waste of time."

"But this isn't really for *us*, though." I look in the direction of Terry, who appears to be imitating someone with palsy to the thunderous laughter of a group of neighbors standing around him.

"Hmm. I suspect that you're correct about that."

"We've never really gotten a chance to talk." I see Monica, on the deck with a tray of hamburger buns in her arms, home in on Spencer and me. She frowns.

"True," he says warily.

I look over at him as he watches a bird flying above us. He is a decent-looking man underneath his awkwardness and apparent inability to put a barbecue-appropriate outfit together. He's wearing dark suit pants, a gray long-sleeve button-up, and expensive leather loafers. His salt-and-pepper hair is shaggy and in need of a haircut, and his glasses aren't nerdy enough to be ironic but are too nerdy to be stylish. He looks tired, slightly agitated, and overall disheveled.

"I've enjoyed getting to know Monica."

"Hmm. The feeling is mutual," he replies carefully.

"And what about you?" I probe.

"What about me?"

"Are you making friends here in Kingsland?"

"I'm afraid I don't have a lot of use for friendship. It has proven to be more trouble than it's worth," he grumbles.

I consider how lonely it must be for Monica to be married to this guy. He's got about as much charisma as overcooked broccoli.

"I thought that maybe you considered Terry and my husband friends of yours."

"Why would you assume that?"

"With your weekly poker game, and all of the work you are doing for Terry," I say lightly.

"I'm not doing anything for Terry," he says defensively. "And poker is one of the best ways to access the critical-thinking portion of my brain. That, and I enjoy taking money from Terry and Gil," he says.

I chuckle. "My husband is not as good at poker as he thinks he is. I'm glad someone is reminding him of that."

I see the corners of his mouth turn up and I see my in with him, finally.

"You can't trust Gil as far as you can throw him. Or Terry. At the poker table or away from it. But something tells me that you already know that."

"I do," he replies.

"Spencer, I've been concerned about something."

His eyebrows furrow.

"It's about Monica."

His body tenses. "What about her?"

"I'm concerned about how much time she and Gil are spending together."

"This is news to me." Spencer looks vexed.

"Well, they were together yesterday."

"What are you talking about? Monica wasn't with Gil yesterday, I—"

"And with their past history, it makes me uncomfortable," I interrupt.

Spencer's mouth twists into a painful grimace and he steps closer to me. His height is intimidating at a distance, but up close, it feels like I've stepped into the shadow of a large tree.

"What do you mean by *their history*?" he asks gruffly.

"I thought you were aware." I bristle. "Monica has been a follower of Gil's for a long time. They met before you moved here, when he was touring for his second book. This was before he was a household name. In fact, she volunteered for his organization and donated quite a bit of money too."

He's barely able to contain his indignation. "I think you've got bad information."

I look away from him and take a sip of my drink. "This is really a conversation you should have with Gil."

"Gil? Why the fuck would I talk to him about this?" He scowls.

"If Monica hasn't brought it up, maybe she'd rather you not know about it. But you should."

Spencer stays quiet and looks at the ground for a few beats before he stares directly into my eyes. I hold his gaze.

"You can't trust them," I repeat, not specifying which of "them" I am referring to. Could be Terry and Gil, or Monica and Gil, or all of them. No answer would be wrong in this case, but I let him do the calculating.

His eyes are completely black and the hair on the back of my neck and arms straightens.

"Monica never met your husband before we came to Kingsland. She would have told me."

"Are you positive about that?" I retort.

"You're lying." He looks thoughtful in his anger. "I just can't figure out why yet."

"Why would I waste my time making something like this up? There are about a thousand conversations I'd rather be having right now than this one."

"As far as I'm concerned, you have fabricated more of the drama that this neighborhood fuels itself on," he says contemptuously.

"There's no need to imagine new drama when there is plenty of actual spectacle happening between your wife and my husband. And between you and Terry. Honestly, that may be the bigger shit show of the two, depending on who you are asking."

Spencer looks as though I've just grabbed him by the testicles.

"What the hell is that supposed to mean?" he says furiously.

"This is a very small community, Spencer."

"I'm aware."

"One with very few well-kept secrets."

"For example?" His face is aflame.

"Like you would never have been acquitted without Terry's help, and that he owns you now."

Spencer takes off his glasses and fumbles with a cleaning cloth. He faces away from me and I scan the party and see Terry and Gil watching us from the other side of the pool and wave at Gil. My husband doesn't react to my wave, but Terry sees me and says something to Gil, seemingly prompting them to make their way over. My heart races.

"Spencer," I say quietly. "Terry is irate and he is not going to let you and Monica leave Kingsland."

"That isn't his decision."

"According to him, it very much is."

"What the fuck are you talking about?" He is a few breaths away from apoplectic.

"That's how he works. He owns you until whatever debt he believes is owed to him is paid off, and then some. Everyone at this party is here"—I gesture to the guests spread around us—"because they *owe him* something."

"I owe him nothing," he says angrily.

"Then you need to stand up to him," I say under my breath as Gil and Terry close in on us, a smirk across each of their faces. I soften my voice and add quickly, "Spencer, please don't say anything to Monica about what I said about her and Gil," I plead.

His attention has already been drawn away by the approaching interlopers. He stares at them, seething.

"Nichols!" Gil says chummily to Spencer, while flat-out ignoring me.

"What are you two conspiring about?" Terry booms, and draws some looks from the nearest guests. Neither Spencer nor I respond.

"You look pretty cozy all tucked in over here. Playing a game of telephone with my missus?" Gil ribs.

They stand watching us, waiting, their arms crossed. Terry looks every inch the bully, and Gil, while softer in his presentation, has started to resemble him in his stance and attitude.

"Just getting to know your wife a little better, Gil. I think she might be a better poker player than you are," Spencer says drily.

Terry releases a roaring laugh and I can feel the attention of the party shift. The ambient chatter falls silent. I don't know where Vicky is, but I can see Monica about a yard from us. She looks stricken.

"I don't know, Gil, you might need to keep an eye on this guy. If past behavior dictates future, he's definitely up to something—"

Spencer's hands are around Terry's neck before he's finished his sentence, and I let out a loud gasp and clap my hand over my mouth. Terry's eyes double in size and he struggles unsuccessfully to break free from Spencer's death grip.

Spencer growls. "I've had it with your bullshit!" He shakes my brother-in-law from side to side like a feral dog with a small animal in its jaws.

"Whoa! Nichols! Calm down," Gil shouts, flustered that things have escalated so extremely. "Ease up!" He grabs Spencer's forearms and manages to get him to unclench his hands from Terry's throat. A few nearby men hustle over.

Terry rubs his neck while he bores holes into Spencer's entire being. Spencer returns the steely gaze, and even though he's released his grip on Terry, he hasn't backed up an inch. The two men are toe to toe.

Gil steps close to them and tersely says, "Gentlemen, this is a celebration, not a confrontation. We need to settle this another time when our heads are cooler."

After a strained minute of silent standoff, Spencer reluctantly backs up. Terry looks around and laughs and puts his hands up in defeat. "Jesus, Nichols, if you didn't like the beer, you should have just helped yourself to some wine."

There is scattered tentative laughter from the spectators and Gil joins in, but Terry's eyes indicate that he is continents away from being amused. He looks savage.

The sound of metal lightly tapping on glass bursts through, and Vicky sings a summoning song from the deck, shifting the crowd's attention from the strained cluster I'm standing in to where she is. She is a colorful vision in the afternoon light while she smiles widely and taps a fork on her wineglass once more.

"Dessert is served, everyone!" People dutifully migrate toward the long table of multiple cakes she's laid out near the sliding doors, knowing from past years that this is the prelude to a series of toasts that people will give about Terry.

"Terry, honey." Vicky summons him with a sweet wave of her arms and I watch my sister enchant the entire party, including Terry, who is reluctant to step away from his opponent so soon.

He turns back to Spencer. "Tomorrow, Nichols," he says hatefully, and huffs off toward the retreating audience.

Gil looks at me with a mix of confusion and disappointment before he follows Terry without saying anything to Spencer. I let everyone get a few feet away before I turn toward him.

"You need to get the hell out of Kingsland, Spencer. Before it is too late."

He doesn't acknowledge that he's heard me or that he's even in the same time and space dimension as I am.

"They are working together and against you," I say seriously.

"I'm starting to think that you might be right," he replies before stalking off in the direction opposite the party.

CHAPTER TWENTY-FIVE

MONICA

SPENCER IS STARING out the kitchen window when I enter. The noise of the running water in the sink obscures my approach and he doesn't even look over his shoulder to acknowledge me.

It is just after three P.M. and I haven't seen him all day. He left the barbecue yesterday without saying goodbye, only sending me a one-line text that he'd gone. When I finally made it home after helping Vicky straighten up after the neighbors dispersed, he was locked in his office. When I woke this morning, his side of the bed was cold.

Spencer absently shuts off the water flow as he continues to gaze out the back, a similarly morose look on his face from our final days in Santa Clara. I stand very still and observe him looking out through the glass at something that I wonder if only he can see. There is a large chef's knife on a cutting board behind him lying next to a half-sliced cucumber, and I doubt he would even react if I brandished it.

"Spence," I finally say.

He doesn't turn to face me, just lowers his head and fixes his gaze sideways on the surface of the counter adjacent to the sink.

"Hmm," he murmurs.

"Can we talk about yesterday?" I take a seat at the table.

"What is there to talk about?" He sighs.

"You going apeshit on Terry, for starters," I say carefully.

"He had it coming. He's lucky that I didn't squeeze harder."

"Spence, you can't just attack the host of the party. *Especially* not Terry."

"Clearly I can. That guy needed to be taken down a few notches."

"I apologized to Vicky and Terry on our behalf after you'd left. Terry still seemed pretty pissed off, though. You should talk to him as soon as possible."

Spencer's eyes flicker upward and I catch something north of irritation. "I wish you hadn't done that," he says.

"Done what? Apologize?"

He nods angrily.

"What did you expect me to do? Act like it didn't happen? Half the neighborhood witnessed it."

"I don't care who saw it."

"I'm trying to fit in here. I'm going to be getting grief about it until Labor Day."

"You'll be long gone before then," he says cryptically.

"What do you mean?" I ask.

"We are leaving this weekend. I've already made arrangements."

"Spence. Stop it." I laugh nervously. "I told you that I would consider it, but that was just a couple of days ago."

"You lost the right to decision-making when you started keeping secrets from me."

"What are you talking about, Spence?"

"It doesn't matter. I just have some loose ends to tie up."

"I'm tired of running every time you get into a war with our neighbors."

He sweeps his arm across the table, sending the ceramic fruit bowl crashing to the floor. An orange and a grapefruit roll in one direction and a peach in the other.

"Calm down!" I cry out.

The bowl lies in three jagged pieces off to the side. I don't move.

"You are my wife and you will go wherever I say," he growls.

"Where are we going?"

He stays silent.

"You aren't even going to tell me where?"

"I can't trust you."

"You are acting paranoid, Spence. I'm worried about you."

"I've got everything under control," he says.

"I'm on your side, sweetheart."

"Then start acting like it."

"Just because I support you doesn't mean that I have to roll over every time you command me."

"This isn't a discussion."

"I don't want to leave Kingsland. I have friends and a routine I like. I am starting to feel like my old self again."

There is a shadowy glint in his eyes. A chill goes through me.

"Your 'old self,' as in the voracious follower of Gil Mathers?"

I tremble beneath the table but keep my composure above.

"Excuse me?" I manage.

"You never mentioned that you knew exactly who he was before we moved here, and certainly not after. I find that very suspicious."

"There wasn't any . . . reason . . . to bring it up," I stammer.

"You don't think moving nearby one of your old boyfriends was a reason?"

"He was not my boyfriend." I shake.

Spencer's steely gaze levels me.

"Not currently?" he asks.

"Not now, not ever." I can barely speak, I'm so overcome.

"Tell me, dear, how am I supposed to believe anything you tell me on this topic when you've apparently omitted so much up to this point?"

"Where is this even coming from?"

"I wasn't sure that any of this was true until the answer was as plain as the lie on your face. And a basic review of your Facebook history yielded a ton of telling information about your involvement in the Gil Mathers universe."

"I was into self-help. It was before we met. What's the problem?"

"For starters, you've been spending so much time over at the Matherses' house, and I assumed it was because of your friends, but it has recently become very clear that there was another reason."

"Did somebody say something to you?" I ask.

"I noticed you acting very squirrelly when Gil showed up here and again at the party yesterday. I realized who the common denominator was."

"Spence, I really think you are making an issue where there isn't one."

"Gil Mathers aside, we are done here. We won't ever talk about this again."

"Spence. Please. You're acting irrationally."

"The truth is, Monica, your personality has become pretty

insufferable since we got here, and with each passing day, you become more like some reality TV character and less like the woman I married. You are too emotionally unstable for this kind of environment."

I'm stunned.

"I'm doing this for your own good," he says with a smirk.

My blood runs cold. I know fighting him is futile. When Spencer makes up his mind, he is unmovable and increasingly cruel.

"I need you to get ready," he says.

"I have our book club tonight," I remind him. "It would look suspicious if I miss it."

"Go. Consider it your time to say goodbye to your friends, without *actually* saying goodbye."

I shoot him a disbelieving look.

"I mean it, Monica—don't say a word about our leaving."

"What about you? Aren't you expected at the poker game?"

"Yes."

"Terry is expecting an apology."

Spencer smiles crookedly, apparently relishing a punch line that only he knows.

"Oh, I'll be going for sure. I have a few things that I need to tell them both. And I'll enjoy taking their money and their pride on my way out."

"Spence. I know I can't stop you from leaving Kingsland," I say gently, "but I'm not going with you."

He snorts. "What? Are you divorcing me? Good luck with that."

"If it comes to that. This is my home now."

"You had nothing when you met me, and you will have nothing if you leave me."

"You can't make me do anything that I don't want to do."

"This may be your 'home,' but it isn't your house. It is going to be pretty hard to blend in with the Kingsland set when you are homeless. Don't forget who keeps you in this lifestyle."

"There are more things than money, Spence," I say calmly.

"If you fight me on this, you are going to be begging me to take you away from here. You'll have nothing left. Trust me," he says, coldly confident.

He stands from the table and pushes his glasses up the bridge of his nose, his menacing expression erasing any long-gone signs of love for me.

"Spencer, I'm staying," I say firmly as he moves past me.

"Start packing," he yells before slamming the front door behind him.

CHAPTER TWENTY-SIX

VICTORIA

"Ter of the dog that bit ya?" I quip.

I've just returned home from running errands to find my husband standing in our kitchen, staring vacantly into the refrigerator, surrounded by the stray gifted bottles of unopened booze strewn about the counter awkwardly, like participants in a game of musical chairs who find themselves without a seat when the song stops playing. He looks bleary-eyed and short-tempered as he sips gingerly from a bottle of Barnes's Brew. My attempt at wordplay doesn't appear to have amused him.

"Huh?" he manages to squeeze out.

"You feeling okay, honey?" I ask. "Pretty long day yesterday."

He promptly waves me off. "I'm fine," he states, as if disappointed by my obvious lapse in judgment. "Just all the pollen in the air, I think."

Terry's always been this way. I think he finds it emasculating to admit to a hangover, and therefore operates as if the laws of human physiology somehow do not apply to him. In each of the years that we've been throwing our Fourth of July bash, he's managed to come down with some ailment or other the morning after, be it a weather headache, a cold, a flu, or, once, food poisoning—from a neighbor's three-bean salad, naturally. But, miraculously, he's never suffered the most common aftereffect of session drinking shitty beer for eight straight hours. I normally find this tough-guy routine grating, but today I decide to will it in the direction of endearing.

"Oh," I say brightly, changing the subject. "I ran into June Hill in town. She asked me to be sure to thank you for yesterday. She and Scott had a marvelous time." It occurs to me that this statement from our neighbor remains genuine largely because she and her husband left early, thereby missing the dustup between my husband and his supposed friends, but I keep the thought to myself. "And she told me that Scott was raving about the brisket all night."

"Good, good," says Terry, a glint of pride brightening his eye. "Glad to hear it."

"Anything I can do to help you out today?" I offer, leaning my hands on the island countertop between us.

"Nah, Vic. I'm good." He shuts the refrigerator door, not seeming too hot on the idea of solid foods at the moment. "Just going to toss all this shit in the garage." He flings his arm in a lazy sweep to indicate the leftover liquor and the stack of unused aluminum serving trays next to the sink. "Then probably tinker around in the office until our game tonight."

I study his face, but the low-lying haze of residual alcohol makes it hard to get a clean read on his expression. "Well, that should be fun," I nudge.

"We'll see." He shrugs. "Guess it'll depend on whether that fucking hothead Nichols wants to go another round with the big man." The thought seems not to disturb him, but rather to raise an attractive prospect of bloodlust. There's a flash in his expression of something primitive.

"Well, I can get a referee over here before I leave for book club," I tease. "You know, just in case."

"Oh right," he says, my comment distracting him only slightly from whatever violent scenario he's concocted in his head. "You're seeing those girlfriends of yours later," he mumbles without looking at me.

"Yes, honey," I say. "I'm getting together with Laura and Mon. Just like every other Sunday." As the words leave my mouth, I realize that they're tinged with resignation rather than annoyance, which saddens me. "That's if I can leave the three of you alone here."

"Please," he blusters. "Nichols isn't going to come over here and disrespect my house again." He polishes off the last of the beer before setting the empty bottle on the countertop and cracking his knuckles. "He only pulled that shit in the first place because he knew that Mathers was there to break it up. Otherwise, I would have wiped the floor with him."

"Or the lawn?" I offer.

"What?" he says confusedly.

"You guys were out in the yard," I explain. "So, I don't know, maybe 'raked the lawn with him' would be a better expression?"

His eyes narrow, but I catch one corner of his mouth perk up. "Well, you're just a regular Kathy Griffiths today," he says, seemingly unaware that he's mangled the name of the comedienne. He steps out from behind the island and approaches me, setting his hands on my hips and pulling me close. His sour breath does him no favors, and I wrap my arms around his back and lay my head against his shoulder as an excuse to avoid the face-to-face. Just as we're settling into a sweet moment, I feel his right hand leave my hip, followed by a sharp smack to my ass.

"Well, that was almost nice," I say, straining to keep it playful.

"Play your cards right," he says slyly, "and we can fool around on the pile of money I'm gonna take off these guys after you get back from your little book club tonight."

"'Play my cards right'?" I say, raising an eyebrow as I gently shove my husband away. "A poker joke, eh? Who's the comedian now?"

"Baby," he says, "when I'm finished with these clowns, I'm gonna be the only one who's still laughing."

I take in his face, and something in the expression transports me. I'm suddenly seeing Terry again on our first date, all those years ago; the look of confidence, the gleam in his gaze, the air of assuredness that reeled me in and left me reeling. The set of his jaw, which I first took for certitude, and which, over the course of our time together, has morphed before my eyes to reveal brashness, arrogance, cocksureness, all the while masking a deep, childlike insecurity. I see him now as I saw him then, and the complicated layers of tumult and strife melt away, and we are who we were before we did all the things that have brought us to this moment. I take his head in my hands and plant a deep, lingering kiss on his lips before I let him go.

"Wow, babe," he says, eyes widening as he sizes me up. "What was that all about?"

I brush his cheek with my fingertips and offer a smile. "Go get 'em tonight, champ." And then I return the favor, reaching around to swat him on the butt.

He laughs as he sets his hands on my hips, keeping his eyes locked on mine. "Oh, don't you worry about that, Vic." He smiles a victorious smile. "Those two aren't even gonna see me coming."

CHAPTER TWENTY-SEVEN

LAURA

"Terry's on a warpath," Vicky says as she refreshes her glass of san-gria. My sister is the first one of us to break through the obvious tension sitting between us.

We are sitting in Monica's backyard admiring the night sky and enjoying the sporadic amateur fireworks. Kingsland's residents have outdone themselves this year, and the sky has been bursting with sparkling color for hours.

As we've been silently watching and nursing our drinks for most of the night, we've let the beautiful weather and explosion-filled sky take the space of our usual endless weekly conversation. The holiday edition of our book club this evening is anything but celebratory.

Monica offers me more in my glass but I look at the time and wave her off.

"Well, this was the first annual Barnes cookout where he got choked out. He must have some strong feelings," I reply.

"I think it's safe to say that the mood at tonight's poker game is going to be tense. I was relieved to walk out of my house this evening."

"Maybe they'll tear each other to pieces and solve all of our problems," I say, and watch their eyes widening.

"Spencer's more angry than I've ever seen him. He was in rare form this morning," Monica says gravely.

A firefly hovers between Vicky's and my chairs, illuminating every few minutes like a tiny warning signal.

"What did he do?" Vicky asks, concerned.

"He told me to start packing," Monica says seriously.

"Well, we know that that just isn't going to happen," my sister says.

"Exactly."

"What did you tell him?" I ask.

"I'm not going anywhere," she replies.

"And how did he take it?"

"As well as Terry took being choked."

Vicky and I nod and sip our drinks.

"How was Gil?" Vicky asks me.

"We haven't spoken since the incident in Libby's room," I say bitterly. "We ignored each other at the cookout. I'm sure he feels like a real hero after yesterday."

"I can't believe he just tore everything down without talking to you," Vicky says angrily. "What was he thinking?" She swats at something in front of her.

"He was thinking about himself," I snap.

"He is so selfish," Monica adds.

"I'm just going to put it all back the way it was."

"Good for you," Monica says. "So, you didn't talk to him before you came over tonight?"

"I haven't seen him all day. I don't even think he came home last night."

"Really?" asks Vicky. "What is that about?"

"Who knows? Clearly, I have no idea who my husband really is. He appears to be shopping for my replacement on an international dating site."

"No," Vicky says angrily.

"I saw it with my own eyes. It was forwarded by none other than Terry."

I glance at Monica to gauge her response. Her eyes are closed and she looks like she's in pain. I see that her hands are gathered into tight fists in her lap.

The crickets seem to increase in volume as the night grows later. There is a gentle breeze running through the trees that sounds like the tide rushing in. I also shut my eyes and try to hold on to the fleeting sense of peace it brings.

"I just want this to be over," Monica says quietly.

"This is probably our most somber book club. Can we try and muster a *little* excitement for the evening?" I say.

"It feels kind of hard to be upbeat about anything right now, given the current state of things," Monica says.

Vicky clears her throat. "Should we . . . talk about the book?"

Monica and I both stare at her, surprised.

"And break our tradition of never *actually* talking about the book?" I say. "I thought we agreed never to do that."

"We did." Monica slaps at something on her arm.

I check the time again, ready to have this night over and done with.

Another round of starburst fireworks illuminates the sky and I can see the lights reflected in Vicky's and Monica's faces.

"It is beautiful, isn't it?" Vicky smiles, and I realize how long it has been since I've seen my sister happy. The round of explosions dies down and we are shrouded in cricket-filled darkness again.

"Makes me miss the summers from our childhood," I say.

"Mmm. Me too," Vicky murmurs.

"Did you guys see that?" Monica says as she straightens up in the Adirondack chair.

Vicky stands and we follow. "See what?"

"I thought I saw someone move over there," Monica replies nervously as she points to the darkest part of her property.

I pull the flashlight up on my phone and wave it in the offending direction. The light sweeps across the grass and the trees. "I don't see anything."

Vicky shakes her head. "Me neither."

The three of us stand in tense silence for a few long minutes, waiting.

"It was probably just shadows from the fireworks," Vicky finally says.

"I guess I'm jumpy," Monica reasons. "I really thought I saw someone."

"Maybe slow down on the sangria," I say.

"It has been a stressful few days," Vicky says. "We're all on edge."

"More like a stressful few years," I say.

Victoria's phone dings and she takes her attention away from us.

"They're finishing up," Vicky says.

The edginess we've been feeling all night feels the most palpable in this moment.

"I don't know if I'm ready to leave," Vicky says.

"I'm going," I say determinedly. "I'm tired of sitting. I need to move."

Monica looks back at me and then at Vicky. "I guess we should call it a night, then."

Vicky finishes her drink and smooths her hair. "Yes, I guess it's that time."

The blast of a particularly loud and bright eruption causes us all to look upward, and we watch the red cascade in the summer sky fall all around us.

We hug each other tightly and head to our respective destinations, moving slowly in the dark, reassuring ourselves that we are ready for whatever awaits.

PART THREE

PRESENT DAY

The only way to realize your true desires is to
wish, believe, and *act*.

The Rule of Three, Sawyer Selwyn

CHAPTER TWENTY-EIGHT

WOLCOTT

"Spencer?" I ask.

"Spencer," she repeats, a twinge of annoyance visible on her drawn, gaunt face. After receiving a call from the hospital staff alerting us to the fact that Gil Mathers had awoken from his coma, Silvestri and I arrived during the early morning bustle in the hopes of interviewing him, only to have it explained to us that Mr. Mathers, after a short exchange with his wife, had promptly returned to a state of unconsciousness. My partner and I had finally managed to sneak in a few hours of sleep prior to being roused by the call, leaving us considerably more well rested than Laura Mathers, whom we now have the pleasure of speaking with in the hallway outside her husband's hospital room.

"And you're sure that was the last thing he said before he went under again?" I wait for her response, notepad flipped open, pen at the ready.

"Uh, yeah," she insists, wearing an expression that suggests she'd love to give me a good whack with the designer purse she's clutching desperately, the veins on the backs of her hands practically bursting through the skin. She seems at once wired and overtired, as if she'd gotten a second wind that'd managed to dovetail nicely with the caffeine from the hospital coffee and the adrenaline roller coaster she's undoubtedly been strapped into. "It was just before he fell into what I thought was cardiac arrest, so it kind of sticks out in my mind."

"Just making sure we've got it all laid out clearly," I explain. "Gives my partner and me a better chance of piecing the puzzle together."

She blinks for a long moment as she exhales, and her eyes return to mine slightly softer. "I understand. And I apologize. Haven't been sleeping much, and this has all been pretty jarring. The uncertainty with Gil is the worst part." She leans in closer, offering Silvestri and me a conspiratorial look. "And between us, I really fucking hate hospitals."

"We're with you on that," I say. "And we're trying to keep this as painless as possible, I assure you."

"Thank you," she manages wearily.

"Now, do you have any idea why your husband would have mentioned Spencer Nichols in that moment?" I ask.

"I mean," she says, the look of frustration returning to her gaze. "Not to do your jobs for you, but it all seems pretty straightforward, no?"

Silvestri leans toward her and tilts his head, a polite smile forming from his lips. "We can be a little thick sometimes, he and I. Mind walking us through it?"

"Jesus Christ," she says, teeth gritted, her calm respite having been relegated to the back burner. "Okay, look. My husband . . ."

I hear the squeak of rubber on linoleum and look over Laura's shoulder to see a passing nurse eavesdropping on our conversation. She catches my glance before dropping her eyes to the floor and continuing down the hallway. "Sorry," I say, returning my attention to Laura Mathers. "You were saying?"

"Look," she begins, newly conscious of her volume. "My husband was found wandering around with a bullet in his head in the vicinity of where they recovered Spencer Nichols's body, right? And this was shortly after the guy they'd been playing cards with was shot to death?" She flips her palms open and nods by way of clarification. "Maybe you guys don't like pieces coming together cleanly or something, but it sure seems like a home run to me."

"It's interesting that you bring that up," I say, allowing for a pause as I assess her expression. She appears already to have decided that whatever I follow up with is going to be the dumbest thing out of my mouth yet, and braces for the inanity.

"Why's that?" she humors me.

"Well, when my partner and I initially spoke with Monica Nichols, she seemed more concerned that her husband was liable to harm *himself* than someone else."

This draws a loud guffaw from Laura. "Oh, she was, was she?" She shakes her head. "Unreal."

"And how's that?" I ask.

"Here's the thing about *our* Monica, okay?" She seems to have even less patience for her friend at the moment than she has for Silvestri and me. "I wouldn't exactly take her impression of her husband as objective fact."

"Hmm." I nod. "And what do you mean by that?"

She sighs and looks off to the side, taking a beat before answering as she seems to measure the weight of the words she's considering. "Monica isn't very self-assured, not very confident. She's kind of meek, especially when it came to her husband. Very deferential. And I just don't think she has a clear sense of what he would or would not have been capable of." She scans the hallway before continuing, then leans in closer. "I know you're not supposed to speak ill of the dead, but Spencer was kind of an asshole."

"Okay." I nod.

"I mean, look. We've all had different challenges with our husbands. Terry could certainly be a handful, and Lord knows my husband can be pretty arrogant." She rolls her eyes as she says this, but her expression is also mournful, nostalgic. "Spencer, though. He was one of those guys who was just really passive-aggressive and controlling. Super manipulative. Gaslit her, that sort of thing." The eye roll comes back for an encore, this time stripped of any tenderness. "She once told me that he'd hired a behavioral coach for her, to help get rid of her accent and 'smooth away her rough edges' or some fucking thing. I'll tell you this: If my husband had ever pulled that with me, I'd have . . ." She catches the thought before it escapes her tongue, and her face goes sour. "Well, you know."

"Sounds like a real piece of business," volunteers Silvestri.

"I'll say." She shifts her eyes to my partner as she loosens a kink in her neck. "And I don't even know what Monica's talking about, with all of this 'self-harm' nonsense. Has she conveniently forgotten how her husband attacked Terry at the cookout?"

This catches my attention, and I flip the notebook to a fresh page. "This is the first we're hearing of this," I say, tossing my partner a look to confirm that we're synched up with our info. "Go on."

"God, this suddenly seems like a lifetime ago." She shakes her head in disbelief, marveling at the tricks time has a way of playing. "So, every year since we've been in Kingsland, my sister and her husband have hosted a cookout for the Fourth. It's mostly a big ego trip for Terry. He ruins a bunch of meat and serves his bitter home-brewed beer, and everyone kisses his ass and compliments Vicky on their big, beautiful house. This year, our husbands are out in the yard talking about something or another when suddenly I look over and see Spencer with his hands around Terry's neck, looking like a man possessed." She crosses her arms in front of her, the recollection jarring her senses. "Gil had to physically pull the two of them apart. It was pretty scary, actually."

"Huh," I say, looking again to my partner before settling back on Laura. "And you wouldn't have any idea of what set their tempers off?"

She averts her eyes for a second before settling on a far-off spot. "I don't know." She shrugs. "The three of them had been acting funny before this all happened. Kind of cagey, secretive, you know?"

"Okay," I say, taking notes. "And was that unusual, in and of itself?"

"Not particularly," she answers. "None of them are exactly world-class communicators, at least not in their marriages, except when they find an opportunity to congratulate themselves on some feat or another—big egos, like I've said. But this was more . . ." She shakes her head as she mulls over the thought. "Yeah, it was the secrecy that stuck out, I guess. And they'd just been kind of tense around one another lately, or even when they were referring to each other in conversation. Paranoid, maybe. Very weird energy."

"I see." I flip the notepad closed, cap the pen, and replace them in my inside jacket pocket. "Well, thank you for talking us through everything. We certainly appreciate it."

"Happy to help," she answers distractedly, her expression betraying the words she's spoken.

"And thank you for setting us straight on Spencer Nichols," I say. "Sounds like he was perfectly capable of violence."

A series of high-pitched beeps suddenly emanate from a room on the other end of the hallway. Within seconds, a flurry of hospital workers whisk past us to attend to whatever's going on down there. Out of the corner of my eye, I catch Laura wincing before she returns her attention to Silvestri and me. The sudden fracas seems to have rattled her, and the words come out shaky. "I'd say he's plenty capable." She narrows her eyes defiantly. "And if you're still unsure, maybe go in there and get a good look at my husband's skull." She taps the side of her own and smirks. "Now, if you'll excuse me, Detectives, I really need to go get some fresh air." And with that, she turns on her heels and storms down the hallway, leaving the two of us in her wake.

CHAPTER TWENTY-NINE

SILVESTRI

As we watch Laura pass the nurses' station and disappear into the hallway leading to the elevator bank, a woman I recognize as the doctor attending to Gil Mathers approaches us, looking back in Laura's direction with a concerned expression before returning her attention to us.

"Dr. Mitali," I say. "Nice to see you again."

"You too," she answers distractedly. "Everything okay there?" She hikes her thumb behind her.

"Mrs. Mathers seemed a little agitated," I explain. "Said she was going to get some air."

She sets her jaw. "Detectives," she says sternly. "I understand that you have a job to do, but I would respectfully ask that you please be careful not to rile up anyone in Mr. Mathers's vicinity. He's in something of a tentative state, and he needs all of the positive energy he can get. It's critical to his recovery."

"We were as gentle as could be," I assure her. "Mrs. Mathers seemed overtired, and rattled by the sudden change in her husband's condition earlier."

"Oh my," she says, and rolls back on her heels, her shoulders dropping. "That *was* a nasty surprise. Poor woman. This must all be so much for her." I notice the doctor nervously working the tip of her thumbnail with her forefinger.

"Have you had much of a chance to interact with Mrs. Mathers?" asks Wolcott.

"I have," she says. "Yes."

"And how would you characterize her response to everything that's happened so far?"

"Well, Detective." She considers the question for a moment. "There's the inevitable shock to consider, as well as her lack of sleep. And that's not even taking into account whatever this has done to her psychologically. She's seemed agitated at times, as you said. A little pushy, maybe." She curls her lips inward. "But no worse than anyone else I've had to deal with under similar circumstances. And I noticed that her sister was here earlier, relieving her from bedside duty and giving moral support, so hopefully she's utilizing her family and network of friends, and not going at this alone."

"I see." Wolcott nods gently. "And can you give us some idea of *Mr.* Mathers's progress at this point?"

"Well," she begins, "we were all surprised that he regained consciousness temporarily. That was an unexpected blip on the radar. But we've been monitoring him closely, and his vitals and brain activity have been encouraging. So, I remain cautiously optimistic. For now, we're continuing to keep an eye on Mr. Mathers's progress to determine when we can safely bring him out of his comatose state."

"Huh," I say. "So, you're essentially controlling his condition right now?"

"As best we can, yes. When a patient suffers this sort of traumatic injury, it's of paramount importance to maintain consistent blood flow to the area and to allow the brain time to properly heal. Once we deem Mr. Mathers to be out of the woods, so to speak, we can bring him back out of his current state safely."

"That's good to know," I say, looking at my partner before returning my attention to the doctor. "Well, we certainly appreciate your time."

"No problem," she says as she hands me a card. "And this is the number to my direct line. Please feel free to give a call if there's anything else I can be helpful with, okay?"

⫴

We're outside the cafeteria on the lower level of the hospital heading toward the exit when a familiar figure rounds the corner, walking in our direction. Wolcott stops just as I do, and the nurse approaches us, an eager look on her kind face.

"Good morning," I say, all sunshine and rainbows. I see her attention shift to my partner and take the opportunity to cheat my eyes to her ID badge. "Lila," I continue. "I'm Detective Silvestri and this is my partner, Detective Wolcott. We noticed you passing by Gil Mathers's room a little while ago." We'd been speaking with Laura in the hallway, and I'd clocked the nurse slowing her pace as she passed us, trying to catch any tidbits from our conversation. I'm hoping she might be able to shed some light on the situation. "Are you attending to Mr. Mathers?"

"I am, yes," she says, eyes wide. "What a poor, poor man."

"A terrible turn of events." I offer a solemn nod. "Listen," I say, dropping the volume of my voice and my head slightly, to take her into our confidence. "My partner and I are concerned about Mrs. Mathers's well-being, in light of her husband's condition." I notice Lila subtly flinch at the mention of Laura. "Have you had a chance to observe her while she's been visiting with him?"

"Some," she says tentatively, then takes a short step to close the distance between the three of us. "I have to admit, I'm a little intimidated by that woman."

"Is that so?" I ask.

"I mean, I feel so bad for her, obviously." Her brow furrows as she takes on the weight of the thought. "But she just seems like someone who's used to getting what she wants, so I guess this is probably even more frustrating for her."

"Huh," I say. "That's a very insightful observation, Lila. Could you give us any examples of the behavior you've seen from her?"

"Well," she says. "She's been bugging the staff about getting her husband moved to a private room, which is kind of beside the point, considering his situation. She keeps asking for a larger bed, which we don't physically have access to. And she's just generally short with the staff. I mean, I feel like she's trying to make an effort, but there's a volatile energy underneath everything."

"I see." I nod encouragingly.

"And even when she was interacting with her husband, when he woke up for a few moments this morning, she seemed aggravated with him."

"That's interesting," says Wolcott. "You were in the room when Mr. Mathers regained consciousness?"

"Oh no," she clarifies. "I was walking past on my rounds when I overheard her talking to him, and then suddenly he groaned and said something back. I was surprised to hear his voice, obviously, and I went to get the doctor to bring her back to check on him, so I only really heard a snippet of their conversation, but she definitely sounded annoyed."

"Lila," I say. "Can you remember any details of the exchange at all?"

"Well," she considers, "he was trying to get out a name, but he was just kind of moaning it. You could tell he was struggling. Then she was trying to explain that she was his wife, because I guess he was disoriented and mistook her for someone else? But she kind of went up on the 'wife' when she said it, you know?"

"I'm sorry," says Wolcott. "How do you mean, 'went up'?"

"Like, uh, her voice jumped in pitch. 'I'm your *wife*.' Like she was annoyed that she had to explain who she was to him. And then she said his name sharply, but that sounded more like she was concerned. And by then I was halfway down the hall."

"This is all very helpful," I say. "And could you make out the name that he called her by mistake?"

"Let me see," she says, squeezing her eyelids together. "It was a woman's name . . ." She nods rhythmically, as if performing some sort of mental excavation. "Probably why his wife was pissed, come to think of it . . ." She opens her eyes, still flashing a look of deep concentration. "Sorry," she says. "My memory's not the best."

"Here's what helps me," volunteers Wolcott. "Start with the letter *A*, and then cycle through the alphabet. Sometimes when you land on the first letter of the name, it jogs your brain into remembering."

"Huh," she says, and closes her eyes again. "He said it slowly. Pronounced each syllable." Her mouth moves absently, trying to retrieve the sounds tucked somewhere in the crevices of her mind. Suddenly her eyes shoot open and a satisfied smile takes over. "I got it," she states proudly. "'Monica.' He definitely said 'Monica.'"

⑾

"So," I say. "Maybe we're looking at some funny business? A little love triangle?" We're back in the unmarked in the lot outside the hospital. This big metal box has been sitting on an open, unshaded stretch of asphalt collecting heat, and I'm blasting the AC to try to keep from melting into the seat leather.

"That'd certainly add a new layer of intrigue," says Wolcott, pulling the heel of his thumb across his damp brow.

"And if there was an affair going on, it might help to explain the double-cross in the clearing out by the woods."

"Good point," he says. "Maybe Mathers knew that Nichols was on to them, anticipated the ambush, and beat him to the punch. Or, you know, to the gunshot."

"I can get with that," I say, throwing the transmission into drive and pulling up behind an outgoing ambulance. I enjoy a burst of cool air from the vent next to the dashboard as I pull out into traffic. "Well, partner. I guess there's the one way to find out."

CHAPTER THIRTY

MONICA

For the first time in days, I'm completely alone in my house without constant phone notifications alongside a soundtrack of unrelenting doorbell chiming.

The intrusions have been a mix of allegedly concerned neighbors and shameless reporters coming right up to the door and peeking into my windows, their cameras and phones aimed in my direction like loaded weapons.

The house feels completely different without Spencer here. I expected things would be heavier and more somber, but they aren't. I should feel guilty for feeling so liberated without him here, but I don't. The absence of him has released a pressure valve and the air feels lighter, even though everything is so dire. My brain flickers with sparks of ideas and a renewed sense of energy, which I suspect may have something to do with evolutionary coping mechanisms. Without Spencer to give me a tutorial about the human psyche during crisis, I'm only left to wonder and possibly google.

I know underneath the shock of him really being dead, there is grief to attend to, and a well of emotional backlog that will overflow when the time is right, but I can't seem to tap into anything other than numbness. Every few hours, like a preset alarm, I have the thought *Spencer is dead. Spencer is dead. Spencer is dead.* And I feel a rush of something, but I'm not sure it is what I'm supposed to be feeling.

I've touched nothing of his since the news of his death, so all the objects related to him are still easily found in well-organized drawers and behind the doors of pristinely arranged closets. But his passing has made me realize how little of ourselves exists out in the open around our house. As I absorb my surroundings on my way out to the patio, I don't find myself destroyed by a favorite coffee mug of his left out unwashed, or well-worn slippers that still bear the imprint of his feet, lying in my path. They aren't there; he would never stand for random out-of-place items. These would be the relics of a lived-in home, not the sterile house where we've been laying our heads for the last year.

Outside, I settle onto the chaise with a glass of lemonade, my book, and a pad of Post-it notes. I've begun writing down quotes to put around the house to keep my spirits up. It was a regular practice I had before I was with Spencer, and now that he's gone, I've decided to rediscover some of the ways I used to self-soothe.

Being outside is another way to stay grounded. I take in the sound of the chirping insects and the dueling lawn mowers to the left and right of me, our neighbors on the same landscaping schedule. I trace a heart into the side of a frosted plastic mug I keep in the freezer for Spence's beer. The tart and sweet juice is refreshing in the afternoon heat, and I close my eyes and let the solar warmth spread through my body.

I've stumbled into a forgotten aspect of myself: complete

independence. After a long period of dormancy, I am once again able to make my own decisions, and my head begins to swim with a multitude of possibilities. I have to close my eyes because the world begins to spin around me, the concept steadily piling anxious thought upon tense realization. I try to focus on the reddish light of the sun through my closed eyelids and feel the cradling heat.

After a period of time, the light I'm basking in is eclipsed by a looming darkness. I open my eyes to the sight of the two detectives obscuring the sun.

I sit up abruptly and knock over my lemonade, the plastic mug clattering to ground, its full contents of liquid and ice spilling out and in between the cracks of the wooden planks as the mug rolls lazily to one side.

"Oh shit!" I blurt, and the detectives barely flinch as I jump to a stand and grab the beach towel from the back of my chair and throw it over the spill. Wolcott steps aside to make room for me, while Silvestri walks slowly around the patio and takes in the surroundings.

"Sorry," I say, flustered. "You scared the hell outta me." My twang is in full effect.

"Apologies for sneaking up on you, Mrs. Nichols. We tried the bell. The side gate was open, and your car was in the garage, so we took a chance."

"You weren't picking up your phone, so we thought we'd swing by to check on you," Silvestri says to the sky as he keeps looking up and around the yard, a mix of awe and wonder across his face.

We are standing awkwardly next to the spill and I gesture toward the glass table surrounded by cushioned chairs. "Why don't we sit over here?" I suggest. They look at each other and nod and I lead the way. They both watch me as I unfurl the umbrella to block out the three o'clock sun hanging high in the cloudless sky.

"Better hose that spot off so you don't get ants," Wolcott advises.

"I'll do that," I say, feeling annoyed. "Can I get you any lemonade or maybe an iced tea or coffee?" I ask, feeling myself beginning to disassociate from the scene and forcing my focus on the men.

"Lemonade sounds lovely," says Wolcott through a warm smile.

"Sure does." His partner nods.

"Be right back," I tell them as I exit into the house. I wipe my palms on the front of my dress out of their sight.

When I fill the glasses with ice and juice and place them on the drinks tray, I watch the men from the window and try to decipher their expressions. Neither is saying anything, and their lack of conversation makes me feel even more agitated. I head back out.

"Here we go," I say brightly as I hand them each a glass. I place a plate of brownies on the table between them. "And here are some baked goods, to go with your juice." I suddenly feel like a mother offering her waterlogged children refreshments after a long day in the pool.

The detectives eyeball the brownies but neither makes a reach for one.

"Are you a baker?" Wolcott asks.

"No, not at all. These are from the next-door neighbors."

"That's thoughtful of them."

"Not really," I say wearily. "They've never come over the entire time we've been here."

"That right?" Wolcott asks.

"Not until yesterday, when they walked right up to the front door to check on 'how I'm doing.'" I throw a look of disdain in the direction of the brownies.

"Not a chocolate fan?" Wolcott asks.

"No appetite," I say softly.

"I gather that this was more of a baked Trojan horse than a genuinely concerned neighbor?" Wolcott asks.

I shrug.

"People's curiosity often clouds their basic consideration for the people who are living through tragedy," he says thoughtfully.

"Apparently," I respond.

"Has the press been bothering you?" Silvestri asks, glancing in the direction beyond the gate, where there were at least two news vans parked the last time I checked.

"Yes, but they seem to have thinned out. Mercifully, they've stopped coming up to the door and the windows after I threatened them. I haven't said anything aside from 'I'm calling the police,' so I think they've gotten bored of me."

"We also had a word with them. They should be keeping their distance," Silvestri says.

The detectives both sip their drinks quietly. I have a thousand questions for them but remain silent.

Silvestri leans back in the sunlight and moves his head around like an overstimulated owl. "You've got an impressive variety of trees. A person could get utterly lost back here in all of this beauty," he says appreciatively, if not a little oddly.

I hesitate, not knowing if this statement is some kind of trick.

Wolcott chuckles. "You'll have to excuse my partner, Mrs. Nichols. He's a bit of an amateur arborist, among other things."

"That's me. I'm a real tree hugger," Silvestri quips back.

I nod politely, unsure of what to make of their banter.

"Mrs. Nichols, we know that this has been an incredibly difficult time and we don't want to add to any of your stress, but the first days following a homicide are the most critical in solving it," Wolcott says carefully.

"Of course. I want to find out what happened to Spencer and why," I say.

"So do we, Mrs. Nichols."

"We have some more questions for you, and we hope you can provide us with as much information as possible, and to the best of your ability," Silvestri adds.

"Whatever I can do to help," I say.

"Good." Wolcott pulls a small notebook from his breast pocket and places it on the table in front of him. There is a blue Bic tucked into it, and from the space made by the pen, I can see many large cursive ink scrawlings covering the pages.

"Mrs. Nichols, could you tell us a little bit about your relationship with Gil Mathers?"

Silvestri's question shoots straight into my solar plexus. Judging by the look the men give each other, my surprise is obvious.

"Excuse me?" I start choking.

The detectives perk up, and Wolcott looks moments away from giving me the Heimlich.

"Sorry," I sputter. "I wasn't expecting that. I assumed you would be asking about *my* husband."

"We'll get there, but we'd also like to know about your relationship with Mr. Mathers," Wolcott says, giving me no sign of reprieve on the subject of Gil.

I feel my face growing hot as I mull over the question. "I didn't really have a *relationship* with Gil. Not beyond 'hello' and 'goodbye' at neighborhood gatherings and in passing when I would be at Laura's house," I answer.

"And how often would you say you were at the Matherses' house?" Wolcott makes a note before I've even answered, which irks me.

"A couple of times a week, I'd guess. We would take turns hosting each other, and during the warmer months we tended to be at Laura's house."

"Any particular reason?" Wolcott inquires, reminding me of Spence's and my last fight.

"I don't know; we liked Laura's pool better, I guess." My irritation has crept into my shoulders.

"Have we struck a nerve?" Silvestri says.

I take a breath. "Detectives, forgive me. I was just thinking about Spence and my last fight. He didn't approve of me going over to Laura's house so much and we had a terrible argument about it." I let the tears come. "I can't believe he's not here anymore."

"Take your time, Mrs. Nichols. This is hard stuff," Wolcott offers.

"It keeps hitting me in the most unpredictable ways." I sniffle.

"Why didn't your husband like you going to the Matherses' house?" Silvestri asks, unfazed by my emotional outpouring.

I sigh. "Because he was overprotective and didn't love me being out of the house without him in the first place . . ."

"And in the second place?" Wolcott probes.

"He wasn't a fan of Gil's. Or Laura or Vicky, for that matter," I say.

"And why wasn't he a fan of Mr. Mathers?" Wolcott asks.

"I'm not entirely sure. I just know that he didn't like him very much. He thought he was arrogant and fake. And his reputation for being a bit of a philanderer didn't help."

"But he played in a regular poker game with him," Silvestri reminds me, and I feel annoyed.

"He did. But I think he made an exception because he enjoyed playing."

"Could the game be the source of the conflict?" Silvestri questions.

I shrug. "Maybe. Spence didn't talk about the game with me."

Wolcott leans in slightly, and I gather he is about to ask me something hard.

"Mrs. Nichols, it sounds like your husband was keeping quite a bit from you. Was that standard in your marriage, or had he become more secretive recently?"

His question frustrates me, because it is one that I had been asking myself many times recently and hadn't been able to come to a conclusion about.

"It's hard to say. I mean, I don't know what I don't know, right?" I say more sharply than I intended. The detectives watch me.

"But if you are asking if Spencer was keeping more from me than usual, I guess the answer is a resounding yes based on how things have turned out." I twist my wedding ring, unable to look at their faces.

Silvestri clears his throat and stands. "Don't mind me, I'm just going to stretch my legs while we talk. And admire these incredible willow trees." He points his chin in the direction of the weepy overhangings swaying gently in the wind.

Wolcott watches his partner walk slowly around the patio along with me.

"Mrs. Nichols," Wolcott says good-naturedly, and I return my attention to him.

"Shifting back to Gil Mathers for a moment, can you tell us more about your interactions with him?"

I feel the agita rising. "I didn't really have any interactions with him. At least none that stand out in my mind as important to what has happened," I respond.

"Well, tell us more about what you and Mrs. Barnes and Mathers would do, when you were spending time together at the Matherses' home," Wolcott says.

I'm really starting to feel overheated. "I don't know what to say. We'd hang out by the pool and catch up on our lives, talk about books and movies and regular stuff."

"And how often would Mr. Mathers be in the mix?" Silvestri is back, asking the question as he eyeballs a bright red cardinal in one of the taller trees.

I look at his partner, unsure about the question. Wolcott sees my seeking and offers an encouraging smile.

"What do you mean?" I respond as sweat trickles down my back.

"Would he hang around with the three of you?" he extends.

"Not really," I answer honestly. "He would be home, but we hardly saw him. He was always upstairs."

"And did Mr. Mathers ever single you out when you were at his home or elsewhere?" Wolcott questions.

I feel a particular type of stress taking hold, like taking an exam I'm underprepared for.

"No. He never singled me out," I say.

"And did the two of you ever spend any time together independently of the group?" Silvestri focuses on my fidgeting hands on my lap through the glass tabletop.

"No," I say firmly. "There was no reason for the two of us to ever be alone."

The detectives glance at each other and I feel myself getting angry.

"Why are you asking me about this? Aren't you supposed to be finding out what happened to my husband?" I snap.

The men both remain relaxed in their chairs.

"Sorry," I mutter. "I think the heat is getting to me."

"No problem. This is very taxing, we know. We'll only ask you a few more questions, if that's okay with you?" Wolcott says sweetly as he lightly taps the end of his pen on his notebook.

"Fine," I say.

"Mrs. Nichols, the last time we spoke, you told us that your husband was 'disturbed.'"

I barely conceal a grimace.

"Yes, my husband has been in a difficult emotional place."

"Can you elaborate on that a little bit more?" he prods.

"If you've read anything about what happened with his company and the last few years of our life, then you have probably already come to that conclusion."

"We'd like your perspective," Wolcott responds.

I curb my frustration. "Spencer is a genius, but that came with a lot of darkness." I struggle with past and present tenses.

Silvestri holds my eye while Wolcott focuses on the glass in front of me. Even so, I can feel that he is hanging on my every word like his partner.

"Darkness in what sense? Was he prone to depression? Or erratic behavior?"

"Both," I say darkly. "He was an inventor at heart, and he was up when he was creating and down when he wasn't."

"Had he ever been treated for any mental illness?" Wolcott asks.

"No, he wasn't treated for anything that I knew of. And he wasn't a fan of the psychiatric profession."

"Was that because of negative personal experience?" Wolcott asks.

"I don't think so. But Spencer doesn't, I mean *didn't*, talk about his past." My voice cracks.

"I know this is difficult, Mrs. Nichols, but anything you can tell us could be helpful in understanding what happened the night of your husband's death," Wolcott says kindly.

I nod, looking down at the table while swiping tears from my cheeks.

"Did he ever have any aggressive or violent tendencies?" Silvestri asks.

I clasp my hands and shake my head. "He was very passionate about the things he cared about. And he didn't like to be told no."

"What form did his 'passion' take at its most heightened?" Silvestri pushes.

"He had a short temper. And we fought. But what married couple doesn't?"

"True enough," says Wolcott knowingly.

"Were you ever afraid of your husband?" Silvestri asks carefully.

"No," I say, barely audibly. "Sometimes," I add reluctantly.

The men are silent and I see them looking me over, not in an invasive way, but with concern. I rub the sweat from the back of my neck and redden when I realize that because my hair is up, they have likely seen the bruising on my neck.

I take another long, deep breath. "Look, Spencer struggled with people telling him how to run his company or how to live his life, and he clearly had issues with authority. I'm not a shrink, so I don't know if he was certifiably crazy, but he was definitely 'touched,' as my grandmother used to say."

"Was your husband having any suicidal ideation recently?"

"He was definitely depressed at times. But he wasn't talking about dying. He was talking about moving out of Kingsland. Getting a fresh start."

"Did you want to move as well?" Wolcott asks.

"I wanted to do what was best for our marriage," I reply tearfully.

"Do you know what prompted your husband's assault on Terry Barnes at the gathering at their house on Saturday?" Wolcott probes.

"I have no idea. I wasn't standing with them and I saw it all happen from a distance."

"Did your husband give you any sense of what had transpired between the men that led him to choke Mr. Barnes?" Silvestri asks.

I shake my head. "No. He downplayed it the next day."

"And did he give you any indication of his state of mind leading up to the poker game that night?" Wolcott asks.

"He was testy and disturbed about the barbecue, but he still wanted to play. He and I argued about moving and he told me that he had already made arrangements for us to relocate. I told him that I didn't want to go. He was definitely unhappy when we parted ways that day," I sputter.

"Do you feel like Spencer was capable of taking another person's life?" Wolcott asks.

I take a sharp inhale and look at the detectives, my eyes brimming. "He was erratic and unpredictable and moody, even before things went badly with Galapagos. But I never thought that he'd be capable of doing anything like . . ."

The words are swelling and stuck in the back of my throat like I'm having some kind of allergic reaction.

"Like what?" Wolcott presses.

"I don't know," I cry out.

"Try," Silvestri says evenly.

I put my hands over my face and sob. "Every day that passes that he's gone, I'm realizing how little I really knew about my husband . . ." I take a heavy breath. "And what he was capable of."

The detectives search my face. Wolcott breaks his concentration first and floats his eyes to the ground, where his face takes on a curious expression. I watch his partner follow his line of vision.

"There's something on the bottom of your shoe." Wolcott says.

I look down and see a fluorescent pink square stuck to my sandal.

"May I?" Silvestri has leaned in to retrieve the Post-it before I can respond. He flips the small square and reads the text on it. "Hmm," he says.

"Whatcha got there?" asks his partner.

"'Tell the story of how you want your life to be, not how it was or how it is.'"

CHAPTER THIRTY-ONE

WOLCOTT

"How you reading this one, you old bloodhound?" I flip down the sun visor in the unmarked to stifle the burst of glare slicing through the windshield. As we're pulling out of Monica Nichols's driveway, I notice Silvestri mean-mugging a reporter camped out across the street. My inquiry pulls his attention back inside the car.

"Well," he says. "I think the truth's in the twang."

"Got a nice ring to it," I say, letting out a chuckle. "What the fuck do you mean by that exactly?"

He cracks his neck. "When we first met Mrs. Nichols, the accent was coming in at around a Tommy Lee Jones level. Just now? That was Willie Nelson, two spliffs in. Seems like something's stressing the widow."

"Yeah," I agree. I use the tip of my tongue to coax a chunk of lemon pulp out from between my teeth. "I suppose that an affair with a friend's now-comatose husband'll do that to a gal."

"I'll say this: For a woman who just lost her own husband, she seemed mighty eager to steer the conversation back around to him."

"And away from Gil Mathers," I say. "I'm with you on that." I come to a four-way stop and let a Maserati cross before pulling out and dropping into the flow of traffic behind it.

"Well," he says, scratching his stubble, "let's look at it from her perspective: She just lost her husband, leaving the sisters as possibly the most solid emotional anchors in her life right now. If Laura Mathers knows about the affair, that could really blow up both of their worlds. And if she doesn't, you can bet that Monica's desperate to keep a tight lid on the situation, wouldn't you think?"

"Sure," I say.

"So," he continues, "having a couple of cops nosing around and asking questions about her big secret ain't exactly going to put her at ease."

"Right." I eye my partner and nod before making the turn out of Kingsland and heading back in the direction of the highway. "No wonder she's sounding like McConaughey at the Oscars."

I hear a hum and catch his hand moving to his pocket in my peripheral. He draws out his phone and taps the screen. "Silvestri," he answers. I adjust the visor to better deflect the stream of sunlight ducking in. "Oh, beautiful," he says. "What do you got?" As I drift into the left lane, I feel the energy in the car change. I glance at my partner out of the corner of my eye and catch the sight of his body tensing up. "Wait, what?" I sense his eyes on me. "That's, uh . . . could you email me that report?" A look of utter confusion masks his face as I catch another flash of him. "Okay, yeah. Thanks." He taps the phone and drops it into the cup holder between us.

"What was that all about?" I ask.

"You're not going to believe this shit," he says, letting out a thin whistle.

"Try me," I say.

"That was ballistics. The slug they pulled out of Gil Mathers's skull?"

"Uh-huh." I nod.

"It didn't come from Spencer Nichols's gun." His phone hums again, and he retrieves it from the cup holder and taps at it. "Wolcott, can you pull into that lot up there?" He points to a shopping center a hundred yards ahead.

"What now?"

"They just sent along the report," he explains. "If I try and read this thing while you're driving, I'm gonna throw up."

I sweep back into the right lane, ride the brake, and pull into the parking lot. I wheel the unmarked into a spot and kill the engine. "All right," I say. "Run me through this."

He holds out his phone for my perusal and scrolls to a spot on the report. "So," he begins. "The bullet that hit Mathers came from a nine-millimeter pistol, but not from Nichols's Beretta." He points to an image on the screen. "See here. That's the bullet that shot Terry Barnes. *That one* came from Nichols's nine. But here," he says, tapping the image next to it. "Different striation patterns on the bullets. Same caliber, different gun."

"So," I say. "There *was* another shooter at the clearing in the woods that night."

"Yes, sir," he says. "It's lookin' that way."

I unlatch my seat belt and turn toward my partner. "Okay, let's take a moment to refresh here." I crack my knuckles and set my elbow on the console between us. "Spencer Nichols was shot with the .40-cal Smith & Wesson we found at the scene. And we confirmed that that gun was registered to Gil Mathers, correct?"

"We did, yeah," he answers.

"Okay. And Terry Barnes was shot with the nine-millimeter Beretta registered to Spencer Nichols."

"Right," he says.

"But it was a different nine that was used to shoot Gil Mathers." I shake my head. "Well, this just got interesting."

"Sure did," he quips, eyes wide.

"So," I say. "We're back to our ambush theory."

"It would seem so, yeah." His eyes go soft and he spaces out for a moment before snapping back to attention. "Wait a minute," he says.

"What's up?"

"I wanna check on something," he says, before dialing a number and pulling the phone to his ear. He holds my stare as he waits for the call to be picked up. "Hey, it's me again," he says into the mouthpiece. "Yeah, sorry to bother you." He clears his throat. "Listen, can you do me a favor?" He looks encouragingly in my direction. "That Beretta you ran for us? Could you tell me how many rounds were left in the clip when it was inventoried?" I nod, realizing that he's going the process-of-elimination route. He holds up a finger and, after a long moment, breaks into a satisfied grin. "Beautiful. Thanks again, brother. Appreciate it." He taps the call dead and drops the phone into the cup holder.

"Yeah?" I ask.

"The clip was only one bullet short," he explains.

"So Nichols never got off a shot in the clearing," I say. "Just the one that killed Terry Barnes earlier."

"And then," says Silvestri, picking up my train of thought, "when they reached the clearing to divvy up the files and the cash, Mathers got the drop on his pal Spencer."

"Right," I continue. "And our mystery shooter plugged Mathers, then dipped off and left him for dead, not realizing he hadn't finished the job."

"Okay, so, premeditated." He sucks the inside of his cheek. "Are we thinking then that Nichols knew that Gil was slipping it to his wife, and set the whole thing up? Had his guy planted at the rendezvous spot, where he'd help Nichols gun Mathers down? But then Mathers got a jump on Nichols before this mystery man could get off a shot?"

"Wait, wait, wait," I say, an earlier piece of our investigation returning to me. "Let's not forget about the tracking software on Nichols's Fastback."

"Oh shit." He taps his temple. "That's right."

"So, do we think Gil *knew* that Spencer knew, and set the whole thing up as a way to beat him to the punch? Had the shooter steal the Mustang, knowing that Spencer would be able to track it down, and used it as a way to lure him into the trap? Then, somehow, in the commotion, Mathers accidentally catches some friendly fire?"

"*Or*," says my partner, "maybe the mystery shooter double-crosses them both?"

"Hmm," I consider. "There's an idea."

"I don't know, man." Silvestri blows out a breath. "I'd really love to have this conversation with whoever it was who pulled that trigger. And based on what we've got so far, I find myself going back to Randall Hemmings as the missing piece to this puzzle."

"Yeah, that file's giving me the itch too," I say. "Wanna go at him again?"

My partner ponders the idea. "Since we're close, what say we drop in on Victoria Barnes one more time. See if she knows more than she realizes about Mr. Hemmings."

"Worth a shot." I shrug, twisting the key in the ignition. "Back to Kingsland?"

"Back to Kingsland," he says, and I turn the unmarked around and pull onto the highway in the opposite direction, back into the sun's invasive glare.

CHAPTER THIRTY-TWO

VICTORIA

"DETECTIVES," I SAY, trying not to betray my surprise at the unexpected materialization of the pair at my doorstep. I'm working to corral the myriad emotions pinballing around inside me, and the last thing I need is to come apart in front of these two.

"Victoria," says Wolcott, a casual air about him. "Glad we got you at home."

"You did indeed." I slip my phone into my pocket and flick a stray strand of hair from my forehead. "Is everything okay?"

"Oh sure," says Silvestri, flashing an easy smile. "Didn't mean to alarm you. We were in the area and had a quick question we were hoping you might be able to help us with."

"Sure thing," I say, suddenly hyperaware of my awkward body language. I drop my shoulders and take a step backward in order to fully open the front door to my guests. "Won't you please come in?"

They cross the threshold and have a cursory glance around the parlor. "Can I get you anything?" I ask as I hurry to the chaise lounge and hastily snap shut the journal lying open against the throw pillow. The sudden motion catches their attention, and I notice Wolcott's eyes sweep to the array of photos spread out on the coffee table in the center of the room. It occurs to me that this feeling of instability I'm experiencing is rooted in the vulnerability inherent in having these two virtual strangers barging in on what is a very intimate, personal process.

"Terry's memorial service is tomorrow," I say by way of explanation. "I was organizing the photo display and trying to write the eulogy, you see."

"We didn't realize," says Silvestri as he begins to fiddle with his hands. I don't rush to quell the discomfiture in the room, instead allowing the detectives to stew in it for a moment. I find that their unease is having the effect of centering me, and I let the quiet stretch out for a beat before I consider breaking the tension.

My mind drifts to the fragmented scribblings in the journal. I've been struggling clumsily with the eulogy, trying to figure how best to tie a neat, tidy bow around the messy set of complications and contradictions that made up the whole of my husband. I fear that I'm thus far failing him miserably.

The sound of Wolcott clearing his throat captures my attention. "Let's talk in the kitchen," I say finally. "Less cluttered in there."

"Lead the way," says Silvestri, the airiness returning to his tone.

They follow me down the hall, Wolcott just over my right shoulder. "Not wasting any time," he says.

"What's that?" I ask.

"The memorial service," he clarifies.

"Well, the coroner's office is refusing to release Terry's body," I say with a deliberate edge. "Part of the ongoing investigation, I'm told. It may take weeks."

"Yeah," responds Silvestri. "There's really no kind of work-around on that one." I swear I catch a hint of satisfaction in his tone.

"Anyway, I've made the decision to just go ahead with it. I've got my sister to think about, and now Monica and the arrangements for Spencer to help out with. And honestly, Terry would have wanted it this way. He hated the thought of anyone beating him to the punch," I explain, half joking. "Even in death."

"I see," says Silvestri, with a slight chuckle.

We reach the kitchen, where I usher them to the stools on the far side of the center island. "You're a coffee drinker," I say, eyeing Wolcott. "If I'm remembering correctly."

"I've hit my limit for the day," he explains. "Another cup of the stuff, and you'll be peeling me off the ceiling. Thank you, though."

I offer Silvestri a refreshment, but he politely declines. "So, Detectives," I begin. "How can I help you today?"

Wolcott sets a hand on the countertop. "When we were looking around your husband's den the other day, we discovered that file with the name 'Randall Hemmings' written on it. Has that name set off any light bulbs in your brain in the time since our conversation?"

I rest my elbows on the space across from them and lean forward. "Still nothing," I say. "Sorry. Terry enjoyed a sizable network, between his business associates and congressional contacts. I simply don't know everyone whom he was connected to."

"Of course," he says, and tucks his hand inside his jacket. He pulls out a cell phone and taps away at the screen. "I'm just going to go ahead and show you a photograph. See if that does anything to jog the old memory." He sets the phone down on the counter, rotates it, and slides it toward me. I get a look at the man in the shot, and my stomach lurches. I'm suddenly back in that room, eavesdropping on a conversation I hadn't anticipated.

My eyes go wide, and I take a deep breath, doing my best to remain composed. "Oh," I say. "*This* guy."

"So," says Silvestri, eyes darting between his partner and myself. "You do recognize Mr. Hemmings."

"I mean, I guess I do, yes." I stand up straight, smoothing the front of my blouse. "When you mentioned the name, it didn't mean anything to me at the time. I didn't realize that this was the man in question."

"I see." Wolcott has reassumed the lead. "And can you tell us how you recognize Mr. Hemmings now?"

"Well," I say, feeling the heat spread through my body. "About a month ago, Terry surprised me with a trip to Palm Springs. Billed it as an impromptu getaway."

"Sounds nice."

"I thought so as well. But my husband's never had a big romantic streak. I should have known there was more to it than that."

"Okay," says Silvestri, studying me closely.

"Terry always had an agenda, you see. Was always playing some sort of angle." The sting of the recollection lingers, but I muscle through it. "So, we arrive in Palm Springs. He's got us set up in a beautiful suite. Very luxurious accommodations. We drop our bags and head down to the restaurant for lunch. Afterward, I decide I'm going to go laze around by the pool. Terry tells me that he's got some work to catch up on but that he'll join me when he wraps up. I head outside and get myself set up on a deck chair, then go for a quick dip. When I get out of the pool, I realize I've left my book upstairs and head back to the room to grab it. When I reach the front door, I can hear a voice on the other side that belongs to someone other than my husband. I'm intrigued, so I open it quietly and sneak in. The suite we're staying in has a partition and some tall potted plants between the entryway and the main space, so I'm able to stay out of sight while I peek in and eavesdrop on this conversation between my husband and a man I'd never seen until that moment." I point to the image on Wolcott's phone screen. "This man right here."

"And Mr. Barnes hadn't mentioned anything to you about this meeting beforehand?" he asks.

"No, he hadn't." I shake my head, feeling the frustration anew. "But as I said, I could have guessed that Terry was up to something."

"Okay," Wolcott urges. "And what can you tell us about anything you may have overheard that day?"

"Well," I recall, "I walked in on the middle of their conversation, but the word that caught my attention was 'tech.'"

"Tech," he parrots.

"Yes," I say. "This man—this Randall Hemmings—was pressing Terry about needing the tech, if he was going to get whatever they were discussing off the ground. I was trying to figure out what he was referring to, and then I remember Terry mentioning Spencer's name, so I figured they must have been talking about the tracking technology that Spence had developed for Galapagos. This Hemmings person seemed very eager to gain access to it."

"Interesting," says Silvestri, again trading looks with his partner. "And how would you describe the tone of the exchange?"

"Hmm," I consider. "A bit tense. Heated, even. It sounded as if this man was trying to leverage Terry, which did not go over well, as you might imagine. My husband was not a person who was used to being pushed around. He seemed to take exception to the general tenor of the conversation."

"Okay," says Wolcott, scribbling notes as I speak. "Any other details or snippets that you might recall?"

"No," I say. "I'm afraid that was it. They'd seemed to have reached an impasse by that point, and I got the sense that Terry was close to ending the meeting, so I snuck out of the room quietly before they had a chance to discover me hiding in there."

"Uh-huh." Silvestri nods. "And did you and your husband ever discuss the incident afterward, between yourselves?"

"We did not." I feel the vein in my neck twitch, and hope that it's not as apparent to the detectives as it feels in my own body. "Maybe that was petulance on my part, but I just thought, *If Terry's not going to bring it up, then neither am I.* Now, of course, I wish we *had* discussed it. Maybe if I knew more, it could help us all get to the bottom of whatever the hell happened the other night."

"Well," says Wolcott reassuringly, "it may still. This information could prove to be very helpful to the investigation. We appreciate you filling us in."

"Of course," I say, as I get a glance at the clock on the wall above the stove. "Oh, Detectives. I'm terribly sorry to rush you off, but my sister is expecting me over at her place in a few minutes. She's taking time out to help me get everything ready for tomorrow, and I don't want to keep her waiting."

"Of course," says Wolcott, straightening up and nodding to his partner. "What time is the service?"

"Two P.M.," I say. "We're holding it at the community center in town here."

"We'll try and stop by to pay our respects," he offers.

"That would be awfully kind of you," I say, nudging them out of the kitchen and toward the front door. "I know you're both very busy with the investigation."

"Well, we'll do our best," he insists as I open the door to them.

"And thank you for your tireless work on my husband's case," I say, offering up a compulsory smile. "I certainly appreciate it."

"It's what we do," says Silvestri. "And thank *you* for the information on Mr. Hemmings. It might just be the piece of the puzzle that helps the whole thing click into place."

"Very happy to help. Goodbye now, Detectives." I close the door before taking a deep, cleansing breath. I step into the parlor, where I gather the images of my husband up off the coffee table and slip them into a large manila envelope set off to the side. I collect the journal from the chaise lounge and tuck it under my arm. I look around once more to make sure I'm not forgetting anything, then grab my purse from the chair and head out the door, steadying myself for this next fire I'm anticipating having to put out.

CHAPTER THIRTY-THREE

LAURA

"IS SOMETHING BURNING?" Victoria asks when she walks into my kitchen.

"How did you get in?" I jump a little as I step into the room from the back deck.

"I had my key," my sister replies. "You didn't answer the door."

"Sorry," I say, distracted. "I was outside."

She sniffs the air. "Have you been smoking?"

"No. But I've been thinking about it," I answer honestly.

She groans. "Don't. Once you start again you'll just have to go through quitting again."

"I know, I know," I say, offering her a tight hug, which she accepts warmly.

"So, why does it smell smoky in here?" she probes as I release our hug.

"I have the fire pit going." I point out the window to the modest flame barely visible in the waning daylight.

Concern crosses my sister's face when she clocks the family photos laid out on the table. "Were you burning something?"

"Just my life, apparently," I deadpan.

She laughs drily. "It feels that way right now, doesn't it?"

"I just felt like lighting a fire. I thought we could sit by it tonight."

She sheds her light button-up blouse, revealing her tanned and toned arms in a silky pale pink camisole. "Isn't it a little warm for that?"

"Not if we don't sit too close."

She nods and eyes my nearly empty glass.

"I opened a bottle. I was getting antsy," I tell her as I move to the fridge, where I pull the half-empty bottle from the door of the fridge.

Victoria reaches into a large tote and places a stack of square glass containers with a colorful variety of plastic lids on the counter. She also pulls a manila folder and her journal out of the bag and places them on the counter.

"What are those?" I point to the mystery containers.

"Food. People have been dropping stuff off around the clock. I have absolutely no appetite, so I thought I'd bring some over."

"Who knew the residents of Kingsland were so charitable?" I say sarcastically.

I look at the food containers and wrinkle my nose. "I'm not hungry either."

I see Vicky home in on the framed photos of Libby on the kitchen table that I've resurrected from storage. She lifts one of her and Libby to her face and smiles.

"It is amazing how much she looked like you at this age," she laments. "I love this one."

"Take it. I have copies."

"Really?" She brightens and holds the frame to her heart.

"Of course. I'm glad it makes you happy."

"Thanks, Laur. I miss her so much." She sighs.

"Me too."

"I haven't seen these for so long," she says as she works her way through the other framed photos and then to the photo album nearby.

"I pulled them out when I was looking for photos of Terry. With Gil in the hospital, I realized that I could take the pictures of Lib out again without a fight. It might sound twisted, but seeing pictures of her out in the open again is making all of this more manageable, somehow."

"That makes sense to me. It reminds me that if we can get through Libby's death, we can survive anything," Vicky responds.

I make an odd face and she looks at me questioningly.

"Sorry, I was having a flashback. I was just remembering that you said something similar to me when Libby died."

"I did?" She turns red.

I nod. "You reminded me that we would be able to get through that terrible time because we'd survived Dad's death and everything that happened afterward. It was helpful then, and it's helpful now."

"In that case, I guess I did. And I stand by it." Vicky chokes up.

I put the glass food containers into the fridge, knowing full well they'll end up in the garbage in a matter of days or weeks, depending on when I ask the housekeeper to purge everything.

"It's good to see these." Vicky refocuses on the photos.

"I found some good ones of Terry and you in the early days. And a lot of Terry by himself." I point to a pile of loose photos on the table dedicated to his solo pics.

"He did love to have his picture taken, didn't he? I think I have plenty for tomorrow, but I will take these just in case." She tucks them into the folder.

"How many people do you think will show up tomorrow?"

"Too many. I've already got a waitlist for speakers." She shakes her head. "It's turning into a three-ring circus."

"Terry's favorite kind," I say. "There were some old pics of Mom and Dad in the stash, also. They're in the Tiffany box." I gesture to the seldom-seen wedding gift from our great-aunt Teresa.

I see my sister hover her hand over the silver rectangle sitting on one of the kitchen chairs and then stop herself.

"I don't blame you. I started looking through them, but I had to stop. It was weird to see either of them, especially the ones where they look like they actually liked each other."

She sighs. "I think I've had too much nostalgia for one day," she says ruefully, and puts the framed photo of Libby to her chest again. "But thank you for this."

"Do you want me to help you put them together in some kind of display?" I ask, and she responds with a pained expression.

"Or I can do it all myself. Then you don't have to stress over it," I add.

"I've got some blowups being done by the printer and they'll be ready tomorrow morning."

"Great. I'm ready," I tell her.

"I'm burnt out right now from all of the planning. I'm already regretting planning this memorial so quickly."

"It's what Terry would have wanted, I'm sure. Do it while he's still front-page news, right?" I say in all seriousness.

"I know. It's terrible, but it's true," Vicky says. "I was also just desperate to do something productive. Planning this felt like the best thing to do with my time."

"It is the right thing to do. No matter what anyone might say," I say.

"Why? Have you heard something?" she asks, alarmed.

"No. But I'm sure someone has or will. You know how this works. Especially with so much unanswered and all of the goddamn media coverage."

"I can't even look at any of it."

"Same," I say.

"I'm not sure what I should be doing tomorrow. I mean, I know what to do. I'm not sure how to be, I guess," she says, showing rare vulnerability.

"Sweetie, you need to be yourself. Nothing more," I say lovingly.

"I'm preparing myself for all of the questions tomorrow," Vicky says.

"There'll be a lot of lips flapping about Gil as well, but I'm happy to tell people to mind their own fucking business," I crack.

"And poor Monica, she'll likely get grilled about Spencer. I'm sure people are speculating about a hundred horrible scenarios," Vicky says sympathetically.

"Has she planned anything for Spencer?" I ask bluntly.

"Monica's not ready to do anything without his . . . body. And the coroner said he and Terry might not be cleared for release for *weeks*."

I pull two glasses from the cabinet and place them on a tray next to the ice bucket.

"Better make it three," Vicky says nonchalantly, and looks away. "Monica's on her way over," she adds.

"I really wish you'd asked me."

"We should talk about everything that has happened," she says firmly.

"I don't know if I'm ready for that," I say, frustrated. "Talking about things is going to make this situation worse." I take the bottle from her and aggressively screw the helix into the cork and compress the arms until the sound of the satisfying pop fills the tense silence between us.

"Fine, three glasses," I say as I pull another goblet from the cabinet and place it on the counter a little too hard for comfort.

"Thank you," Vicky says.

"I guess I better make it three bottles, then," I say as I trash the first empty bottle, stick the now open one in the waiting ice bucket, and then fetch another bottle of rosé and place it in the refrigerator.

"It could be a long night. I, for one, would really like to know what, if anything, the detectives have found out. I feel totally in the dark."

"I am with you."

"Laur, they came by my house today," Vicky says, on edge.

Before I can press her for information, the doorbell chimes.

I pour myself a glass and make no move to answer the door.

"I'll get it," she says, annoyed.

In the few moments I have before Vicky returns with Monica, I feel an emotional waterfall churning.

Monica looks skittish when she steps into the kitchen. "Hi, Laura," she says anxiously. It dawns on me that the last time we'd been in person, Spencer hadn't been found yet. A ripple of pity runs through me.

"Hi," I say. Vicky is right behind her and shoots me a look of pleading.

"How are you holding up?" I say as I move to hug her. We stand stiffly in a half embrace.

"I don't think I've fully absorbed it. I keep waiting for him to walk through the door."

The three of us stand in an uncomfortable silence for a second before Vicky breaks through.

"I'm glad we are all together again," she says heartfully.

"Me too," Monica replies. "Laura." She steps toward me, shifting from one foot to the other. "I want to apologize." She pulls at the skin on her arms and I see red welts forming on her pale skin.

"For what, exactly?" I ask.

"For everything. For what I told you about Gil last month. It was a huge thing to put on you."

I feel the weight of my misdirected anger and can no longer deny how much of it belongs to Gil, not her.

She continues in my silence. "And for how I handled things with Gil . . . I didn't keep up my end of the bargain. I can't really explain what happened. And you told me that you didn't want details."

My heart backflips. "I *don't* want details." The thought of Monica confronting Gil makes me nauseous.

"I really fucked things up. But I want to make it right."

I look up at her and then at my sister, their faces open and hopeful.

"I think this moment calls for a truce. We need to trust each other and forgive any lingering resentments," Vicky interjects.

"Apology accepted. Let's move on," I say.

"Thank you," Monica replies, her tone grateful.

Vicky clears her throat gently. "Why don't we go outside and talk? It's getting dark enough that we can enjoy the fire Laura has started."

⫸

The first twinkling of starlight is emerging. Our glasses have been filled, bug spray has been passed around and applied, and chairs have been arranged and rearranged. We are finally situated in the three reclining chairs facing one another a few feet from the fire pit.

"How are you doing, Vicky?" Monica asks gently. "It must have been horrible to find Terry that way."

I watch my sister's body language, knowing that she is an expert at keeping her emotions locked away, even in the presence of the people closest to her. She was conditioned by our mother, who considered vulnerability low-class.

"It was incredibly gruesome and completely traumatizing. Nothing prepares you for something like that," she says. "I think the detectives are expecting me to be hysterical."

"That's not who you are."

"Everyone processes grief differently."

"Finding Terry brought me back to when I found Dad," Vicky directs to me, and I see Monica's mouth open slightly.

"I didn't realize you were the one . . . ," she trails off mournfully. Vicky looks at her and nods.

"Yes. I went to his house to check on him. He'd . . . fallen . . . and had been dead for a few days," Vicky says matter-of-factly.

"Oh God," Monica says.

I don't tell Monica that Vicky has been the member of our family who has had the dubious task of seeing her loved ones dead not just twice, but three times. When Libby was shot, I couldn't bring myself to identify her, and Gil was MIA. Vicky stepped in for me. My gratitude and awe for my sister being so strong in the face of each of these horrendous experiences humbles me. But I worry for her emotional health, having seen so much death without falling to pieces like most people would have.

Vicky changes the subject. "The detectives told me today that they'll be stopping by the memorial service tomorrow. I told them that they were welcome."

"Really?" I ask. "I guess that's a good thing. They are doing their jobs."

"How much more do you think they are going to ask?" Monica asks miserably.

"They'll be asking questions until they figure out why this happened, I would imagine," Vicky says, her eyes focused on something in the dark grass.

Fireflies flicker in random patterns around us and beyond into the reaches of the yard where the dark corners make way into the trees.

"It's their job to find out who did this, and the more we can help them, the sooner this will be over," I say.

"It would be useful if they shared their leads with us," Vicky says. "I'd like to know what direction they are leaning in."

"I've been getting a lot of questions, but not very many answers," I commiserate.

"Same. They came by today and were asking a lot about Gil," Monica shares.

"What about him?" I ask.

"About what my relationship with him was," she replies.

I see Vicky shift uncomfortably in her chair. "They are likely trying to figure out why Gil would have hurt Spencer," she says.

"And what did you tell them?" I ask Monica pointedly, the reflection of the flames dancing alongside her cheek.

She looks at me for a full second without saying anything, and I feel a little surprised by the chilliness of her stare. "I told them the truth," she says finally.

"Which is?" I ask harshly.

Vicky purses her lips.

"That there was no relationship between us," Monica says.

Vicky looks at her wine and pulls her feet under her before speaking. "All we can do is tell them about our husbands and let them figure out what happened that night. We have to be patient."

"*I'm* still trying to figure out what happened that night!" I say, feeling the wine fast-tracking me through patience to indignation.

"We all are, Laur," Vicky says, shushing me with her tone. "Clearly, things got out of control. We just need to stick together and not lose our minds right now."

"I'm trying," Monica says, barely above a whisper.

"The detectives were asking me about Randall Hemmings today," Vicky says. "I told them about Palm Springs."

"Do they think that your trip has something to do with the shootings?" Monica asks.

"I'm not sure. But they asked about a file on Hemmings they found in Terry's safe."

The summer night sounds play out around us.

"Is Hemmings a suspect?" I ask.

"Maybe? They didn't exactly fill me in on their thoughts on the topic," Vicky answers. "He's a shady character, but who knows what they'll actually find on him."

"Who did Terry keep company with that wasn't shady?" I say.

"They should be interviewing the whole neighborhood. Given the number of nearly convicted men living in Kingsland—" Vicky says quietly.

"And with grudges against one or all of our husbands—" I agree.

"It could be anyone," Monica says.

"So, we really have no clue what they think happened that night?"

"They haven't told me anything," Monica says.

"Gil is probably the most likely suspect. When he wakes up and is able to talk, this will all be very different."

"*If* he wakes up and can talk," I say bitterly.

Monica looks like she's about to speak and then stops herself. She takes a gulp of wine and looks off into the fire.

"How is Gil doing?" she finally asks.

"He's in a coma," I say coldly. "But he woke up for a few minutes yesterday and spoke."

Vicky's and Monica's eyes double in size. "Oh, Laur, you didn't tell me that."

"Oh my God!" Vicky exclaims.

Monica's eyes are brimming in the flicker of the fire. "What did he say?" she whispers.

"Nothing intelligible," I lie. "And he was unconscious again before I could get the doctor into the room."

"I have a feeling that he will wake up again," Vicky says steadily, and looks at me, her expression filled with so much emotion.

"So do I," I agree, and begin to cry in spite of my best attempts to keep it inside.

"And when he does," I continue seriously, "things are only going to get more complicated."

CHAPTER THIRTY-FOUR

SILVESTRI

"Straight to voicemail," I mouth to my partner across the desk as I wait for the outgoing message to wrap up. Captain Evans gives an offhand wave as he passes us, heading in the direction of his office. "Yes, Mr. Hemmings," I speak into the phone. "This is Detective Dennis Silvestri of the Stony Brook Police Department. We spoke the other day regarding your friend Terry Barnes. Some new information has surfaced in Mr. Barnes's case that I'd love to speak with you about at your earliest convenience." I leave my number, as I'm sure he didn't bother to make a note of it during our previous conversation. "Please get back to me as soon as possible. I'll await your call." I drop the cell on top of a stack of folders and lean back in my seat.

"Tone was a bit curt," Wolcott ribs me, tapping the tip of his pen rapidly against the sole of the shoe he's crossed over his knee. "You still chafed about him hanging up on you the last time?"

"Nah," I say dismissively. "I'm not interested in holding grudges, pal. Just interested in shooters."

"I'm with you on that, Silvestri. We got any other lines to this guy?"

"Well, I dug up some contact info for a personal assistant of his." I flip a page in the file set open atop my desk and locate what I'm looking for. "Let me give her a shot." I dial the number and am once again transferred to voicemail, where I proceed to leave a message for the young woman on the other end of the greeting, her youthful tone shaded with ennui. "Let's see if we have better luck there," I say before setting the phone back down and returning my attention to my partner.

"I'll tell you the thing that's chafing *me*," says Wolcott, eyes shifting back and forth as if he's reading the eye chart at the optometrist's office. "Something about this whole configuration seems off."

"How so?" I ask.

"Well, they've got this little back-scratch circle going, right? Barnes, Mathers, Nichols, and now Hemmings. One guy's doing a favor for another guy, who's doing a favor for the next guy, and so on?"

"Okay," I say.

"When we spoke with Barnes's widow earlier about their Palm Springs trip, didn't you get the impression that Hemmings was putting the clamps on Barnes for the tech from Nichols? Like there was some tension there?"

"Sounded that way," I agree.

"Which makes me think that Nichols was pushing back some, no? Maybe he didn't like the idea of sharing. Or he had some issue with Hemmings personally, or with whatever Hemmings intended to do with the technology he'd developed?"

"Sure," I reason.

"Okay, so bear with me here." He uncrosses his legs and sets his elbows on the desk, his focus now pointed. "With the way we're looking at the logistics, we're thinking that Nichols put Hemmings up to ambushing Mathers and shooting him in the clearing that night."

"That's the thought," I say.

"So assuming that *is* the case, why would Nichols cozy up with the guy he was trying to keep *away* from his tech?" he asks. "Seems like one of those head-scratchers to me, no?"

"I see your point." I turn the thought over in my mind and sift through the strands. "Maybe Nichols used that as the condition for handing it over. A little quid pro quo. Leverage."

"Hmm," he ponders. "Okay, so Nichols and Hemmings decided to get slick. Went ahead and cut Barnes out of the equation altogether. Eliminated the middleman, as it were."

"That could fly." I nod. "And then Hemmings double-crosses Nichols. Lets him catch a bullet from Mathers before Hemmings puts *him* down. Walks away from the whole mess assuming that all the loose ends have been tied up."

Wolcott appears to run the sequence back in his head, feeling around for loose threads. "And he just leaves the cash behind?"

"If he had Nichols's tech." I consider. "Maybe he wasn't that concerned with the money?"

"You think Nichols handed over the goods before Hemmings had even done the deed?" He shakes his head and cracks a grin. "That's amateur hour right there."

"Listen," I say. "It's not as if we're dealing with a pool of criminal masterminds here. These are a bunch of entitled rich guys clearly in over their heads. Shit, maybe the guy just panicked and left the cash behind."

"Yeah, maybe," he reasons. "I mean, otherwise, if Hemmings isn't even sweating the prospect of leaving a hundred large just sitting there—if that's such small potatoes to this cat—then I'd *really* like to know what the hell he's got up his sleeve as far as Nichols's tech goes."

"That's you and me both, brother." My eyes return to the paper-work in the file, but the text is beginning to blur. I've looked over these documents so many times that the words have managed to lose their objective coherency.

"The other question I have now is Mathers," says my partner, coaxing my attention back to our spitballing session. "Even if we get in his ear after he wakes up, how much is he going to be able to give us if he's been cut out of the loop by these other guys?"

"Right," I agree.

"Hey." Wolcott's now tapping his pen against the surface of the desk, his mind restless. "When are they scheduled to bring Mathers out of the coma, anyway?"

"Sometime over the next few days, I think. I asked the doctor to give us a heads-up whenever they get a time locked down."

"Okay, good." He looks past me, his eyes unfocused and floating. After a moment, the pen stops tapping and my partner's stare finds me. "Do we think Randall Hemmings is gonna show up at Barnes's memorial service tomorrow?" There's a trace of glee in his voice, as if he's daring the very thought to prove itself true.

"Ooh," I say, the sheer brazenness of the idea tickling me. "Some set of stones that would take, if he's behind it all."

"Doesn't seem to be a guy who's lacking nerve," muses Wolcott. "And who knows? Maybe he'll even get a kick out of it. Like return-ing to the scene of the crime, in a way."

"Well, having had the pleasure of speaking to the guy, I can tell you that he enjoys no shortage of arrogance. And who knows?" I feel a burst of excitement at the prospect. "Maybe this son of a bitch serves himself right up."

Wolcott grips the knot of his tie with one hand and gives the length of fabric a tug with the other. "Break out your classiest mourning attire, Silvestri." He squares his shoulders, a glimmer in his gaze. "We're gonna bump that RSVP from a maybe to a hard yes."

CHAPTER THIRTY-FIVE

MONICA

As SOON AS I walk into the vestibule from the downpour outside, I recognize the sound of people talking about me. The wagging tongues halt after a blur of double takes when I enter, and I keep my head held up, as much as I want to turn and run. I look over the crowd, and one eternal pause later, their attention settles back on one another and the cadence of somber conversation resumes.

Even though I've prepared myself for the worst, a deep gnawing of otherness reverberates in me as I step into the fray. I don't see Vicky or Laura anywhere among the hundreds of darkly clad mourners in tight circles in the grand hall of the Libby Mathers Memorial Community Center, generously built and donated by none other than Terry Barnes. As I maneuver through the crowd to an open spot underneath the photograph of Libby in her school uniform, I notice that Terry's name is as big as hers on the large brass plaque bolted to the wall beneath.

I've only been in the building a handful of times before. They were all Kingsland fundraisers for nondescript causes, which were really just excuses for the residents to roll out their red-carpet-worthy duds and drink too much top-shelf liquor on Terry. The center is probably the most overly lavish and amenity-filled building of its kind that I've ever seen, with floor-to-ceiling marble, cathedral ceilings, a full-size theater, a state-of-the-art gym, and an Olympic-size swimming pool.

I hand my umbrella to a kind-faced woman in uniform who has appeared out of thin air, and she gives me a coat-check number in return. I thank her with a smile, slide the paper ticket into my purse, and survey the chittering throng.

A startling yelp echoes from the direction I've just been, and I see an impeccably dressed woman in six-inch heels being held up by a silver-haired man in a navy suit and a pocket square.

"I could have broken my neck!" she exclaims loudly while glaring at the woman I've just handed my umbrella to.

I spot liquid pooled at my feet and realize I've been dripping water from the front door to where I was standing. A short woman in uniform, seemingly out of the shadows, quickly swipes it away with a small towel before I can make a move. My face flames up as I move from the spot quickly and into the center of the room.

Three hundred and sixty degrees around me are faces and mouths contorted into smirks and frowns. The ambient noise of a hundred hushed conversations overlapping and the collective buzzing makes the room feel like it is tilting on its axis.

"Mathers is on life support . . . not unlike his career . . ."

"I'm glad I have an alibi for that night . . ."

Every few seconds, suppressed laughter ripples around the room and I shudder.

". . . publicity stunt? . . ."

"Victoria looks incredible as always. You'd think she'd look a little less perfect today . . ."

Every direction I turn, I feel more boxed in by the chorus. I expect no one's sympathy or condolences today, but I put up a shield around me just in case. These people are here for Terry, or the spectacle. No one is here for Spence, or me.

"Did you see how many congressmen are here? . . ."

"Someone told me that Nichols attacked Barnes the day before . . ."

The competing snippets of conversation carry and meld with the disquieting conversation running at top volume through my own head. I try to block everything out with no luck.

". . . shot ten times in the heart . . ."

"Is it true he is being cryogenically frozen? . . ."

"The wine is fantastic, at least . . ."

I move through the bodies with my head down and my arms folded tightly across my chest.

"God, can you even imagine, she was the one who found him . . ."

"The killer was in the house with her . . ."

I can't locate Vicky anywhere in the sea of people. I'm feeling hot and dizzy and worry that I might not be able to contain the scream that is threatening to escape my body.

"The family is cursed . . ."

Someone to the left of me gripes loudly to a passing caterer with a tray of full red wineglasses about there not being any white. The waiter looks indifferent and keeps moving toward the main room, where it seems the majority of the attendees have congregated. I spot an opening and push through to a space off to the side of the room.

Along the periphery of the crowd there are professional poster blowups of Terry and a number of photo collages with a collection of pictures spanning baby pics through shots as recently as the Fourth of July barbecue. No one is looking at the photos.

I peer closely at the group of shots from just days earlier and start to shake. In one of the prints, I can see Spencer in the foreground. A sickening chill runs through me. He is off-center and out of focus. Gil is also in the shot, with his head thrown back mid-laugh and standing off to the side of the main subject of the photograph. True to form, front and center is Terry, his hands in the air dramatically. The realization that two-thirds of the people in this shot are dead, and one is barely alive, turns my stomach.

"Why does it always rain at funerals?" someone behind me muses.

"This isn't a funeral, dear. It's a memorial service," a deep voice responds.

"What's the difference?"

"You need a body for a funeral."

I move away from the photos and toward a spread of crab legs, shrimp cocktail, oysters on the half shell, and an array of other seafood. There are also numerous untouched growlers of Terry's homemade beer, Barnes's Brew, on ice, which people are passing by without a second glance to get to the seafood bar. Well-dressed multitasking mourners are making small talk with one another while filling small plates and balancing them with their wineglasses and scanning the room for who has just arrived. The only difference between this event and any other I've attended here is the gloomy color scheme of the clothing and the lack of Terry Barnes setting the average volume slightly above a scream.

I walk toward the main hall and grab a glass of white wine and gulp it down fast before I reach the doorway. It is surprisingly delicious for event wine, and I feel its effects almost immediately.

There is a group of well-dressed men blocking the entrance, their backs a mix of expensive summer suits and dark sports jackets. The space beyond is packed with people, their voices a blend of whispers and soothing tones. The absence of happy laughter is a stark reminder of the reason why we are all here, and when an errant chuckle erupts, it startlingly rips through the gloominess.

I am grateful for my shorter stature at this moment. I can hide in the shadows of the pack of Terry's mourners. I lean against the wall and none of the men in front of me turn or acknowledge my presence.

"Bloody awful," an older man with an English accent says. "Shot right in his home." I can see the backs of the men's heads shaking. "I wouldn't believe it, if it was anyone other than Barnes."

"And Nichols was in a park or something?" someone asks, and I shrink a little. "With Mathers?"

"I've heard a lot of conflicting stories. All terrible."

"Who do they think did it?" asks another.

"My money is on Mathers," a third man replies.

"I wouldn't have pegged him for a killer, but he's always been a bit of a wild card."

"True. I spent some time with him during that week in Saint Lucia in 2000. The man was a maniac."

"He isn't dead yet."

"Saint Lucia! That was epic! You were there? I don't remember you, mate."

"Funny, I don't remember you either," says one, chuckling lightly.

"It was that kind of weekend."

"Barnes did throw a good party, I'll give him that."

They raise their drinks and I have to restrain myself from smacking the glasses out of their fat hands.

"To the king of the lost weekend." They toast.

As I push through them, the tallest of the three abruptly drops his smirk when he sees my face.

I move through the crowd and spot two familiar faces: the detectives. I see Silvestri propped up against a wall studying the mourners a few yards away. Wolcott is walking slowly around the border of the main floor before he slides into the space right in front of me. My heart does a two-step and I freeze in place, praying he won't spin around and use the opportunity to question me. Luckily, he seems more interested in the cluster of people talking in front of him.

The group of mostly men and one extremely dour-faced woman are locked in a tight circle and don't seem to notice either of us.

"I can't believe he didn't show up," a man with bad acne scars says.

"He's on the East Coast right now. I saw him at the screening a couple of nights ago." The woman's frown lifts momentarily before resting back into solid misery.

"Not like ol' Randall to miss an opportunity to rub elbows with the DC crew. There is a lot of glad-handing to be had here," a man in a seersucker suit, looking better suited for a derby, says as he scans the room.

"Or to miss drinking Terry's good stuff," adds a ruddy-faced man to his right.

Wolcott seems absorbed enough in what the men are saying, and Silvestri seems focused enough on someone in the other direction, that I've gone unnoticed. I move away from the detectives quietly.

I see Milly talking with a group of women that I recognize from the neighborhood and turn away, but I feel her long-nailed hand on my arm before I make it very far.

"Moooniiicaaa," she says dramatically. "How are you doing?" She is head to toe in black with dramatic makeup and a tight topknot bun atop her pinhead. "This must just be a nightmare for you. I am just so beside myself, I can't even eat or sleep. I've been at Vicky's side *every* minute since it all happened." She draws curious looks from the people around us.

I don't say a word and let my eyes bore into hers. She shifts uneasily on her Louboutins.

"Fuck off, Milly," I say harshly before breaking away from her, leaving her stunned and a few people in earshot slack-jawed.

I catch sight of Vicky making her way to the dais as the crowd's murmurings begin to quiet. I watch my friend, statuesque in a stunning indigo silk dress with capped sleeves and a beautiful Gucci scarf around her shoulders.

I feel someone sidle up next to me and I see that it is Laura holding two glasses of wine. She wordlessly hands me one and I take it, relieved for the company.

"You look like you need this," she says.

I accept the glass and take a large sip.

"Vicky opened Terry's special wine collection for this."

We sip together in silence, both intently watching Vicky.

"He would have lost his mind if he was here and realized she'd gone into his stash. He loved that wine more than her," Laura says.

"I thought it tasted too good for a catered event," I say.

"Just pace yourself. You don't want to be carried out of here and give the gristmill any more material," she says disdainfully.

I take another sip and look at Laura. "How are you?" I ask her.

She keeps her gaze on her sister, who is waiting for the crowd to quiet down completely.

"Never better," she says, her sarcasm as full-bodied as the wine.

"Any update about Gil?" I ask, bracing myself.

"He's improving. I think they'll bring him out of the coma soon." She whispers this directly in my ear as the room around us grows silent. My heart races.

Vicky clears her throat and begins to speak.

"Dear friends and family, thank you for being here today. It brings me great comfort to see so many familiar faces in this room. As most of you know, I'm not one for public speaking, so I promise to keep this short and sweet."

The audience is completely rapt, with all eyes on her. I see a few stragglers entering the back of the main hall when I look over my shoulder and realize how crowded the place has become. It looks like there are at least three hundred people packed into the space and I begin to feel claustrophobic.

"We are gathered together to celebrate the life of Terrence Charles Barnes—Terry, as all of you knew him—a devoted husband, son, friend, colleague, and public servant. Though taken from us far too soon, Terry carved a bold path and left quite a legacy in his wake."

I'm finding it hard to keep focused on Vicky's words and am distracted by the hundreds of microreactions happening all around me. I glance at Laura and wonder if she's having the same experience, but she is laser focused on her sister, a look of stoicism chiseled across her face while Vicky continues to mesmerize the room.

"My husband was many things: stubborn, opinionated, outspoken, occasionally temperamental. Now, I know what you're probably thinking: *Vicki, did the man have any flaws?*"

Vicky expertly pauses as a wave of tentative laughter moves through the room and grows louder as more people respond. I catch sight of Wolcott and Silvestri, now both on the outskirts of the crowd, intently watching the audience, not the speaker. Their focus distracts me, imagining that they are scanning each face for any clue of what might have happened to Terry, Gil, and Spence. I redirect back to Vicky, who isn't missing a beat.

"But in all seriousness, Terry contained multitudes. He was a passionate human being who advocated for the things he believed in and stayed the course in the face of adversity. He was fiercely loyal to those in his camp."

I watch a few people in front of us exchange dubious glances with each other and a woman pinch the man next to her in the back of the arm when he mutters something to her under his breath.

"Terry served faithfully as a member of Congress, always paying the office the respect he felt it deserved. And he built this community that is Kingsland as a haven for those who'd erred along the way, but who he felt were deserving of a second chance in life." Her voice is strong but emotional.

"His dedication to, and advocacy for, this principle of salvation was just one of the many displays of compassion that my husband exhibited, close to the vest though he may have kept them. Terry was always willing to lend a hand to a friend in need, whether it was providing a business opportunity as a way to help someone get back on their feet, or even donating the assistance of his legal team to those embroiled in woes of their own. He was always happy to provide a boost to anyone who he felt could use a leg up."

Someone snickers and another person shushes them somewhere behind me. I'm amazed at how clear, confident, and composed Vicky is able to be and wonder if she's conscious of all the commentary happening in the room.

"It's crazy to think that it was only days ago that many of you joined us at our home to help celebrate the independence of this great nation of ours. It was one of Terry's favorite events of the year, and I'm so glad that he was able to spend that time with those closest to him, enjoying the warmth of spirit and comfort of community that meant so much to my dear husband. In the short time that I enjoyed with him afterward, he spoke of the happiness it brought him, a feeling that I sincerely hope you all shared as well."

Vicky's voice trembles for a second and I watch in awe as one perfect tear rolls out of each eye and down her flawless cheeks. The entire room is holding their breath. Whatever their opinion of Terry, the gravity of what has happened to him, and to her, appears to have fully taken hold of everyone.

"As we leave this celebration of life today, please take a moment to keep Terry present in your hearts and minds, and to acknowledge the indomitable spirit that guided him through life, all the way to the end. I sincerely appreciate everyone coming here to show your love and support, and please know that my dear husband held you all in as high esteem as I do. Thank you so much."

Vicky smiles appreciatively at the room and a few scattered bursts of applause break through the heavy silence before stopping short after realizing that this isn't a clapping-appropriate occasion.

"She was amazing," I say to Laura, who is still looking at the dais even though Vicky has moved from her place to rejoin the group.

"She always is," Laura agrees.

"The detectives are over there," I say to her softly.

"I know."

"I wonder what they think about all of this," I say, looking around the room at the cast of characters surrounding us.

"I think they are wondering what everyone else is," she says.

"What's that?"

"If Terry's killer is in the room right now."

CHAPTER THIRTY-SIX

WOLCOTT

"Well, that was a bust," says Silvestri, wrestling with a large umbrella as we step out the front door of the community center and pause off to the side of the walkway. "At least as far as Hemmings is concerned."

"Yeah, conspicuously absent," I agree, still distracted by the oversize vented monstrosity that my partner is attempting to wrangle. It looks like the type you'd find out on a golf course, and I can't for the life of me ever remember the guy using anything other than a loose plastic bag to shield himself from the rain anytime we've been caught in a downpour. "Hey," I say, eyeing the mass of bodies fanning out on the walkway. "You notice anything strange about the demographic around here?"

He cocks an eyebrow. "Aside from the twenty-year age gap between most of the couples?"

"Well, yeah." I chuckle. "You kind of expect that. But the diversity of the wives, I mean. This whole place looks like a bunch of old white guys tripped and fell into a Benetton ad."

"How 'bout that," he says, cracking a grin as he looks over the throng. "We've got a real woke crowd around here, I guess."

"Something like that," I deadpan.

Silvestri's scanning the stream of mourners emptying out of the building when I notice his eyes lock on a petite blond woman. "Hey," he says to me. "Isn't that Barnes's neighbor? The one we spoke with the night of?"

"It sure is," I say. "Kind of a Chatty Cathy, wasn't she?"

"Yeah, she's the one who hipped us to the Palm Springs trip initially."

"Right you are."

"Let's go say hi," he says, stepping onto the pathway to intercept the woman as I dig for my notepad and follow his lead, finally realizing his strategy in bringing the umbrella along.

The woman seems momentarily startled as Silvestri offers her cover from the storm, but relaxes as she recognizes us. "Detectives," she says, and thanks my partner for the gesture.

"Hello again"—I locate the name in my notes just in time—"Mrs. Addison-LeFleur. Sorry to be meeting under these circumstances."

"Oh, call me Milly," she says, swatting my arm gently for the transgression before letting her hand rest against the sleeve of my jacket. "It's just so tragic." Her display of solemnity seems to be rooted more in perceived expectation than genuine emotion. "All of this."

"It certainly is." I nod in agreement as I pat the hand squeezing my forearm. "A tough week for Kingsland."

"So senseless." She looks around to confirm a clear coast before continuing. "I've never liked guns. Never. To think that this latest tragedy was observed today in *this* place, which is only here as the result of more gun violence. The irony is just too . . . I mean, what are the chances?"

"That's a fair point," I remark. "Say, Milly, you strike us as the observant type." She appears to take my carefully chosen wording in the spirit of a compliment, and her face brightens.

"I do like to know what's going on." She beams.

"Sure, sure," I say. "And I wondered if you'd noticed anything out of the ordinary since my partner and I last spoke with you."

"Hmm," she considers. "Like what?"

"Well," says Silvestri. "You seem to be the eyes and ears around here. Anything jump out at you? Anything unusual, maybe concerning the wives?"

"I'll say this." Her eyes widen as she leans closer. "When I spoke to Monica Nichols earlier, she nearly bit my head clear off."

"Is that right?" I ask.

"Just completely out of the blue," she explains. "I was trying to ask her how she was holding up. And she told me to *eff off*."

"I see."

"Now, I know the poor thing is going through a lot emotionally right now, what with having just lost her husband, but I simply can't understand why she'd be directing it at me. I've shown her nothing but compassion ever since they got here."

"Hmm," says Silvestri. "Could there be anything else going on that might be contributing to her stress?"

She draws her head back, her eyes shifting between the two of us. "I feel like you're getting at something, Detective."

I scan the crowd to make sure we're out of earshot, to offer her the full cloak-and-dagger experience. She's practically frothing at the mouth, dizzy with the intrigue of it all. "Milly," I nearly whisper. "We've heard rumors—and these are *just* rumors, mind you—that there may have been something going on between Monica Nichols and Gil Mathers."

It's all she can do to contain the squeal of delight bubbling in her throat. "You know," she coos, "I've always thought there was a kind of charged energy between those two."

"So," says Silvestri, "the idea doesn't surprise you?"

"I couldn't say for sure, Detectives. And far be it from me to gossip, but it does make sense, now that I think about it." Her eyes float off as she considers the implications behind this new nugget of speculation. "Wait, do you think this could have something to do with the *murders*?"

"Well," I say, "that's exactly what we're trying to get to the bottom of, with the help of vigilant neighbors such as yourself."

"Detectives." Now it's her turn to check for eavesdroppers. Confirming that we're a safe distance from the throng, she allows for a dramatic pause before continuing. "Between us, I've picked up on some tension between Monica and Laura recently. And those husbands of theirs are a little strange. A little, I don't know, off. If those two *were* having an affair, it could help explain some things." She seems lost in her own fog of curiosity. "Now that I think of it, there could have been all manner of mischief going on between those homes."

Suddenly, the sound of an aggrieved bellow cuts through the air, interrupting our clandestine exchange. I follow the noise to the parking lot on the far side of the building, where an irate man stands shaking his fist as a distressed woman attempts to calm him.

"Excuse us, Milly," I say. "We'll have to pick this back up later."

"But . . ." She stands there frozen, mouth agape, as we cross the lawn to the lot to check out the disturbance, catching snippets of stirrings and murmurs along the way. As we approach the man, he's firing off a string of expletives to no one in particular.

"Sir," I begin. "Detectives Wolcott and Silvestri, Stony Brook Police Department. What seems to be the problem?"

"My car," he says, turning to us in a helpless daze. "My brand-new fucking car."

Sensing her husband's despondency over the crippling loss, the woman interjects. "It was a Bentley Flying Spur," she explains. "In Moroccan Blue. Spent a fortune on the thing. He just got the delivery two weeks ago. We parked it right here before the funeral, and when we came back out, it was gone."

"Memorial service," states the man firmly.

"What's that, darling?"

"I already told you," he snaps. "It wasn't a funeral; it was a memorial service!"

"Oh, for chrissakes, Kenneth! Really?!"

Amid the couple's bickering, I catch my partner's eye and we exchange nods. I get the distinct impression that he's formulating the same idea that I am. He steps aside to call in the theft, and as I retrieve my notepad and jot down the make and model of the stolen set of wheels, a possibility we hadn't paid much mind to begins taking shape inside my head.

CHAPTER THIRTY-SEVEN

SILVESTRI

"Mr. Addison-LeFleur," I say, letting my eyes sink into the kid. "May I call you Bryce?"

We're in the interrogation room back at the station talking to Milly's son, who's been arrested in connection with the stolen Bentley. A pair of uniforms responding to the APB that Wolcott called in spotted the car pulling onto the highway a few miles outside Kingsland and gave chase. After a brief high-speed pursuit, Bryce and his pal dumped the Bentley at a rest stop and attempted to escape into the woods on foot. The other suspect got away, but the officers apprehended young Mr. Addison-LeFleur and kicked him over to us as part of our active investigation.

The kid's all attitude, limbs splayed lazily about the chair, his demeanor dripping with insouciance. I suspect he's watched one too many Tarantino flicks. The lawyer in the two-thousand-dollar suit seated next to him is making up for the lad's poor posture. My partner, positioned in the chair across from them, is a study in articulated stillness. Meanwhile, I'm skulking behind Wolcott, just to make

Bryce work a little to figure out which one of us he should be focused on.

"Call me B," he says, tossing off a casual nod.

"Tell us," begins Wolcott, ignoring the request. "Who was your friend in the car with you? The fitness enthusiast?"

"Don't know who you're talking about," the kid answers, throwing in a smirk for good measure.

"That's how you wanna play this thing?" my partner asks.

"Detectives," interjects the lawyer, checking his watch to remind us of all the better things he has to do with his time. "What are we really talking about here? This was nothing more than a youthful prank."

"A little off on the word choice," I remind him. "In fact, Mr. Addison-LeFleur recently turned eighteen, making him an adult in the eyes of the state. So, shall we kick things off with the grand larceny charge he's facing for the car theft?"

"Come now," counters the lawyer, maintaining his casual tone. "You've got my client on joyriding, at best."

"Your client engaged two of our officers in a high-speed pursuit before dumping the stolen vehicle and attempting to elude them on foot. Does that really sound like a joyriding charge to you?"

"Detective, please. Grand larceny, as you well know, relies upon the suspect's intent to *permanently* deprive the owner of the car in question."

"And how do we know that wasn't Bryce's ultimate goal here?" asks Wolcott.

"Consider my client's past history, which you'll agree has never gone beyond the *misdemeanor* charge of joyriding."

"So," I say, "he *is* copping to all those other car thefts, then?"

The lawyer shoots me a look as he takes a moment to regroup.

"This is a young man with absolutely no criminal record, as I'm quite sure you're both aware."

"Hey, when you can afford the best . . ." I throw him a wink. "Isn't that right, Counselor?"

"Flattery aside, Detective." He clears his throat, unamused. "The family would be more than happy to offer financial remuneration to those inconvenienced by Mr. Addison-LeFleur's . . . recreational choices."

Wolcott turns his attention from the lawyer to focus directly on the kid. "Bryce, let me ask you something."

"Shoot," he says, pointing a finger at my partner.

"Do you happen to remember a hunter-green '68 Mustang you might have taken out for a spin a few nights back? I mean, that particular car would be nearly impossible to forget."

The lawyer leans in to consult with his client, but before he can get a word out, the kid's flipped a hand in the man's face. "Dad, chill the fuck out!" he shouts, surprising the hell out of me. "You're such a fucking lame." Bryce shakes his head and reengages with Wolcott. "Yeah," he continues, settling back into the chair while lacing his fingers over his stomach and flashing a smug grin. "Sure sounds like it could be my work."

"Hmm," my partner says, reaching into a folder and pulling out a photograph. "This jog your memory at all?" He flips the photo onto the table in front of our suspect.

It takes the young man a moment for the image of Spencer Nichols's corpse lying in front of the Fastback to register. Once it does, Bryce shoots straight up in his seat, hands grabbing the edge of the table, eyes popping out of his head as if someone's just dropped a cartoon anvil on him. "What the . . . fuck?!" he stammers.

Wolcott doesn't bat a lash. "Someone helped themselves to a ride in this fella's car the other night, and when he took exception, that same person tried to make a Pez dispenser out of him." He taps a finger near the bullet wound in Nichols's neck in the photo.

"Detective!" the father interjects.

"So," continues Wolcott, breezing over the objection. "We've got this guy in the morgue on a slab, and a friend of his laid up in a hospital bed in a coma with a bullet hole in the side of his head." He takes a healthy pause to let the details sink in before turning his attention to the lawyer. "We'd just like to know if your son—er, *client*—can speak to these events at all."

"I, I, I . . ." The kid's face has gone eggshell, and he's looking desperately at counsel, pleading for help in fishing him out of the horror show he's unwittingly waded into. "We didn't have anything to do with that. Holy shit!"

"Detectives, please." The father is making a visible effort to keep his agitation at bay. "My client has absolutely no knowledge of this unfortunate turn of events."

"We didn't steal the Mustang!" Bryce whines, an octave above his normal tone. "I was just trying to, to . . ."

"Trying to be a big man?" I ask. "Trying to show off for us?"

"Yes," he says, sheepishly avoiding eye contact with the rest of the men in the room. "Kevin and I just wanted to stick it to all these rich, uptight assholes with their sports cars. We were walking through the trails in the woods one day and realized that we could sneak into our neighbors' yards and boost their rides." He looks to his dad, eyes overflowing with embarrassment. "We knew when all of these events were taking place around the neighborhood, and we took advantage. I'm sorry."

"Bryce," says Wolcott, cocking his head. "Could you clarify about the trail in the woods?"

"Yeah," the kid says, jittery with nerves. "There are these walking paths behind the houses all over Kingsland. You can sneak around back there without anyone seeing. It was stupid of us to do. We were just bored, I guess."

"Detectives," his father pleads. "My client has quite obviously been traumatized by the details of this tragic situation and bears no responsibility here. Now, are you planning on charging him with a crime?"

"That'll be up to the owners of the vehicles that Bryce and his pal borrowed without permission," I explain. I turn to the young man and let him squirm for a long moment before I speak. "How about it, kid? Think it might be time to find yourself a new hobby?"

"Yes," he yelps, just south of hyperventilating. "Holy shit, yes."

⑊

"Hell of a *Scared Straight* routine," I say to Wolcott in the hallway after we've exited the interrogation room. "I think you might have spared the young pup a tragic life of crime."

"Yeah," he grumbles, a mix of boredom and resigned frustration coloring his tone. "You think we can go ahead and cut young Master Addison-LeFleur from our list of likely suspects?"

"I'd say we should send someone in there to mop up the piss dripping from the chair he was sitting in."

"Seems like his old man is plenty used to cleaning up the kid's messes," says Wolcott, allowing a clipped laugh to escape his mouth. "Man, do I weep for the future."

CHAPTER THIRTY-EIGHT

WOLCOTT

"L<small>ET ME CHECK</small> this real quick."

We've just returned to our desks when Silvestri pulls his phone from his pocket and plops down into his seat to listen to the voice-mail he missed while we were busy in the interrogation room. I hang my jacket on the back of my chair before sitting against the edge of the desk and rolling my shoulders.

"Ooh, here's something." He perks up.

"What's that?"

"Hemmings's assistant called back." He hits R<small>EDIAL</small> and puts the phone to his ear. "Let me see if I can catch her." After a moment, I hear the soft sound of a voice on the other end of the line. "Yes, is this Julia Tagan? . . . Miss Tagan, this is Detective Silvestri returning your call . . . Would you mind if I put you on speaker, so that my partner can join our conversation?" He removes the phone from his ear, taps the screen, and sets the cell on top of his desk. "Thanks for getting back to us."

"No problem, Detective. Sorry it took me a minute."

"Not at all," he says. "Let me introduce you to my partner, Detective Wolcott."

"Ms. Tagan," I say. "Nice to meet you."

"You as well."

"So, we understand you're currently employed as Randall Hemmings's personal assistant?"

"Well, not exactly 'currently.' I just quit."

"Is that right?" asks Silvestri, flashing me a look. "And can we ask you about the circumstances that led to your leaving the position?"

"Um . . . listen, I won't get in trouble for talking to you guys even if I signed an NDA, right?"

"Correct," he explains. "Any agreement you may have signed does not preclude you from speaking to law enforcement."

"Okay, cool. In that case, I quit because the guy's a raging asshole."

"Ms. Tagan," I say, stifling a laugh, "could you be a bit more specific?"

"God, where do I start?" There's a pause on the other end of the line before she lets out a sigh. *"Well, Randy's definitely a low-key creeper. He's just got a shady kind of vibe, you know? Like, he never came straight out and harassed me, but he'd be suggestive, and then when I called him on his bullshit, he'd gaslight me. Act like I was crazy for misinterpreting him."*

"I see."

"And it wasn't just me. I saw him pull the same kind of stuff with actresses, too. Plus, he was kind of all over the place in his day-to-day. Conducted himself sloppily, you know? I'm pretty sure he was coked up most of the time."

"Uh-huh. And when did you officially terminate your employment with Mr. Hemmings?"

"Yesterday. That's why I was a little late getting back to you guys. I went out last night to celebrate being free of the sleaze. A little hungover still, if I'm being honest."

"Gotcha. And was there a specific incident that led to your quitting?"

"Yeah, the other night was kind of the last straw. We'd gone to the premiere of a new film he'd produced that was screening at a festival in New York. Afterward, we zipped out of there to hit the after-party at the penthouse of one of the investors—some of these money guys, good Lord."

"That right?"

"Oh, man. Let's just say they were in perfect company with Randy. Anyway, we get to this apartment, and there are drugs and booze and all the usual stuff, but someone's managed to get their hands on a bunch of ayahuasca, and Randy decides that he wants to join them on the trip. Next thing I know, some idiot in a pair of tuxedo pants and beaded moccasins is dancing around on top of a marble coffee table playing shaman while these dickheads are sprawled all over the carpet, puking into buckets.

"It was then that I realized I was nothing more than a glorified babysitter for an adult train wreck with a trust fund and an expense account. I took the position in the first place so that I could learn the industry and eventually get films made that empowered women and had something to say about the plight of society, and I'm stuck cleaning up this guy's vomit? No, thanks. There's got to be a better way to go about it."

"Changing the system from within," I say. "That's a noble goal, Ms. Tagan."

"Yeah, we'll see. Of course, I'm out of a job at the moment, so, you know, back to square one."

I ready my next question, certain that her response is going to land us in the same position. "And what night was this?"

She performs a quick bit of arithmetic before answering. "Sunday night, it would have been."

"We see." I look at Silvestri, his resignation mirroring mine.

"Sorry, I've just been rattling on. What did Randy do, anyway?"

"Well, we were actually checking to see if he'd been involved in an incident that took place late Sunday night out on Long Island."

There's a stretch of dead air before she speaks again. *"Wait, did I just alibi him?!"*

"Yeah." I wince. "I'm afraid you did."

"Shit! I'm sorry to hear that. If it makes you feel any better, I'm sure there's something floating around out there that you can get the guy on."

"Miss Tagan, we certainly appreciate your time. And best of luck in your career. We'll be keeping an eye out for you."

"Aww, thank you, guys. And seriously, if there's ever anything I can help you nail this prick with, I'd be more than happy to."

"We'll let you know," says Silvestri before wishing her a good day and ending the call. He pinches the bridge of his nose with his thumb and forefinger and blinks repeatedly before shaking his head like a dog fresh out of the bath. "Wolcott, we never got anything useful from that tip line, right?"

"No," I confirm. As is standard procedure, the department set up a hotline for individuals to phone in potential leads to aid in our investigation around the shootings of Barnes, Mathers, and Nichols. Normally, we'd use those leads to help put together a list of potential suspects, but in this case the crackpot quotient has been off the charts—it seems that these three engendered an incredible amount of animosity, and according to the concerned citizens who have phoned in, anyone from their own disgruntled ex to several high-ranking members of Congress could have had a hand in the murders. "Nothing that stuck."

"Okay," he says, blinking hard. "My turn for the caffeine run." He pivots on his heel and makes off down the hall, leaving me with a lot of paperwork and little in the way of clarity.

I push myself away from the desk and take a few laps around the room, attempting to shake off our previous suspicions involving Randall Hemmings and look at things afresh. I return to my seat and set out in a neat row across my desk's surface the contents of the files Terry Barnes kept on his associates. I then retrieve my notepad and begin to flip through the various pieces of information I've jotted down over the course of our investigation.

As I scan the sea of text before me, I relax my eyes and let my focus expand as one might when observing a cluster of stars in the night sky, allowing the alignment of constellations to gradually reveal themselves. I visually sift through the particulars; the bits of compiled intel referencing two men—one dead, the other lying in an uncertain state of limbo—and the wives of those men. I mentally shuffle through the conversations my partner and I have had with those involved in the case, and the subtleties and slips we've picked up on along the way.

My attention is drawn to the mention in the file of the charitable organization that Monica Nichols headed up for a time. I run a Google search and turn up a video of her delivering a keynote address to a roomful of people in which she discusses her own exposure to sexual misconduct, and how the experience inspired her to found the organization on behalf of assault survivors.

As the video plays, I reach for the copy of *The Rule of Three* that I've been consulting since the title was first mentioned to us and open it up to the very beginning. I read the words on the page, and their context begins to reconfigure itself before my eyes in a way I'd not considered earlier.

As I take in the sum of information before me, that old familiar itch takes hold and a pattern begins to form, the various pieces slotting together into a semblance of logic, a picture taking shape and coming into increasingly sharper focus. A shot of adrenaline pings through my gut as the sense of clarity deepens.

My partner rounds the corner and sets a cup of coffee before me, and I greet him with a burst of charged excitement.

"Silvestri, the neighbor that we talked to, at the memorial service?"

"Milly?" he asks, surprised by my sudden change in energy.

"Yeah," I confirm, abuzz with exhilaration. "Remember that thing she mentioned, about chance?"

"Huh?" he says.

"Let's take a walk, partner. I want to go check something out."

CHAPTER THIRTY-NINE

LAURA

I PAGE MINDLESSLY through *The Rule of Three*, which sits heavy in my lap. My eyes settle on a line that makes me laugh out loud. *You do not face reality; you create it.*

I purposely didn't finish it, but I find myself regretting that decision. I wonder how different things would be if I'd challenged the selection, or pushed back at Vicky for having the stupid club, or if I'd skipped the book club meeting altogether. What if I'd convinced Gil to stay home with me that night and not go to the poker game? What if I'd tried a little harder with him to make things work?

I'm familiar with the self-torturing game of what-ifs; I've been playing it relentlessly my entire life, but especially since Libby was killed. Each barbed wagering of what would have been different if I'd kept her home from school that day digs a little more deeply into my heart.

In the middle of the book, where I stopped reading, is a bookmark, a photograph of Libby. It is a photo I've transferred from one book to the next, a ritual bookmark for everything I've read since she died. In the picture, she is a wide-eyed, smiling infant in my arms, not a care in the world. It is a perfect image of what motherhood felt like for me at its most pure. In our faces, happiness and possibility are suspended in photographic amber. It is exactly what I need to comfort myself—easily tucked away, yet retrievable when I need to hold her in my hands.

When I lift the photo to my face, my eyes drift to the text beneath. *The longer we choose to dwell in self-pity, the deeper we become entrenched in toxic negativity.*

I snap the book shut and my phone springs to life on the pillow next to me.

"Mrs. Mathers?" I recognize the doctor's accented voice on the other end.

"Yes." My heart is in my throat.

"I have some news about your husband."

"What is it? Has something happened?" I hold my breath.

"We'd like to bring him into consciousness," she says, the odd phrasing sounding like something in the pages of *The Rule of Three*.

I sit up in bed and move my feet to the floor, a burst of energy surging.

"Is he ready?" I ask.

"Yes. His vitals have remained stable and we've successfully reversed his swelling and brought his oxygen levels back to normal."

"How was he able to just wake up the other day?" I ask.

"It happens sometimes . . . not often . . . and we don't know exactly how." She sounds a little flustered. "But it is a good sign that he was able to try and speak right away."

"You don't think it's too soon to bring him out again?" I ask shakily. "I read something on the Internet—"

"Mrs. Mathers, now is the right time," she interrupts.

I am stunned silent even though I fully expected this call eventually. Gil Mathers is nothing if not a fighter.

"This is *good* news," she says, a confused timbre in her voice.

"Forgive me," I say, buoying my tone. "I guess I'm afraid of getting my hopes up. This is incredible news."

"I understand," she says.

"When will Gil be awake?"

"We've scheduled the anesthesiologist for ten A.M. tomorrow."

I look at the alarm clock on the bedside. In less than twenty-four hours, Gil could be back.

"Can I be there?" I am flooded with feelings.

"Not during the procedure. But as soon as we've determined your husband's stability, you can see him."

"I'd like to be with him when he wakes up," I tell her. "I think he'd be better off seeing me before a bunch of strangers, don't you?"

"Mrs. Mathers, it isn't a guarantee that Gil will be fully functioning. Neither are there assurances that his memory or his motor skills will be normal, or functional at all."

"Meaning what exactly?"

"Some people come out of a coma without any mental or physical disability, but most require at least some type of therapy to regain mental and motor skills. Your husband may need to relearn how to speak, walk, and even eat."

I take in a sharp breath.

"In some cases, patients are never able to recover completely. They may regain some functions but transition into a vegetative state."

"I thought you said all of his vitals were good." An edge has crept into my tone.

"They are, and his Glasgow score and EKG are strong and he's showing all of the signs of a strong recovery. That being said, we just won't know what we are dealing with until he's conscious. Not to mention that the last time he was really awake and aware was when he was being attacked. So his most recent memory will be that trauma."

My stomach plummets thinking about what it will be like for Gil to wake up in the hospital bed and remember what brought him there. He'll finally be able to tell us what happened that night.

"I was planning on coming by this afternoon to see him. Will you be there?" I ask.

"I've just finished my daily rounds, but we can talk this evening by phone if you'd like. And I'll be there tomorrow when they bring him out and will walk you through his progress afterward."

"Thank you, Doctor," I say, and release the phone before she has a chance to respond. I am on my feet and half dressed before the call disconnects.

⫴

I barely feel the ground beneath me as I hit the path and struggle to lock into a steady pace. My body feels as out of sorts as my brain does as I hurtle toward Monica's house.

All I can think of is Gil and our last interaction. I know it will only get more painful when he's fully conscious and trying to piece things back together. I almost called Vicky but decided against it. She'd discourage me from what I'm about to do, and while I love my sister more than anyone else on this earth, her ironclad sense of what is right sometimes gets in the way.

When I reach her back door, I can see Monica sitting at her large kitchen table, a mug in one hand and the book in the other. She looks frozen mid-thought.

I tap lightly on the glass and she breaks her trance, looks up, and starts at the sight of me. I try the door and find that it is unlocked and easily slides open.

"You should really lock your doors," I tell her as I step inside and pull the door shut behind me and flip the lock.

"Apparently," she says flatly before snapping out of whatever dark mood I've caught her in and slipping into a sunnier version of herself. "Where is that vigilante neighborhood watch when I need them?" she cracks.

"I'm not sure how much good they can do. I'm afraid the real criminals are inside." Monica smiles wryly and raises her mug. "Cappuccino? I just fired up the machine. I think it's too early for wine."

I shake my head. "I'm just here to talk."

I sense her foreboding, but she retains composure as she offers me a seat. "Let's talk."

"They're bringing Gil out of the coma tomorrow," I say without moving.

"Really?" She visibly tenses.

"His doctor says he's ready."

I sit down. I reach for her hand. "I've been thinking a lot about this."

"I'm sure you have." She looks down at my hand. "I have too."

"I think it would be best if you were there."

She gently retracts her palm, the color returning to the area that I've been squeezing.

"I don't know, Laura," she says softly. "How would that look?"

"You should be the one Gil sees when he wakes up," I say.

"What do I say to him? What is it you want me to do?"

"You need to end this, once and for all, so that the three of us can move forward with our lives."

"How do I even get in? I'm not immediate family," she asks.

"I've spent so much time coming and going, I can tell you how to sneak in without being noticed. Anyway, no one ever suspects women like us of doing anything wrong. And if you get caught, just say you got lost."

She sits very still, quietly pensive.

"That is what we agreed on, Monica," I remind her.

"A lot has changed," she scoffs. "So much has gone wrong."

"Please. For our friendship," I say, more gently. "Him or me?"

She closes her eyes and takes my hand again. "Of course I choose you," she says, her voice cracking.

"Good," I say. "Prove it."

CHAPTER FORTY

MONICA

THE LIGHT OF my e-reader burns bright in the darkness of my parked car. I scroll through the digital copy of *The Rule of Three*, looking for a mantra to help carry me through my first face-to-face with Gil since he was shot.

When I find a line that motivates me, I say it aloud three times: "Once you take action, freedom will be yours." As my voice fills the car, the fatigue and grief of the last week make way for wired motivation.

I've parked in the far corner of the hospital staff parking lot next to a dumpster, as far away from any security cameras as possible. Once I'm out of my car, I spot an overturned shopping cart a few feet from where I am. I scan the area to make sure that I'm alone and quickly put the cart right side up and roll it toward the section of employee parking. There are a number of pricey vehicles, undoubtedly belonging to the MDs inside. After checking my surroundings once more, I give the cart a hard push right into the bumper of a black Maserati and hastily backpedal as the car's alarm blares.

From the shadow of a nearby tree, I watch a security guard inspect the ruckus before I slide into the entrance while he's distracted. I dash past his unmanned post and into the stairwell. As I move up the first of seven flights, I focus my thoughts on seeing Gil. Memories of the first time I met him invade my ascent.

Before Gil Mathers was a household name, when he was hocking his self-published books in hotel conference rooms for groups of fifty people or fewer, I tagged along with a friend to his "Prioritizing Personal Power Summit." My friend claimed that Gil Mathers and his program had completely changed her life. I probably should have asked her what she meant by that.

Gil's well-rehearsed monologue of overcoming a childhood of shameful dysfunction and dark secrets hooked me. Now a self-made millionaire and "thought leader," Gil had shown me what I could become after feeling directionless in my life. I hadn't gone that day looking for a guru, but I left inspired, and with an armful of books and a ticket to his next seminar.

As I reach the third-floor landing, I start to feel my lungs burning.

By my fifth Gil Mathers event, he'd graduated to ballrooms. His following had quadrupled in size. I'd walked across hot coals and lost ten pounds of water weight in a sweat lodge. I'd participated in samurai war games and character-building acts of humiliation. When he asked for the first volunteer to get their head shaved onstage to prove that their worth was not reliant on their appearance, I was the first to volunteer.

By the tenth event, I'd already decided to quit my job at the investment firm office where I'd been languishing. I didn't really need the job and had agreed to it only to satisfy my father's requirement that I made an honest living before my trust fund was available, which happened the week before the head-shaving weekend, when I turned twenty-six. The partners weren't unhappy to see me go after I showed up for work looking like I'd come fresh from boot camp. Their and my parents' judgment didn't matter; I was orbiting planets of self-growth way outside their understanding and started volunteering for Gil's organization full time.

My breathing is starting to feel labored, so I slow my pace slightly and take a minute to catch my breath on floor five.

Once you take action, freedom will be yours, I say to myself.

Things in my life didn't get better as promised in all of Gil's slick marketing, but I was determined to prove wrong everyone in my former life who said I was throwing my life away.

No matter how many of the events I showed up for, or how much more money I spent to "level up," I still couldn't get into Gil's inner circle of anointed ones. There was always another level to reach and another tier to pay for. I would expect that the amount of money I was doling out would equate to VIP treatment and the elusive top-tier understanding that was teased by Gil, but it never did. Even after I became a "platinum investor" in his organization and put almost my entire bank balance from my trust into it, he never positively singled me out in the way he did so many other devotees. I deserved to be acknowledged and to have all the promises he kept dangling start to materialize.

By the end of my funds, I was desperate to talk to Gil about my investments in his organization, which had failed to yield any returns. I had no income because I was working sixty hours a week for the Gil Mathers team so that I could continue his seminars, and living in a communal housing situation with others like me. His gatekeepers never let us get close enough to him to have an actual conversation. The only thing I hadn't done was pay to have a face-to-face with him, and it was the only way I could see getting a chance to get my money back. His promise was that after one hour of one-on-one time with him, we would enter the next dimension of self-realization. Desperate, I shelled out my last ten grand to secure an exclusive VIP spot in the "Spartan Warrior" retreat after-party.

I text Laura and press my ear to the access door and hear the sound of the front-desk phone ringing until it stops and a muffled voice speaks. I count to ten and hold my breath as I pull the fire door open, waiting for the alarm to sound and feeling great relief when, as promised, it doesn't. I open and slide through the door and down the hall, catching the reflection of the nurse on duty in the glass-encased elevator bank, directly across from her station. Her back is turned.

Inside Gil's room, the sounds of the machines around us and on the other side of the curtain whir and beep in stereo.

He looks small and old and so meek compared to when I first met him.

"I told Laura everything," I whisper into his ear.

Gil's eyes move steadily back and forth beneath his eyelids before I turn my back to him and move toward the closet. Once inside, I retrieve a spare pillow.

I return to his side, my hands gripping the rough industrial fabric so tightly, all of the color has drained from them.

Ten minutes into the party, I knew Gil Mathers had no interest in me or in the financial help I'd given him. He barely registered my name when I introduced myself, even though I'd literally been in the first row at more than fifty of his events and he'd cashed just as many of my checks. Every time I tried to talk about my losses, he would change the subject, ply me with drinks, or look over my head to see who else was at the party he could flirt with. Quickly his detachment flipped into predatory focus on a young woman who I found out had been invited to the reception along with her friends for free after one of Gil's managers approached them after the show. They couldn't have been more than seventeen. As Gil started whispering into her ear, I saw him ask his security detail something, and shortly after, everyone but the girl and the friends she'd brought with her were cleared out of the room.

In my blind rage, I'd barely made it back to my hotel room when I realized that I'd left my phone in the suite. When I knocked, no one came, but a bellman walked by just as I was on the verge of tears and, seeing my eyes, asked me if he could help. I explained that I'd locked myself out and he opened the door and wished me a good night. Rave music was blaring, and neither the girls dancing in the low strobing lights nor Gil and the girl, who were intermittently making out and snorting white powder off a copy of Gil's book in a corner, noticed me standing in the doorway. I was shocked that this was really who this person I'd devoted so much of my hope, time, and money to was. He was not a guru or a savior; he was a predator and a fraud.

I started filming.

⫯⫯⫯

His chest continues its steady rhythm under the hospital sheet. I hover over him, shaking violently. His neighbor's machine has started to beep alarmingly.

"You have to be stopped before you ruin anyone else's life." I squeeze the pillow so hard my knuckles crack.

Angry tears fall from my cheeks as the beeping on the other side of the curtain escalates. I can feel the warmth wafting off him as I eclipse his face with the pillow.

His roommate's machines are beeping so loudly now, it sounds like the car alarm from earlier has gone off in this room.

I am startled backward when the door bursts open and a number of nurses descend. I think they've come to rescue Gil until they rip back the privacy curtain and begin to examine the man currently flatlining in the next bed.

One of the attending nurses shouts in my direction and a crash cart is rolled in. "Miss, please, you need to wait outside."

Stunned, I exit the room. As I lean against the wall, tearfully trembling, I make out two figures moving toward me and I think they are Terry and Spencer coming for me.

I blink, slowly registering my surroundings.

"Mrs. Nichols," says Detective Wolcott. "Fancy meeting you here."

Detective Silvestri doesn't say anything as he scans me from top to bottom, resting his gaze on the pillow I'm hugging tightly to my body.

Stunned, I hear the words fall out of my mouth before I know what I'm saying.

"I got lost."

CHAPTER FORTY-ONE

LAURA

IT'S AFTER MIDNIGHT and my sister looks haunted. The memorial service feels so far away now, but in reality, it has only been a few hours since we were able to wrest ourselves away from Terry's mourners.

"You don't have to hold everything together anymore; it's just me now," I say softly, tugging at her shoulder. She barely looks up. She has my copy of *The Rule of Three* on her lap, but it remains closed. She's been sitting in silence looking at the darkened TV screen for the last twenty minutes and hasn't moved an inch. Her phone has finally stopped its nonstop vibrating.

"It tends to be more entertaining if you turn it on." I halfheartedly hand her the stack of remotes.

She breaks from her trance and half smiles.

"Please don't."

"Phew. Gil has these fucking things wired in such a way, I don't even know how to turn the damn thing on anymore."

"I can't take any more news coverage," she says through a loud yawn.

"Me neither." I stare off into space beyond the screen too. "We just have to wait it out. They will get tired of us and move on to the next thing like they always do."

I take a seat on the opposite edge of the couch so that I can stretch out my legs and nudge her thigh with my toe.

She sighs wearily. "I just want this to be over."

"I know. Me too." I check my phone for any sign of Monica.

"Thank you for convincing me to stay."

"There's no way you stay in the house alone right now."

"Not even after the crime scene cleaners have been through." She shudders. "I have the painters coming tomorrow to fix the walls in his office, but I don't know how much it will help the *feeling* in there."

"I want you here for as long as you want to stay. You don't ever have to go back. We can hire people to pack it all up for you and sell it and you can start over completely."

"I can't even begin to wrap my head around that right now."

"Baby steps."

"I don't even know where to begin."

"I'll help. You've been doing so much. The memorial service was impeccable. I don't know how you pulled it all off so quickly."

"I was in some fugue state. I don't remember any of it."

"You are a force of nature, Vicky."

"So many people have touched me in the last twenty-four hours." She rubs her arm distastefully.

"Not me. People seem to be scared." I try to nibble on a piece of pita bread before giving up and putting it back on the tray.

"You know what the really scary thing is?" she says, pulling her hair away from her exhausted face.

"What?" I lean in, happy to have a less guarded side of my sister emerging. It makes me feel better about my own vulnerability.

"All of those stories people were telling about Terry at the service? It all sounded like they were talking about someone else."

"He was someone different to each person," I reply.

"It was hard to tell his friends from his enemies in that crowd," she says darkly.

"I think there is a very thin line dividing those two camps." I tread lightly.

"True. When I was doing the eulogy and looking around the room, I had the thought that any one of the people in that hall had motive to take Terry out. He either knew secrets about nearly every one or was owed favors. Or both."

"I think people showed up to make sure he was really dead," I say.

Vicky purses her lips but doesn't say anything.

"You did a good job with your eulogy," I praise her. "Mom would have approved."

"She did love Terry," she says. "I suppose I wasn't really describing the real him either."

"It was exactly what you had to do. You don't have to do that any longer, though."

"Could I really have known *so* little about him?" she muses.

"Don't doubt yourself now. We've been through this," I say patiently.

"Right."

"You could say the same for me. And for Mom. Look at how much she didn't know about Dad. Think about how many things we found out about him *after* she died too. No wonder her heart gave out. It was too much to process. I'm sure so much more will be revealed about all of them the longer they are dead."

Vicky looks pained at the mention of our parents, but I don't relent. "There's a definite pattern in this family."

"Secrets." Vicky shifts uncomfortably and I can tell that this is getting too deep for her comfort level. But I do what I always do and push.

"And lies," I say. "Terry was the king of both."

"You never liked him, did you?" she says without a trace of resentment.

"No. But I never hid it, did I?"

"No, and it was what made him desperate for you to like him. He could never win you over. He loved a challenge almost as much as adulation."

"Did *you* like him?" I ask her gently.

"I can't remember."

I touch her leg with my foot again. "What's done is done. Don't make yourself crazy by rehashing what was."

"You sound like this book," Vicky says drily, and I grimace.

"God. I guess that's better than sounding like Gil."

"What about Gil?" The consternation in her voice pushes my anxiety up a few notches.

I haven't told Vicky about Monica visiting Gil, but it has been too long to have not heard anything from her and I'm beginning to panic.

I am amazed when my phone interrupts my response hesitation with a text notification. My heart halts as I read Monica's message.

22:3:32

Vicky's eyebrows are frozen in raised anticipation.

"Hey, Vick, let me see the book for a minute?" I say, forcing calm neutrality.

She furrows her brow but promptly hands it to me.

I find the page I want and read it twice. My blood pressure soars.

"What is it?" Vicky asks, immediately concerned.

"Nothing." I clear my throat a few times, unable to free whatever is blocking it.

I look at the text again and don't respond to my sister.

"I need to get to the hospital."

"Is he awake?" She jumps to her feet. "I'll come with you."

"No," I say sharply. "I need to be alone with him."

"Okay, Laura." I see she's hurt, but time is running out. I grab my car keys.

"What's going on?" Her concern for me is etched in the creases around her eyes.

I pause on the doorknob and take my key fob off the crown keychain and place the heavy charm on the entryway table, the diamond sparkling in the hallway's chandelier light. Vicky's eyes go to it and then back to my face.

"There's something I need to take care of. Don't wait up."

⫷⫸

It is almost two A.M. and the only signs of life are artificial, the machines clicking away as I walk carefully down the corridor. With each cautious step, I hope that whoever is monitoring the hospital's security cameras is otherwise occupied.

Gil's room feels oddly spacious when I tiptoe in and gingerly shut the door. It takes me a few minutes to adjust to the darkness and register the absence of his roommate. The privacy curtain has been pulled open, giving a cavernous feel to the space.

"I guess you got your private room after all," I whisper. I feel a pang for the man he'd been rooming with—whose name I never learned—and his family.

In the closet where I saw the nurse stocking extra blankets and pillows earlier in the week, I feel around and discover that there are no pillows, so I opt for a blanket. Feeling the synthetic material and realizing its porousness in my hands, I put it over my face and breath, the flow of air through the cheap fibers confirming what I suspected. I return to the closet and find a commode wrapped in a large plastic bag. I unsheath it, place it back into the dark cubby, and walk over to his bedside with the bag in my hands.

I don't think about anything other than what I need to do. There is no space for hesitation or doubt. This must be done for us to have any chance at a happy life.

I barely look at his face as I slide off the ventilator mask and quickly place it on my own face to keep the machine's alarm from going off from the inevitable pressure drop. I smell his familiar breath in the mask and think that this is as close as we'll get to a last kiss.

Once the machine appears to be stable, I lift Gil's head with the back of my right hand. His breathing has picked up pace without the oxygen, and this rattles me slightly as I pull him closer.

I keep waiting for my emotions to overtake me as I cast a last look on Gil's drawn face, but now all I can see is Libby, lying in her hospital bed, brain-dead, only being kept alive by a machine long enough for us to say goodbye. I channel how Gil was in that moment when I so desperately needed him there for me, and for Libby. But he was somewhere else too.

I pull the plastic bag over the top of his head and slide it down his face and cinch it at his neck. The cool flow of oxygen in the mask on my own face feels inappropriately calming as his body begins its natural fight against suffocation, even in unconsciousness.

I place my hands firmly around his neck to keep the bag taut as the long pitch of the EKG begins to flatline. I close my eyes and say, "Let go," over and over until his body stops seizing.

The sound of my name being called and the heavy pressure on my arms and shoulders rips me away from my husband and out of my daze.

There are frantic people and harsh lights all around me. I try to speak at the sight of the bag being pulled from his head, his oxygen being pulled from my head and replaced on his, but the steady machine tone of his heartbeat restarting is the only sound I can make out while I'm pulled into the hallway and my hands are pulled firmly behind my back.

CHAPTER FORTY-TWO

WOLCOTT/SILVESTRI

"Mrs. Barnes," I say, before correcting myself. "I'm sorry. Victoria."

She greets the address with a tight, wordless smirk. She's sitting next to her lawyer across the table from me. When they first arrived, this guy could barely be bothered with going through the motions of polite formality. The Panerai peeking out from under his shirt cuff nicely complements the pair of freshly polished wingtips that easily eclipse the monthly sum of my mortgage payments. I'm often self-conscious about my use of the word "irony" but am willing to bet that utilizing the deep legal bullpen of the man whose murder you've helped plot in the hopes of getting yourself acquitted of that very crime falls under the dictionary definition.

Silvestri's in the room down the hall with Laura Mathers and her lawyer, handling that interrogation. I'd guess the mood in there is as humorless as the one I'm dealing with, though my partner does have a knack for injecting levity whenever possible.

"Victoria," I begin. "I'm going to be straight with you. We walked in on your sister in the act. We've got her dead to rights. Now, she can take the full weight of this on her own, or you can help her out by filling us in on how it really went down."

"Detective," the lawyer protests on her behalf, "my client will be neither intimidated nor cajoled—"

"I've gotta give it to you," I say, briskly ignoring him. "You ladies nearly pulled it off." She does an admirable job of holding my gaze stoically. "You really sold the whole grieving-widow act." I draw out the pause, to give this next bit a nice, long runway. "Even the tracking devices that Terry planted on you and the gals didn't manage to implicate you, somehow." She indulges in a deep breath and a slow, deliberate blink but otherwise manages to maintain a neutral expression. "I'll admit," I continue. "We took our focus off the three of you pretty early on."

⫼

"It was Milly who got us curious again."

Laura grumbles under her breath. I watch her jaw unclamp, but counsel dissuades her from speaking on the matter with a quick flourish of his hand. I guess mum's the game plan for today. The lawyer turns his attention to me and his eyes engage mine and hold firm as if he's trying to win a staring contest. I toss him a dismissive grin to indicate I'll be having none of it, and return my focus to his client.

"We had a conversation with her outside of Terry's memorial service, where she made a couple of comments that stirred our curiosity. The first referred to chance; specifically, the odds of two people in the same family falling victim to the same type of violence." I watch the emotion catch in her throat and decide to move right along. "The second was an offhanded remark about all the mischief you ladies could be getting up to between your houses. The comment didn't fully click with us until later, after her son, Bryce, filled us in on the trails in the woods that connect the homes in Kingsland."

⫶

"The nurse attending to Gil mentioned that he'd called out Monica's name when he awoke from the coma briefly, which initially had us assuming an affair between the two of them, but after the conversation with Milly, we went back and took a closer look at those files your husband kept on the Nicholses and Matherses. And wouldn't you know it: The closer we looked, the more a pattern began to form. The pieces started falling into place.

"Your husband was a big gun advocate, and your niece became the tragic victim of a mass shooting. On top of that, Gil Mathers has a past history of committing sexual assault, and your friend Monica Nichols headed up a charity organization that aided *survivors* of sexual assault. Now, I know love can overlook a lot of things, but that seemed like a pretty extreme blind spot.

"So, we started reassessing our earlier assumptions. Maybe, we thought, when your brother-in-law spoke Monica's name from his hospital bed, he wasn't calling out for his mistress. Maybe he was calling out the name of the person who'd tried to murder him."

⫶

"Planting Hemmings's file along with the husbands' was a nice touch. We started down that road, and he's certainly the kind of guy to raise a few red flags. When we got the ballistics back from the shooting in the woods and realized there was a *second* nine millimeter in the mix, we assumed it was his. Until he got alibied out, that is.

"At that point, we had to rejigger the math on the guns, and something occurred to us: There was a tight window of time on all three of the shootings that night, and if someone were trying to make it look like the same gun was used in two places at once, getting their hands on the same caliber weapon would be a handy way to go about it. Who knows; maybe we'd just assume it was the same nine millimeter and not look too closely at it. Of course we did, and then it became simple arithmetic: three different guns; three different shooters."

⫿⫿⫿

"This was all circumstantial, of course. We still needed a way to play the theory out. Luckily, we were able to get Dr. Mitali to help by pushing up Gil's resuscitation date . . . at least in her phone call to your sister." The color is rising in Victoria's face, and I notice she's white-knuckling the edge of the table. The veneer of calm collectedness I've never seen her without threatens to flake away before my eyes. "That little ploy seemed to force your collective hand," I continue. "And after Monica's close call, Laura walked right into our trap."

⫿⫿⫿

"After we arrested you, we were able to poke around in your phone. Found a couple of interesting tidbits there. For one, you forgot to delete the confirmation email from the app that does the timed Instagram posts." I watch Laura's face tighten. "Now, why would you need to delay a post, unless you were trying to, say, establish a timeline toward an alibi?" I let the question hang in the air for a moment, with no expectation of receiving an answer.

"Which brings us to *The Rule of Three*." I crack a thin smile as I shake my head. "My partner and I were pretty tickled when we realized you ladies were utilizing a self-help book as the inspiration to plot a triple homicide. That was a first, in our experience. And it took us a minute to correlate the number code in your text exchange with the page from the book—that was my partner's hunch. But once we did, it all came clear." I pull up the page on my phone so as not to butcher it in the recounting. "Okay, Monica's last text to you: '22:3:32.' Chapter twenty-two, third paragraph, thirty-second word. Here goes: 'When chasing your desired goals, remember this: Where a rash heart first fails, a sober head later succeeds.'" I let the realization of her misstep sink in before speaking again. "I get it. Monica couldn't finish off Gil in the hospital that night—and you couldn't risk him talking when he woke up—so you had to step in and handle things yourself."

Laura's eyes narrow, and I can practically feel the rage vibrating off her, a kettle climbing toward a boil. But she remains silent under her lawyer's watch.

ılı.

"Now, Victoria," I say. "I'd like to ask you about Monica Nichols. My partner and I haven't had any luck tracking her down since she left Gil's hospital room last night." I give the pause after my remark some room to breathe. "She hasn't been at home, and there doesn't appear to be any sign of her having packed up and taken off." I watch as a look forms on Victoria's face that I take for genuine surprise. Heartened, I push on. "It's as if Mrs. Nichols just up and disappeared. *Or* as if someone disappeared her. You wouldn't know anything about that, would you?"

She remains silent as her lawyer interjects, but I swear I detect nervous doubt sneaking its way into her expression. I let the silence stretch out as she seems to consider this new development, and I wonder in the moment if she's beginning to consider what her own sister might be capable of without her.

⊸⫙⊷

"You get anything?" Wolcott and I are back at our desks after wrapping up the interrogations for the day.

"Nah." He shakes his head. "Crickets all the way. You?"

"Same. Those lawyers are keeping a tight rein on the program."

"Bet." He blows gently on his coffee. "Although I'm not sure how you wriggle out of getting caught in the act of suffocating a comatose man."

"Never underestimate the finest defense money can buy," I say, feeling the sneer take shape.

"We'll see." He takes a deliberate sip, then shakes his head.

"You do have to find it funny, though."

"What's that?" asks Wolcott.

"The fact that the book that gave them the idea in the first place led to the whole plan unraveling."

We'd been at our wit's end yesterday after hitting yet another wall with the stolen-car lead. I'd gone to get us a coffee and a tea, and when I'd returned, a light bulb had gone on in my partner's head. He'd had his copy of *The Rule of Three* cracked open and excitedly showed me the first rule: *The spiritual path is not a solo one; choose carefully who you decide to walk it with*. It took me a moment to grasp what he was going on about, but he explained it as we left the station and drove to Kingsland to confirm his hunch.

The mention of the figurative path in the book had dovetailed in his brain with Bryce's comment about the literal paths in the woods behind the houses in the neighborhood, and with Milly's mention of the mischief she'd suspected the women to be capable of. When we'd arrived and stealthily nosed around the area between the houses of the three women, the connection was confirmed, and our theory was on its way to being proven right, with a little help from the very people who were trying their best to throw us off the trail.

With the interrogations taken care of, our next order of business will be to reach out to the FBI to turn over Terry Barnes's laptop. Once their techs have a chance to examine the tracking app Terry was utilizing, they should be able to get a better handle on the scope of the criminal activity involving Barnes, Nichols, Mathers, and Randall Hemmings. And while Hemmings's hands proved to be clean insofar as the murders were concerned, my partner and I remain convinced that the feds will turn up a dirty pair of mitts on the guy with regard to the tracking tech as they figure out exactly how that piece fits into the larger puzzle.

"I gotta tell you, pal." I enjoy a sip of tea as Wolcott eyes me. "I don't think I can remember being this excited for a good night's sleep."

"You got that right," he says, glancing at his watch. "And it'll sure be nice to wake up back in the real world again."

CHAPTER FORTY-THREE

LAURA

"This is the end," Vicky says, as we pull into a spot outside the gates of Kingsland Memorial cemetery.

"Depends on your perspective," I say.

Vicky side-eyes me as we step out of the car. The sun is high in the cloudless sky and the temperature is a perfect seventy-five degrees. Being outside, unencumbered and alone with my sister, feels miraculous. It is mid-September, a year and two months after the deaths of Terry and Spencer and the near death of Gil. Vicky and I have been in custody, under house arrest, and on trial for fourteen months. As of today at three P.M., we are free. Relatively speaking.

We link arms and ignore the paparazzi with long-range cameras pointed in our direction at the security gate of the property. Our expressions rest in unmoving solemnity, but inside, we are light, happy, and liberated.

"You were incredible on the stand. I always knew you were good under pressure, but that was an Oscar-worthy performance, Vick. I think everyone on the jury fell in love with you."

"Not that we ended up needing it," she says.

"Still. I barely made it through my cross-examination without cursing out the prosecution. You were all dignity and class."

"I just thought about all of the pain they caused and what they were planning. And I thought about Libby and everything that you've had to go through." A few tears roll down my sister's beautiful face. "My feelings were honest. And I have no regrets."

"Me neither." I squeeze her arm, feeling an unexpected wave of emotion rising. She sees that I'm on the verge and looks toward the photographers behind us, who can't come any farther into the private property.

"Let's not give them the satisfaction. Crying shots go for more money, I'm sure." She flicks her tears away. "The last thing we need is more media commentary on our mental conditions."

"Does it matter anymore? We've been acquitted," I say.

"Only on a technicality. Everyone still thinks we did it."

"Good. Maybe the next crop of misogynistic sociopaths who think they can control and treat women like possessions will think twice."

"Let's not get too cocky. There'll be appeals," Vicky presses.

"Your late husband was wrong about so many things, but I'll agree with him on having the best legal defense team on the planet," I say. "We'll be fine."

"It worked just like we knew it would," she says.

"Not that it was easy," I lament.

We are both beyond relieved to be done with the monotony of being housebound alone. We've missed each other terribly. The frantic circus of the court proceedings of the last six weeks was jarring and dicey at moments, but at least Vicky and I were able to be together during the trial after being separated for so long.

"Honestly, at this point, how many murderers have we seen walk free, thanks to Terry and his legal mafia?" Vicky says bitterly.

"Too many. Now we have time to try and make some of those cases right."

"Absolutely," Vicky says knowingly.

"And unfortunately for the offices of LeFleur, Stermer & Schelling, we know where Terry's rainy-day dirt is buried."

The soothing sounds of nature around us fill in the blanks as we continue walking, deep in our own thoughts.

"If I didn't know better, I would think this was a golf course," I say as we pass a babbling brook flowing lazily past perfectly green grass and weeping willows.

"I think that was kind of Terry's point."

"Golfing is as exciting as walking through a cemetery?"

"Or that golf was like death."

There is only one grave so far in Kingsland Memorial. It sits at the top of the hill like a barbican overlooking the houses of Kingsland a quarter of a mile from where we are walking. It is a garish black marble mausoleum reminiscent of the Lincoln Memorial, complete with a life-size likeness of Terry standing outside the structure watching over his creation.

"Of course he included burial plots in the deluxe package," I marvel.

"Even in death, Terry wanted to keep tabs on everyone," Vicky deadpans.

"I don't think he planned on being the first one in, though."

"He will likely be the only. More houses went up for sale this week. I'm hearing that almost half of the original Kingslanders are gone so far."

As we move toward the eyesore on the hill, the feeling of being watched from afar nags.

"I think it's time we moved on from Kingsland too, don't you?"

"Agreed."

We unlink arms as we ascend the marble stairs leading to the entrance of Terry's eyesore.

Vicky surveys the cemetery property all around us. "Monica should be here."

"In Terry's cemetery?" I say.

Vicky frowns. "You know what I mean.

"Everyone thinks that we killed her," my sister says.

"Monica had to be out of the picture for this all to work," I say.

"According to the gristmill, she's buried in pieces somewhere along the trails."

"That's awful, and completely unimaginative."

Vicky shoots me a disapproving look.

"I also heard that we took her out on Terry's boat and threw her in the ocean."

We both shake our heads. "As if I'd ever step foot on the *Seaduction* ever again. I hate that boat so much," Vicky says.

"At least the DA's case against us has fizzled."

"No body, no crime. Everyone knows that."

"People in Kingsland are afraid of us."

"The husbands are. But the wives are grateful. After the FBI revealed that they all were being tracked, Roger LeFleur's divorce cases quadrupled. The women know that we are the reason the police found out about the tracking."

"And the *trafficking*." We both shake our heads.

We stop to watch a crow that has landed near our feet and is pecking at something in the grass.

"I miss Mon," Vicky says softly.

"She served her purpose."

Vicky raises an eyebrow. "Oh, Laura."

"What? You liked her more than I did."

"Say what you will about her, Laur, she helped us escape this insanity. I'm grateful she and Spencer came to Kingsland."

"If only she'd been able to keep up her end," I say bitterly. "Luckily the case was done before Gil had a chance to testify."

"Even if he *had* taken the stand, the lawyers had a hundred ways to discredit him. And he never saw me that night."

"Plus, even if he did claim to see Monica, they won't be able to find her to ask her about it," I add. "It is amazing what a difference a few centimeters can make. Gil is a lucky motherfucker."

"Lucky for him that the detectives were waiting for you that night in the hospital," Vicky says disapprovingly. "Less so for you. I still can't believe you went there to kill him without telling me. That wasn't part of the plan and really stupid."

"I knew you would have tried to stop me. And I had to take care of what Monica couldn't," I say resentfully.

"Holding on to the past will keep you from ever moving forward," Vicky says.

I side-eye her. "Are you quoting the fucking book?"

"It is true, though, isn't it? If you keep replaying what didn't happen that night, we'll never be able to reap the benefits of what did happen."

I am dually irritated and amused by my sister's wisdom.

"What *really* happened that night?" I ask Vicky.

"Really? Now?" she moans.

"We've stayed silent for so long." I take a breath. "When Gil turned up alive, I almost cracked."

"Me too. But the risk that someone would hear us, or that we were being recorded, was enough incentive to keep quiet."

I gesture to our surroundings. "And if ever there was an appropriate backdrop . . ."

"Okay." She takes a breath. "We thought everything went smoothly until Gil turned up alive." I hear the weariness in Vicky's voice. "I shot Spence and Monica shot Gil, as planned. As far as we could tell, Gil and Spence didn't see us coming. We waited for them in the bushes, and when they pulled up, Monica got Gil from behind, and I got Spence from the side. When we put the gun in Spence's hand and looked over Gil, well, they both looked very dead."

"Neither of you thought to double-check?" I say, a year-plus resentment resurfacing.

"There was a lot of blood and we were thinking about footprints and fingerprints. We didn't want to move around the scene too much—"

"That was the point of the gloves and wearing Hemmings's favorite shoes in his size—"

"—which wasn't that easy, by the way. We were both slipping around in them, even though they weren't that big—"

"Hemmings did give off major small-shoe energy at the barbecue."

"We thought we heard a car coming so we got out of there as fast as we could," Vicky says, annoyed.

"I guess Little Miss Texas was not such a sharpshooter after all," I grumble.

"Laur. It worked out. It's over, isn't it?"

"Easy for you to say. You're free of Terry. You got your wish. Gil is going to haunt me for the rest of his life, especially with his *comeback*." I groan.

"At least you got your divorce, and with the prenup that he fought so passionately against, he can't touch our money, or you, ever again."

"It would have gone better if it had been just you and me."

"What do you want me to say?" Vicky says, frustrated. "It needed to be the three of us, Laur. It kind of was her idea anyway."

I balk. "You're giving her way too much credit. Way before Monica blew into town, we knew what problems Gil and Terry were. I wanted to kill them both after Libby died."

Vicky's brow furrows. "I don't know if you ever said the word 'kill' back then."

"You wanted to get rid of Terry at the first whiff of him taking kickbacks," I say.

Vicky's face turns a deep shade of red.

"Well, you wanted to put a hit out on Gil after the video went viral. And all of the payoffs that followed when the other women started coming out of the woodwork."

My adrenaline shoots up at the reminder.

"What about Terry siphoning our family's trust money into offshore accounts?"

"How about Gil's line of nutrition shakes that caused kidney failure and all of the ensuing lawsuits?"

A small smile cracks Vicky's sour expression and I can't contain my own grin breaking through.

"Terry's beer," we say in unison.

"We should have killed him as soon as he said the words 'dry hops.'"

We lean on each other, trying not to laugh too hard.

"Anyway, Monica was the catalyst," Vicky brings us back.

"Palm Springs was the catalyst."

"Are you really going to argue about who should get credit for this?"

"I'm not arguing. I'm just setting the record straight," I say.

"Then *I* was the catalyst. I knew we had to do something after Palm Springs, when I heard Terry tell Hemmings about his plan for

Spencer's implant tech," Vicky recalls, reliving the horrific day. "Hemmings was bragging about his 'members only' dating site being the number one source for Kingsland husbands to find their wives *and* mistresses. 'One-stop shopping,'" she recounts bitterly. "He compared the women getting nano implants to pets getting microchips for when they run away from their owners." Her eyes are on fire.

"What Terry said wasn't any better," I say, still in disbelief from the first time I heard it.

"'The women of Kingsland will be the perfect case study for the new tech before we roll it out to the girls,'" Vicky imitates Terry, and we both cringe. "'This is the ultimate upgrade.'"

"Thank God you heard that part of it and figured out he was already tracking us," I say angrily as we reach the summit and stand before the massive chiseled door to the crypt.

"I know, Laur. I still can't believe it. We were the first. Terry's guinea pigs."

"And Gil fucking knew the whole time," I spit. "That's why he always seemed to know where I was," I scoff. "And I used to think at one time we were so in sync."

"I know. Me too. I thought the same about Terry."

"We were just the first generation of Terry's tracked women. Once he got wind of Spencer's technology, it was only a matter of time before he upgraded us. Think about all of the wives of Kingsland who didn't even know they were being tracked."

"Or the husbands who paid Terry for the tracking access to their own wives."

I squeeze my sister's hand.

"To think, if I had never forgotten my copy of *The Rule of Three* in the hotel room, I never would have found out what Terry was involved in," Vicky says. "Where would we be now?"

We both pull Terry's crown keychains from our purses at the same time and hold them in our hands one last time before Vicky enters 0505 into the electronic keypad of the tomb and the heavy door slowly swings inward.

"The safe combo?" I ask, and she nods. "That figures," I say.

We step inside the frigid structure and gasp when we see the pile of Cartier crown charms piled on top of his crypt.

"Look." Both our eyes fill with tears.

"How did they get in?" I sniffle.

"Clearly, the women of Kingsland are resourceful, no matter how much their asshole husbands underestimate them."

In one synchronized motion, we place the Kingsland key charms atop Terry's final resting place. We stand in silence, breathing together, the dark holding us in cold stillness.

"You'll never be able to keep tabs on us ever again, you fucker," I say.

Vicky stares at the dark marble slab. I can't decipher her face.

"Vick? Are you okay?"

A smile breaks through. It is a beautiful, freeing sight.

"And we'll always know exactly where you are, Terbear." She pats the top of the vault.

"I get it, Laur," Vicky says as she turns to me slowly.

"What?" I say.

"'Depends on how you look at it.'"

I look at her expectantly.

"It isn't over. It's just beginning," she says, smiling.

"Exactly right, sis."

"And wherever Monica Nichols is," Vicky says with a hand on her heart, "I hope she's finally found some peace."

EPILOGUE

GIL

"Welcome to the Help Yourself in-conversation speaker series. Tonight we are joined by two incredible authors and internationally recognized giants in the field of inspiration and self-improvement.

"Please give them a warm welcome as they come to the stage: Sawyer Selwyn, the author of the multimillion-copy bestseller The Rule of Three: How to Radically Change Your Life with the Law of Action, *and Gil Mathers, motivational speaker and bestselling author of numerous books, including his just-released self-help memoir,* Dying to Become Me: Transformative Lessons from the Other Side."

I step out from the wing and into the light while the opening strains of Phil Collins's "In the Air Tonight" blast. As I glide to my seat at center stage, I wave in the direction of the wildly clapping fans.

Draped in lace and gauzy white robes fringed with feathers, Sawyer Selwyn looks ridiculous as she enters from the opposite side to thunderous applause and a standing ovation. All the starstruck women in the front row with dream catchers around their

necks swoon when she walks to the edge of the stage to acknowledge them.

Finally, after a few minutes of endless applause, she makes her
way to center stage, where I am waiting.

I take Sawyer's extended hand, her hundred silver bangles on each
wrist twinkling in the stage lights. She beams at me and I break from
her extraterrestrially dark eyes and peer around the twenty-five-
hundred-seat theater. Being back onstage is electrifying and I feel
confident that the people who have come to see Sawyer Selwyn tonight will leave as fans of mine.

"So, Gil," Selwyn purrs in her hard-to-place European accent, "it
has been two years since your wife tried to suffocate you to death
after a shooting attempt by her friend landed you in a coma. That is
quite a life path you've been on."

The crowd murmurs excitedly.

"It sounds like a made-for-TV movie when you spell it out, Sawyer, but it is all true."

"There is no question that you've been to hell and back." She takes
my hand. She makes me extremely uncomfortable and not just because she's currently occupying the top spot on the bestseller list,
which is rightfully mine.

"It has been a long, hard journey to be able to sit here with you
right now, but dying twice was not the most challenging part."

Sawyer takes a sip of water. "Evidently, you are a hard man to
kill."

"I've got six lives left. I plan to use them wisely."

The cat lovers, of which there are many apparently, clap wildly.

"Just a few short years ago, you lost your only child in a horrific
school shooting. The nation rallied around you and your family, and

you kept up the work you'd been doing in spite of that tragedy. But not long after, you had a pretty public takedown. You were revealed to be misogynistic, hypocritical, offensive to your most loyal followers, and some say predatory. Your biggest critics have accused you of using your fame, wealth, and influence to live above the law."

"That is all true. I needed to be exposed. I wasn't just living above man's laws, Sawyer. Your book showed me that I was living above universal law as well," I pander.

"And the second rule of *The Rule of Three* tells us that whatever energy a person puts out to the universe will come back to them threefold." She lets this hang.

I clear my throat.

"So, my question for you, Gil, is what energy had you been putting forth that came back to you so extremely? And are you still living in that energy, or have you truly changed? Or is your book an attempt to exploit public sympathy?"

"That sounds like three questions, Sawyer." The audience laughs lightly.

I smile through my rage. Sawyer looks at me sanctimoniously, waiting. I feel no remorse about the private investigator I have digging into her past. It would only take one or two little seeds of doubt about her background leaked to Twitter to get her canceled.

"We reap what we sow. I am living proof of that universal law in action," I say, taking my time. I'm relieved to see the front row attentively nodding. "I was definitely projecting terrible energy out into the world, and with my extramarital choices especially. I have deep remorse about my acts all those years ago. I was a man in grief and pain and not fully awake to my own human defects."

"Do you believe that you deserve public redemption? After your video leaked, a number of women came forward and alleged that you abused your power for sexual favors. It is a big leap for people to start taking advice from you again after those revelations."

"I just want to say that most of those allegations were categorically false. But if I ever made anyone uncomfortable, I am truly sorry. I realize now that I wasn't really listening to the women in my life."

Sawyer looks ready to pounce. I'm not surprised that she's brought me onstage to humiliate me, but I've been preparing for this.

"Sawyer, believe me. I am fundamentally changed. My heartset, which is like a mindset, but much more powerful"—I place both hands over my chest—"has fundamentally shifted. I am no longer the self-centered, low-frequency man that was on that video."

Scattered applause peppers throughout the space.

"How does it feel that no justice has been brought against your alleged perpetrators?"

"Well, before I talk about that, I need to thank you. I wouldn't be here today if it wasn't for your powerful book. So, I guess in a large way, you are responsible for my life-after-death experiences." She can ask about the trial as much as she wants, but I will continue to weave around the things I don't care to talk about.

"Another satisfied customer of the universe's infinite wisdom." She puts her hands in prayer formation. I hope the entire hour isn't this whack-job bowing and praying. She is as fake as the hard-to-place accent she is hiding behind.

I scan the sea of smiling fans who are watching us with a desperate intensity, waiting to be altered.

The same old energetic pulsing in my throat and chest begins to hum hard and I know I can win them over.

"So." Selwyn leans in to me and uncrosses her long legs before recrossing.

"Let's talk about your resurrection."

⫘

"You've got a seven A.M. pickup tomorrow for the *Today* show, followed by *Kelly and Ryan*. Then the car will take you to JFK for the five P.M. to La Jolla for the *Super Soul Sunday* taping. Did you get my email about wardrobe options? NO purple."

I barely look up from the stack of my books I am signing backstage as Margarite, my assistant, runs through tomorrow's schedule.

"Got it," I say as I shake the numbness out of my hand. "No purple."

Margarite clears her throat.

"*New York* magazine still wants a comment on your wife and sister-in-law's mistrial. I told them 'no comment' two times already, but they are relentless."

"Ex-wife," I say curtly.

"Sorry."

"I still have no comment."

"It's crazy," she says under her breath. "Jury tampering by the prosecution? *And* mishandling of evidence by the district attorney's office? Does that shit really happen outside of the movies?"

"Anything can happen when you have the Terry Barnes legal team," I say.

"That's what I mean. How did the legal team that represented both of the victims end up defending the accused?"

She's a sharp kid, even if she doesn't know when to shut up.

"They were the ones with the money all along," I say, sotto voce.

"And what about their missing friend? Do you think your ex-wife really killed her?"

"Margarite, enough."

I sign the balance of books and hand my pen to her.

"Your next interview is waiting for you in the lounge," she says.

"Fuck me. Can we move it?" I rub my temples.

She shoots me an exasperated look. "It's *Vanity Fair*."

I perk up. "I thought they turned us down."

"They did, but then I got a call yesterday that they were sending someone to the event and for a sit-down with you afterward. Could be a feature if it goes well." She exhales loudly. "I really wish you would read the updated itineraries when I send them."

I feel my second wind setting in at the thought of a feature story "Just get me a lot of caffeine and I'll be good as new."

"Nuh-uh, I'm clocking out. I've been up since five A.M. You are perfectly capable of getting yourself coffee." She gives me an impatient look.

"Fair enough." I know better than to push her.

As we walk to the entrance of the lounge, Margarite says, "See you bright and early!" before booking out of the revolving doors.

I scan the crowd at the bar and the people seated on cushy chairs and couches at small candlelit tables. There is the usual mix of suits and a few loud women in their cups next to a roaring fireplace. I don't see any men sitting alone or looking in my direction.

I haven't paid any attention to the details of this journalist's name or any other basic information that might aid me in finding him.

I am about to send an annoyed text to Margarite and pull up the itinerary when I feel a tap on my shoulder. When I turn around, I am face-to-face with a gorgeous woman with breast-length straight black hair, stylish dark-rimmed glasses, enormous hazel eyes, and stop-sign-red lips. She is so close to my face we are in kiss-or-kill territory.

"Mr. Mathers," she says confidently, and I feel an ancient stirring below the belt. My libido has been one of the slower biological returns post-coma, and I'm invigorated by the sensation.

"You are a woman." My foot is in my mouth faster than I can close it.

She frowns. "Does that matter?"

I blanch at my insensitive outburst, and to a reporter, no less.

"Sorry. I'm Gil Mathers." I extend my hand. "Pleasure to meet you."

"I know. I'm Dawn Graham." Her grip is strong.

Dawn takes a small step back from me and I take in the full view of her body. She frowns again and I lock my gaze to her face.

"Shall we find a place to sit?" I offer.

Three grinning women walk past us, each holding my book, and wave at me as they make their way to the bar.

"I was hoping we could talk somewhere quieter. I don't think we'll get any privacy here."

"Good call. We can go to my suite . . ."

Dawn nods and leads me to the elevator bank by the arm before I can finish. When the doors open and we step inside, we are surrounded on all sides by dark mirrors.

"Have you noticed how dark this hotel is? I can barely see two feet in front of me."

"Hmm," she says as I press the button for the top floor. We stand in a thick silence, the energy sparking between us like socks dragging on a carpet.

Our arms bump against each other as we walk down the hallway and to the door to my room, where I retrieve the key card from my suit pocket and wait for the satisfying click and green light. When we enter I see a bottle of Dom Ruinart that I assume is a gift from the hotel or my publisher.

"Make yourself comfortable," I tell her as I put my wallet and phone on a side table next to an enormous aquarium filled with bright-colored angelfish. "I'll just be a minute."

"I'll admire the view." She holds my eye before she crosses to the large windows overlooking Central Park.

"I'm assuming we aren't doing any photos tonight. I'm a little worse for the wear." I look down at myself.

"You look great to me," she says smoothly.

In the bathroom, I grin at myself in the mirror. I strip and do a quick shower to rinse the day off and douse myself in cologne and fresh deodorant. From my toiletry bag, I pull out the bottle of Cialis and place one in my mouth.

Back in the suite, Dawn has made herself comfortable and is seated on the couch with two glasses of champagne poured. She has an iPhone on the table with the audio recorder ready to go.

"I figured you might need a drink," she says.

I sidle onto the couch next to her.

"What should we toast to?" I ask.

"To second chances?" she says cheerfully.

"Cheers." I take a large sip and let the bubbles work their way around my mouth.

"Your event with Sawyer Selwyn was impressive. You seemed to win over a very skeptical audience and in the face of some difficult questions."

"Thank you. I'm glad the audience was receptive to my message."

"Your energy is different from your last tour," she says knowingly.

I make an effort to keep my eyes on hers. "Have you been following my career long?"

She has a peculiar smile when I ask this.

"You don't recognize me?" Her expression is indecipherable.

"Give me a minute," I stall. "I'm terrible with faces. Was it at one of my events?"

"More than one." She laughs lightly. "I've been following your career since the beginning."

"A little more champagne and I bet you my recall will come back online."

She pours me another glass. I feel my tired muscles releasing into the couch and lean back and yawn.

"I'm not boring you already, am I?" she teases.

"Not at all. I just feel really comfortable with you." I feel my body melting into the upholstery. "Feel free to fire away with your questions," I push.

The sooner we get it out of the way, the sooner we can go to bed.

A serious expression overtakes her face. "There have been rumors that Terry Barnes and Spencer Nichols were involved in the sex-trafficking ring that Randall Hemmings was just indicted for. And that Vicky Barnes and your ex-wife and Monica Nichols found out about it." She searches my face and I feel it growing hot.

She continues. "Were you involved with that?"

My heart speeds up.

"I don't want to talk about that," I say shortly.

"I'd like to get your side of the story before—"

"Dawn." I rest my hand on her arm and remove it quickly when she gives me a withering look.

"I operate on the philosophy that if we don't leave our past where it belongs, it will destroy the future," I say, irritated that she appears distracted. "Aren't you going to start recording?"

"I never forget anything," she says pointedly.

"I thought this was going to be a feature about my book," I say testily.

"I'm interested in why you think it happened. And since the case ended before your testimony—"

"If that's what you're interested in, you can read my deposition. I hear it has been leaked online."

"I read both and I was surprised how much was missing."

I've started to feel nauseous. "What do you mean?"

"There was quite a bit of revisionist history," she says coldly.

When I try to sit up taller on the couch, I only sink in deeper.

"If you would excuse me for just a minute," I say, trying to stand.

"The book is garbage." She smirks. "It is derivative, schlocky, and your worst one yet."

I double over as a wave of stabbing pain hits me.

"Oh my God," I gasp.

"Are you okay?" Dawn says, her words trailing off. "Maybe you should cool it with the champagne."

"Yeah," I say weakly, and see my empty glass. I feel like I've drunk way more than two glasses. I scan the room for my phone. I should call Margarite from the bathroom to get this woman out of here. And maybe get an ambulance. The last thing I want is a reporter present for that.

I stand up and am immediately baffled as to why my cheek is against the carpeted floor.

"Uh-oh," Dawn singsongs. "Looks like you're having some trouble there."

"My phone. I need it."

"Hmm. I think I saw it in the fish tank."

"What?" There's a terrible pressure in my chest.

Sure enough, when I'm able to pull myself a few feet closer to the fish tank in the entryway, I see my iPhone submerged. I lift my head from the floor and look for the room phone and see that it is un- plugged and moved out of my reach.

"I think I'm having a heart attack." I gasp as the pain expands to an alarming degree.

"You aren't having a heart attack," she replies unsympathetically.

"It might be a bad reaction to my pills," I manage.

"What did you take?" she asks, confused. I can't speak and just point in the direction of the bathroom.

I close my eyes and hear her walking away. Then laughter.

I watch her pointed boots move closer to me until I'm nose to toe with her. I roll onto my back and look up.

"Well, that's a twist."

"Hmm?" I gurgle. The pain is excruciating.

She shakes the bottle of Cialis. "Laura never mentioned these." She begins typing on the screen on her phone and lets out a little whistle. "Uh-oh."

"Help." My chest feels like it is going to explode.

"If I had known, I never would have used so much ketamine. I'm afraid this is going to be much more painful for you than I had planned on."

Cold sweat is breaking out all over my body and the pressure has mushroomed to my head and my bowels.

"Ketamine?"

"Oh, Gil, you arrogant dickhead." Dawn kneels down next to me. Her voice is different, her glasses gone, and her big eyes look surpris- ingly blue now. She tugs at her hair and removes the long silky black wig, making way for a mass of curly blond underneath. She gets all the way down to the floor and lies next to me. A flicker of this face getting her head shaved onstage flashes in between the searing pains in my chest. Another image of her nagging me at the VIP party flickers in my memory.

"Monica Brightling?" I say, realizing that I knew Mrs. Nichols before she was Mrs. Nichols.

"You finally made the connection," she says, satisfied.

"Please, help me."

"For so many years, I thought you were the one who was going to help me." She props herself up on one arm as I moan in pain.

"But it was the opposite. You were the cause of my biggest problems, Gil. You stole all of my money. You brainwashed me for years. And I never would have married Spencer if it wasn't for you."

"Monica. Call 911 . . . please," I beg weakly.

"Before you die, I'd like to set the record straight. I know you were led to believe that your brother-in-law was responsible for the video leak, but I just can't let Terry fucking Barnes get the credit for it," she practically spits.

"Oh God," I sputter, clutching my stomach.

"The night of the VIP party, your response to my saying that you'd stolen my money was that I needed to sign up for your course on financial codependence. I could have murdered you then," she says furiously. "You told me that if I don't change my problems, I'm choosing them."

"You bitch," I try to force, but nothing comes out.

"And when I came back into that hotel room that night and saw your true colors, all of those seminars about taking responsibility for my own life and making fearless choices finally clicked."

She nods, and even though I can barely focus, I can see how insane she really is. I'm shocked that someone so forgettable in my life has wreaked so much destruction.

"Gil, you really inspired me that night."

Her eyes are empty as she stares into mine until I can't keep them open any longer. I feel her breath in my ear and I feel something more peaceful than sleep creeping in.

"Threefold, asshole."

MONICA

After almost a year and a half of running, I am finally here.

Planning for this moment brought me through the darkest periods of that time. I'll wait here until I'm satisfied that he isn't going to wake up, but this time, I know that it is finally done. I have hours before anyone is going to miss him, and if he has a third miraculous recovery, I've got an arsenal of weapons that can quickly correct any more comebacks.

I hadn't planned for the booster effect of the Cialis on the ketamine I spiked his champagne with, and the irony is priceless.

I pull out my book and read *The Rule of Three* in the quiet of the room, Gil's body unmoving at my feet. The familiar line at the top of the page makes my eyes well with tears of relief. *Everything in your life, you've attracted. As you hold the power to create, you also hold the power to destroy.*

I hope that somewhere, not far from this room, Vicky and Laura are planning their new lives, free of the scrutiny and heartache they've experienced for so much of theirs. I can rest easy knowing that once word of Gil's death reaches them, we'll be even.

By now, the district attorney's office will have received an untraceable video link, a short proof-of-life clip showing that I am alive and well, holding up a copy of today's *Wall Street Journal* with the headline about the sisters' acquittal, the trackable location and time stamp encrypted beyond any traceability, naturally.

I shed fresh tears thinking about the friends I won't ever see again and what we've been through together. There were so many important bonding and commiserating sessions, but the most significant one was the week that Vicky returned from her trip with Terry.

"This idiotic book says that whatever consumes your thoughts is what you will eventually get in life," Laura mockingly read when she picked up Vicky's copy, half read on her Palm Springs trip. "If that is true, then Gil and Terry would be dead ten times over."

I waited for Vicky to say something, but she'd remained quiet.

"I've murdered Spencer with my thoughts about a hundred times over," I chanced.

Laura and I laughed. Vicky began to cry. Laura looked as surprised as I felt by the rare display of vulnerability.

"I just wish he was out of my life for good," Vicky said defeatedly. "Out of everybody's lives. He's evil."

We'd been lamenting about our husbands over the last few months, but always with a tone of snark. This night was very different.

"I need to tell you about Palm Springs," Vicky whispered before she filled in the parts of the trip she hadn't shared when they'd returned a week earlier. She recalled stumbling upon the conversation between Terry and Hemmings in the hotel room and discovering their scheme to traffic women using Spencer's tech. Gil had caught wind of the plot and had blackmailed Terry into forcing Hemmings to pull industry strings to help him get famous again. She recounted each horrid detail of the conversation, from the mention of Terry receiving kickbacks from the gun lobbyists to ease restrictions on firearms purchases, to the dawning of the gruesome revelation that both Gil and Terry exploited the school shooting that claimed Libby's life as a way to get themselves back into the news cycle.

"What fucking animals," Laura had screamed.

The mood in the room darkened considerably.

"We have to do something. This is insanity. Women are going to suffer."

"Women already have," Laura said bitterly.

"We have to stop them."

〜

The following week, when we resumed our book club, I came with a plan and armed with the words of the book.

> The third Rule of Three states that the only way to realize your true desires is to follow the three steps of the rules: wish, believe, and *act*.

"So what?" said Laura, who'd been opposed to discussing a self-help book from the beginning. Understandably she had a particular animosity toward anything in the genre.

"This is going to help us," I said seriously.

"I don't need any help from a book," Laura defended.

"Let's hear her out," Victoria said.

Ultimately, Laura agreed because the success of *The Rule of Three* was driving Gil crazy with jealousy and she relished the idea of carrying the copy around the house to torture him. Vicky had been quiet when I read more from the book.

Control what consumes you. Your thoughts become things; your fears become problems. Be your own solution.

Though we'd traded our marital resentments, I needed Vicky and Laura to see them for what they were: justifiable motives. I told them that we'd never be happy if we didn't do something life-changing for all of us. And our husbands were only going to continue to drain us in every possible way.

"We need to kill them."

The sisters were silent as I laid out the configuration that would reduce the possibility of last-minute capitulation. Laura would kill Terry, Vicky would kill Spencer, and I would kill Gil. And after that initial night, we would never speak about it again.

After a long silence and pensive looks between the sisters, Laura spoke first. "Okay, Monica, let's say we agree to this. I get that you hate Terry and Spencer, but do you really care enough about Vicky and me to risk your freedom for killing Gil? I don't think I've seen the two of you even speak to each other once."

If I wanted to make them trust me, I had to tell them everything.

Neither Laura nor Vicky said much after I told them that I'd been a devotee of Gil's and lost all my money and was disowned by my parents because they thought I'd joined a cult. I wasn't welcome back in Galveston by any of my former friends. I'd bet everything on a man who deemed me so insignificant that he didn't even recognize me when I came to Kingsland. And I confessed to Laura that it was me who'd leaked the video on Twitter that brought Gil down.

Vicky looked stricken and sick, while Laura appeared out of body.

"You realize that you didn't just ruin his life when you did that," Laura said angrily.

"I'm so sorry for that. I didn't know you then. It ruined my life too. When Gil was canceled, I had no job, no money, and no one to look to for help. For better or worse, Gil was the person in my life who gave me purpose. I was young and didn't know that I could be that for myself, yet. And when I met Spencer a few weeks later, I was desperate, homeless, and out of options," I told them.

"You're blaming Gil as the reason you ended up with Spencer?" Laura said. "Are you hearing this?" she'd asked Vicky.

Vicky stayed quiet.

"Cause and effect," I said. "And it came back to me threefold when Spencer was indicted. We lost everything. I went through the same thing you did, Laura!"

"It is a remarkable coincidence that Terry recruited you to Kingsland, where Gil happened to be living, given your history with Gil," Vicky said finally.

"There are no coincidences, only opportunities." I quoted the book.

What I didn't share with the sisters was that I'd helped push that coincidence along. I'd been keeping tabs on Gil for a few years and knew he was living in a wealthy community for social outcasts. When it became apparent that Spencer was on the same trajectory, I dug deeper and saw that Terry's legal team had repped a number of Kingsland's once-esteemed residents. I had no idea when I made a call to the law offices of LeFleur, Stermer & Schelling that it would set off such a life-changing chain reaction.

When Gil laid eyes on me at that first Kingsland event and had absolutely no recognition, I was furious and humiliated. But I knew the opportunity had been presented to me to teach him a lesson. Meeting the sisters and learning about all the deplorable things that their husbands had gotten away with—even before the Palm Springs trip revelations—inspired a "three birds, one stone" plan.

"What if we get caught?" Laura had finally said. "Isn't it always the spouses?"

"Not if the spouses have airtight alibis, no motive, and the victims have many enemies." I could see the wheels turning in both of their heads.

"And we have the perfect scapegoat," I'd added.

"Hemmings," Vicky wisely said.

"Yes. That fucker has to go down too."

"How do we do it?" Laura pressed.

"I think the punishment should fit the crimes, don't you?"

"Guns," Vicky said softly.

"Exactly," I replied.

"I don't want to go to prison," Vicky said.

"We actually know people who've gotten away with murder. Most of them were defended by Terry's legal team," Laura said.

"Kingsland isn't exactly the kind of place that a triple homicide happens and isn't scrutinized. There's no crime here," Vicky countered.

"*Except* for the spate of car thefts. There is an emerging criminal element here, one that could likely escalate."

"This is crazy. There's no way we'll get away with this."

"The people who get caught are the ones who slip up and talk about it," I said.

"We don't speak a word about this once it is done."

⊸⫴⊸

Fourth of July weekend seemed perfect because people would be distracted by the holiday festivities and the all-day drinking would make witness recountings murky. The sound of fireworks would be a good cover for gunshots. We had to prime the husbands leading up to the big party at Terry and Vicky's for maximum tension and conflict. Individually, we planted seeds of doubt about each other's motives and betrayals so that the barbecue would be rife with tension between the husbands. As far as everyone in Kingsland knew after that cook-out, Spencer Nichols wanted to kill Terry and Gil.

Milly was integral in the lead-up to the murders, as we knew she'd help spread far and wide that there was trouble in the Nichols household after the yoga class with me once she'd seen my bruises. We knew she was always in earshot and used it to our advantage before and after the shootings to make sure people were looking in the right directions.

That night, after Vicky got her usual text from Terry that the game was disbanding, we each put on gloves, snuck out the back, and used the trail to head to her place without being seen.

Laura hid around the side of the house while Vicky and I drove Spence's beloved Mustang out to the woods. Spence's and my ongoing argument about his obsessively tracking everything guaranteed that he'd be able to find his way to the car with the software he'd installed in it, a move that seemed contradictory given his practice of leaving the car's keys in the visor. And Gil fancied himself a cowboy, so Laura figured he'd be up to help save the day. If he hadn't, we had a backup plan to get him after Spencer at Laura's.

As soon as the men left in Gil's car, Laura snuck inside, shot Terry, planted the Hemmings file in the safe, and left the painting covering the safe slightly crooked, to tip off the cops. Meanwhile, Vicky and I were lying in wait for Spencer and Gil, in the bushes in Gucci loafers like the ones we'd seen Hemmings wearing in most of his online red-carpet shots, in size nine (info we got by calling his assistant and claiming we were from the designer and wanted to send a comp pair to Mr. Hemmings). We shot them and planted the guns. Then we met back at Laura's house to get the keychains with the trackers we'd intentionally left behind to solidify our alibis and took the trails to our respective homes without being seen by a soul. Vicki called the police, then I called the police, and we all waited for our new lives to begin.

⫙

The night we agreed to murder one another's husbands, Vicky raised the obvious and glaring issue with our book club selection.

"Aren't we going to suffer three times over for taking their lives?"

I'd already considered this. "I've lost my fortune, the charity I founded, and my social standing. By my count, I've paid threefold for other people's shitty actions without the perpetrators suffering any consequences."

"I don't believe any of this self-help 'the Universe made me do it' stuff anyway," Laura responded cynically.

"Couldn't we just go to the authorities?" Vicky asked.

"You know they'll get away with it. They always do," I replied.

"And if they don't, Terry will make us pay for the rest of his life," Laura said.

"Haven't you both suffered enough, though? You've had no privacy for your entire lives. You've lost your freedom, your marriages, your daughter and niece. Who knows how different things would have turned out, if Terry hadn't taken that money." Vicky and Laura looked at each other, processing silently.

"How much more do we lose before we put a stop to it?" Vicky said to Laura.

"Rule of three?" I asked the sisters.

"Wish," said Vicky.

"Believe," Laura replied.

"Act," I finished.

I took Vicky's hand in my left, and her sister's in my right.

ACKNOWLEDGMENTS

Writing our third book during the Covid-19 pandemic made us even more appreciative of the love and support of everyone in our lives. We couldn't have made it through the past eighteen months without the encouragement and counsel of so many special people and we are indebted to each of them for getting us through this unbelievable time.

It takes a fleet of talented people to make a book and we are so lucky to have an incredible team at Dutton. We are so grateful for our wonderful editor, John Parsley, and to Cassidy Sachs for being a constant source of support. And major props and thanks to the publicity and marketing wizards: Amanda Walker, Jamie Knapp, Caroline Payne, Katie Taylor, Kathleen Carter, and Stephanie Cooper. Special thanks to Christine Ball, Madeline McIntosh, Allison Dobson, and Lauren Monaco and the PRH sales team for their enthusiasm for our books. And to David Litman for the stunning jacket design, art director Christopher Lin, and thank you to production and design dynamos Susan Schwartz, Ryan Richardson, LeeAnn

Pemberton, Hannah Dragone, Tiffany Estreicher, and Nancy Resnick.

A huge thank-you to our remarkable agent, Christopher Schelling.

Thanks to our film agent, Pouya Shahbazian. And to our foreign rights and translation team: Chris Lotts, Nicola Barr, Lara Allen, Jacob Roach; thank you for all your work on our behalf.

To our incredibly supportive families: Thank you for helping to foster our love of books and for encouraging us to follow our passion.

A big thank-you for all the inspiration, motivation, and support from our dear friends. Many of you are writers, artists, performers, and creators, and you motivate and energize us. We couldn't write these books without you.

Thank you to Anthony Palieri for his way with a turn of phrase.

Huge thanks to all the authors, readers, bloggers, bookstagrammers, booksellers, and librarians who make this wonderful literary community all that it is.

And special thanks to Brian for getting me home safely.

And to Fiona for lighting the way.

ABOUT THE AUTHORS

E. G. Scott is the shared pseudonym of authors Elizabeth Keenan and Greg Wands, whose books include the internationally bestselling debut *The Woman Inside* and the follow-up, *In Case of Emergency*. Elizabeth lives in Pennsylvania and Greg lives in New York City.